The Widow on the Honeymoon Cruise

C.A. Larmer is a journalist, editor, teacher and author of four crime series, two stand-alone novels and a non-fiction book about pioneering surveyors in Papua New Guinea. Christina grew up in PNG, was educated in Australia, and spent many years working in Sydney, London, Los Angeles and New York. She now lives with her musician husband, two sons and their very cheeky Bluey on the east coast of Australia.

Sign up for news, views and giveaways:
calarmer.com

ALSO BY C.A. LARMER

The Murder Mystery Book Club series:
The Murder Mystery Book Club (Book 1)
Danger On the SS Orient (Book 2)
Death Under the Stars (Book 3)
When There Were 9 (Book 4)

The Ghostwriter Mystery series:
Killer Twist (Book 1)
A Plot to Die For (Book 2)
Last Writes (Book 3)
Dying Words (Book 4)
Words Can Kill (Book 5)
A Note Before Dying (Book 6)
Without a Word (Book 7)

The Posthumous Mystery series:
Do Not Go Gentle
Do Not Go Alone

The Sleuths of Last Resort:
Blind Men Don't Dial Zero
Smart Girls Don't Trust Strangers
Good Girls Don't Drink Vodka

PLUS
After the Ferry: A Gripping
Psychological Novel

An Island Lost

C.A. LARMER

The Widow on the Honeymoon Cruise

The Murder Mystery Book Club
(Book 5)

LARMER MEDIA

Published by Larmer Media
Northern NSW, Australia
calarmer.com
ISBN: 978-0-6452835-9-4

Cover design by Nimo Pyle
Cover photography by master1305 @ iStock
Edited by D.A. Sarac, The Editing Pen
& Elaine Rivers (with thanks)

For Peter Ashton

A NOTE FROM THE AUTHOR

This series was originally published under the title *The Agatha Christie Book Club*. To avoid confusion and broaden future storylines, like this one, I have since renamed the entire series *The Murder Mystery Book Club*. I apologise for any confusion.

You will find that past content remains largely unchanged, so, too, the core book club members, including beloved sisters Alicia and Lynette, vintage fashionista Claire, palaeontologist Perry and ditzy librarian Missy, as well as Alicia's beau, Detective Liam Jackson.

In this instalment, the gang draw inspiration from a modern murder mystery, and are joined by two new members as well as a cast of colourful characters—good and bad. There's also the usual dark humour, twist-laden plot, and some very cheeky red herrings.

Happy sleuthing, mystery lovers…

PROLOGUE

The sun was as brutal as a blowtorch, the sky a blistering blue, as a small crowd gathered on the promenade deck of the MV *Living Large*, hands to mouths, eyes unblinking, sweat pouring from stretched brows. They were watching a man with a dripping ponytail bash away at a woman draped across the dive platform. He had her wetsuit ripped open and was hammering at her chest.

"One… two… three… four…"

When he got to thirty, he dropped back on his haunches as another man threw himself on the woman's purple lips, releasing two powerful puffs of air. Both of them futile. And so the desperate dance continued.

Thirty chest compressions.

Two breaths.

Nothing.

Thirty chest compressions.

Two breaths.

Nothing.

At some point the captain tried to drag Ponytail away, but he would not leave the dance floor. Not yet. Not until he knew for certain. Only after twenty long minutes of trying did he finally retire, falling back in an exhausted huddle as gasps sang out around the group.

"No!" somebody screamed.

"Keep going!" yelled someone else, but the first officer was already placing a towel gently over the woman's body, and the captain had now turned to face her passengers.

"I am so, so sorry," she began but then stopped as she saw it, the look of relief that fluttered across someone's face. More than that, it was a vision of undiluted delight,

1

as though they'd just been handed the keys to the superyacht. The expression was fleeting, just a fraction of a second, but the captain had clocked it.

And, conveniently for the victim, so too had Claire Hargreaves, one-time member of Australia's nosiest book club.

CHAPTER 1
Two Days Earlier...

The black helicopter landed just in front of the bridge at the bow of the luxury cruiser, like something from a tacky action movie, and Claire watched with delight, one hand holding fast to her wide-brimmed vintage straw hat lest the rotor blades whip it off and towards oblivion. Or Papua New Guinea at least.

The *Living Large* was anchored just off Lizard Island in tropical far North Queensland, and no one was going to be sending the zodiac to fetch her hat today. Not even her lovely new husband, Simon Barrier, who owned both the superyacht and its dinghy and could send it any which way he chose. He was too busy reading the fluttering pages of the *Financial Review* and barely looked up from his deck chair as the chopper made its brash descent.

But Claire was watching, and she was mesmerised. It took many minutes for the blades to slow and the cabin door to swing wide, and she gasped again as a couple alighted, the man, short and stocky in a baby-blue linen suit, the woman dressed in flowing winter white, her long, bleached hair matching that shade, her body towering over him like a billowy cloud even as she bent down to avoid the stalling blades.

"It's James Wynter!" Claire called back to Simon. "You know? Heir to the media empire."

Finally he looked up. "Really? That short fellow? In the crumpled suit?"

"I think you'll find it's a very expensive crumpled suit, but yes. That must be his new wife, Indya, beside him. She's just twenty-two and a supermodel, you know."

He shoved the paper under an overloaded charcuterie

board and stepped towards her. "Well, I don't think you're allowed to have buckets of money and an ugly wife. It's against the rules." He smiled at his joke and added, "And I should know. I can't believe you said yes!"

"I can't believe we got the wedding together so quickly and are now on our honeymoon," added Claire, pulling her feline eyes from the helipad and back to her new husband.

Tall with a mop of black hair and a crumpled look himself, Simon was well into his fifties so wasn't keen to muck about, and it didn't take a psychologist to understand why thirtysomething Claire had rushed to the altar so quickly this time. Her first engagement, to a very unavailable Chinese man, had lasted four years and ended in tears.

Still, she did worry about the rushing part...

"Thank you for organising this at the last minute," Claire added, one hand waving across the sun deck at the top of the two-hundred-foot-long motor yacht.

He winked. "It helps when you own the vessel. But I am so sorry. I thought we'd be all alone on the high seas, and the blasted thing has filled right up."

The dream *was* to have it all to themselves—at least that was the intention when Simon asked his dynamic executive assistant, Queenie Dobson, to book it soon after he'd proposed to Claire.

The *Living Large* was part of his company's massive hospitality network. Living Large Enterprises also owned boutique hotels in multiple cities, luxury getaways in remote locations, and this custom-built cruiser that explored the Great Barrier Reef under the command of Captain Elizabeth Flinders. She'd been on board since its maiden voyage two years ago, although this was only her second trip as top dog, and was ably assisted by First Officer/Chief Engineer Gary Andrews and Chief Stewardess/Purser Pasha Patel. There was also an award-winning Italian chef called Sergio, a Filipino butler called Freddy, and a British marine biologist/expedition leader by the name of Dr Roland J. Brown.

This particular voyage was not part of the boat's usual itinerary, but the captain had happily added it to the schedule. And Simon had been happy enough, too, when his business partner suggested opening it to paying guests to help soften the costs. There were six staterooms after all, perhaps they could lure some like-minded honeymooners? And so the idea of a boutique honeymoon cruise was born, and here they were just a month after conjuring the idea, almost fully booked.

The wealthy Wynters had just joined them by chopper, and another couple had arrived earlier via a scheduled morning flight from the mainland. A third couple were due to jump on board midway through the cruise, during a stopover at the northerly port of Cooktown, leaving just two empty staterooms. No wonder his partner waved them off with a satisfied smirk!

And it really was a wonderful way to celebrate your nuptials. Not only were the cabins pure luxury—boasting king-sized beds, spacious spa baths and their own private balconies—but the superyacht also sailed the secluded northern end of the reef, far from the zinc-creamed hordes who descended daily from the coastal port back at Cairns. That's where Claire and Simon had jumped aboard, and at least they'd had two glorious nights alone before the other couples arrived, and she was glad the whipping breeze masked her sigh as she watched this new lot make their way across the bow and vanish beneath the bridge.

"But that's not all," said Simon. "Captain Flinders just informed me we'll be setting off slightly later this evening as we have another couple joining us tonight—and they've booked *both* remaining cabins. One of them must snore."

He chuckled and Claire tried to chuckle along but couldn't quite muster it.

Simon added, "That couple is on a chartered flight to the island now, I believe, and will be on board just in time for the captain's official welcome drinks." He sighed.

"Not so much our own private Idaho as a full ship I'm afraid."

Claire regained her smile. "That's what happens when you provide such an irresistibly beautiful venue. You really only have yourself to blame."

He laughed. "It doesn't matter anyway. We're sure to have a lot of fun and none of your nosey book club within a two-thousand-kilometre radius. So it'll be a corpse-free adventure too."

"Touch wood!" She tapped the gleaming handrail beside her as her mind drifted to the club.

Claire wasn't gunning for a corpse, but she wouldn't have minded having the gang here if she were being honest, maybe a puzzle or two to solve. She had officially stepped away from her beloved Murder Mystery Book Club, having taken up a position with Simon's company, and she missed their camaraderie and complete inability to walk past a question without answering it—often with terrifying consequences. Claire thought then of the first time she'd met Simon at the luxury rainforest retreat she now managed, of the shock of discovering first one, then a second murder victim, of the way they had pulled together to not only solve the crimes but survive a terrifying bush fire raging towards them.

It wasn't hard to forget all that drama while out here in the calm Coral Sea, but she would not forget the book club so easily...

~

Back in Sydney, Lynette Finlay's expression was stormy as she glared at her recipe book. The club co-founder had been smashing through, looking for ideas to cook for the following day's book meeting, when she'd stumbled upon her Earl Grey teacake—Claire's favourite.

"Everything okay?" asked her sister and co-founder, Alicia, glancing up from a laptop where she'd been editing content for a popular puzzle magazine (Code Crackers! Crosswords! Sudoku!).

Lynette scooped her long blond tresses into a messy topknot. "I can cook up a feast, sis, but it's just not the same without her."

Alicia knew who she was referring to and agreed. "We all miss Claire, honey, but the two new members have been good, yes?"

Despite her initial reservations, Lynette could not disagree. The book club had all grown to love the wealthy widow Ronnie Westera after their last deadly adventure, and it hadn't taken long for their newest member, Queenie Dobson, to fit in. Queenie was just twenty-three, and her knowledge of Agatha Christie left even their resident Christie afficionado and librarian Missy Corner feeling inadequate.

But still, they weren't Claire.

"I'm so glad Claire and Simon found each other," said Alicia, her eyes trained on her sister.

Lynette rolled hers and turned towards the pantry. "I don't need a man to be happy," she retorted, reaching for some flour.

"I never said you did."

"Ah, but your eyes spoke volumes." Lynette scooped a cup from the jar and sieved it into a large bowl. "You can stop feeling sorry for me please. I've got my business course and my cooking, not to mention you and Max. You're my family."

The sisters' black Labrador heard his name then and came bounding in, tail wagging, and Alicia slipped him a treat while Lynette pretended not to see, just as she pretended not to be ever-so-slightly worried. Max was now getting on in age, and Alicia had a boyfriend of her own, a homicide detective called Liam Jackson. It would only be a matter of time before those two set sail on their own honeymoon, and where would that leave Lynette?

She bent down and gave Max a proper hug.

Perhaps we could stow aboard with them, hey Maxie? she thought, her mind wafting back to the missing book club member.

How lucky Claire was to be sailing one of the seven natural wonders of the world. How serene and peaceful it all must be...

CHAPTER 2
Fireworks at the First Sundowners

There was tension in the air as Captain Elizabeth Flinders raised her champagne flute to officially welcome the guests, and Claire knew that if Liz had arrived fifteen minutes earlier, she'd have a better idea why.

It was just on sunset. The passengers had all gathered for the Captain's Cocktail Party, as requested, in the air-conditioned lounge bar on the promenade deck. It was one of three guest decks and also housed a fully-equipped galley kitchen, the six staterooms, and an open activities area at the stern that boasted a hydraulic dive platform and myriad water toys. Above them was the bridge deck, home to a state-of-the-art, *Starship Enterprise*-style command centre, the captain's ample quarters and the helipad, and above all that, the sun deck with its enormous jacuzzi, cosy cocktail bar and "alfresco dining experience". The crew's quarters, storage area and engine room were hidden well below, a world away from the dazzling lounge bar they were now in.

Dubbed Nemo's Lounge, with good reason, it was decorated in lurid shades of burnt orange, startling white, and black velvet trimming. There was floor-to-ceiling reinforced glass on two sides, a glittering cocktail bar in the centre, a baby grand piano, a Bose Lifestyle surround system and gigantic flat-screen TV for movies and presentations, and shockingly bright downlighting.

Squinting around now, Claire couldn't help sighing

wistfully, her mind tripping back to the last cruise she took on the *SS Orient* with all its subtle shades and dim lamps and deep, weathered oak. That ship was the antithesis of this vessel—as old-fashioned as this was modern—and she knew which she preferred, but she kept that to herself.

Simon had been so chuffed about the booking!

The other couples were also inspecting the room and each other. Despite the wealthy Wynters' clamorous arrival, no one had actually met, and this was a chance for the passengers to not only introduce themselves but to toast the official start of the journey, which was just getting underway, the yacht now swaying and listing as it made its way from Lizard Island towards the open sea. They would sail for another hour, then stall the engines in time for a calm dinner under the stars on the top deck, as was the usual practice.

As Simon handed her a crystal glass of champagne, Claire felt her heart flutter again and wondered how she'd got so lucky. What more could she possibly ask for than a husband who loved and spoiled her? Really, he was all that she needed...

Releasing another contented sigh, Claire glanced about. She had now taken a sneak peek at the yacht's manifest, but it didn't take an Agatha Christie fan to deduce who was who. The young media couple—the Wynters—were now dressed entirely in black and seated far too close to the piano, which was currently being crucified by the chief stewardess Pasha. Pasha was also the yacht's entertainment director and general dog's body, assisting everyone from Captain Flinders to their butler Freddy who, according to the brochure, also doubled as a waiter and barman, although he was nowhere to be seen this evening. It was Pasha who poured the champagne and was now hammering away at the baby grand like she was trying to smash her way through it.

Large and deeply tanned, with black curls and a bleached smile to match her tailored white uniform, Pasha began to warble as badly as she played, but James and Indya Wynter didn't seem to notice. They had eyes and ears only for each other and were laughing at some shared joke—hopefully not Pasha's corny rendition of "Piano Man"!

Every few minutes young Indya would produce her phone, snuggle closer to James, swish her glacial-white hair back, and snap a selfie. Claire noticed it was an older model iPhone like hers and wondered if Ms Wynter would upgrade now that she'd married into one of Australia's wealthiest families.

The other couple had to be the Dudley-Pines. They were older, late thirties perhaps, and clearly gym junkies. He was straining the seams of a Hugo Boss tuxedo; she was wearing a slinky silver dress several sizes too small, her muscular shoulders foreboding beneath thin spaghetti straps. Those two had eyes only for the Wynters and seemed to be watching them closely, the sunset through the windows no match as it morphed from orange to pink to purple.

The captain had not arrived at that point, and Simon rose to start the introductions when an audible gasp came from across the room. Pasha's fingers paused on the piano, and they all looked around to see a new couple standing at the top of the short staircase that led down into the bar.

This was the mysterious fifth couple, the one who had booked both staterooms last minute, and they were certainly a sight to behold. Not your typical newlyweds, they were both well into their seventies—he sporting a large bald head and an even larger belly, which was also squashed into an expensive tuxedo; she whippet thin with long, pearly grey hair, bright red eyeglasses, and a shimmering pink dress that fell all the way to the lush carpet and clashed badly with the orange decor.

They were standing at the top of the stairs, arm in arm, wide grin on the woman's perfectly pencilled lips, a strained smile on the man's.

"She looks familiar. Who is that?" Claire whispered to Simon just as James Wynter leapt to his feet and answered for him.

"Mother!" he yelled out, bounding across the room and up the stairs in three easy steps. He stopped inches from the woman, eyes wide. "Wow. This is a pleasant surprise! I wasn't expecting you."

The elderly lady reached towards him and held him in a grip so tight her knuckles began to whiten.

"Really, Jimmy?" she said when she finally let go. "I don't see why. You do know how much I adore my cruising."

"Of course, Mother, but it is a *couple's honeymoon* cruise, you wicked, wicked woman."

James tsked at her, winked knowingly at the man beside her, and then, finally, glanced back and across to his new wife.

Indya was still seated at their table, clutching her champagne with both hands as if trying to strangle it. It was only then that James saw what the others had witnessed from the moment the older couple made their grand entrance. Indya had paled to the colour of her hair and had a look of repulsion in her large brown eyes.

James gulped and turned back to his mother, who seemed not to notice.

"It *is* a bit cheeky of me," she croaked out. "But when you mentioned it, I thought, come on, Elsbeth Wynter. You can find yourself a plus one. That's when I convinced Boulder to step up."

She nudged her companion with a bony shoulder and he chuckled like a naughty school boy.

James was now chuckling along, waving a hand downwards. "In that case, you'd better come and join us for a glass of bubbly, right, Indy?"

But there was nothing right about any of this, not for young Indya. The colour returned to her cheeks as she released the glass, grabbed her iPhone and stood up. Then she swished her long hair back with a flick of her head and strode up the stairs towards them as they began their descent.

But there would be no tight hugs for her. Indya didn't even glance at her mother-in-law as she swept past and out of the bar, leaving nothing but the lingering scent of Chanel No. 5 and a roomful of shocked expressions.

James seemed most shocked of all. "Goodness," he said, turning back to his mother. "I... I'm so sorry, Mother. I don't know what's got into Indy."

"Perhaps a touch of seasickness?" she suggested, a wicked glint in her eyes. "Leave her, Jimmy. I need one of those promised champagnes, and it better be French."

James nodded and looked like he was about to follow his mother to the bar when he must have thought better of it and said, "Sorry, um... you head down and I'll be back in a tick!"

Then he rushed after his wife.

Halfway along the narrow corridor that led between the lounge and the staterooms, James slammed into Captain Flinders, toppling the peaked cap from her head in the process.

"Oh, goodness me!" said Liz, propping it back over her glossy chignon. "Everything okay, Mr Wynter? I think you and your wife are going the wrong way."

"Sorry!" was all he managed as he brushed past her and away.

"But... but there's welcome cocktails in the lounge!" she tried again. "And we've got our all-important safety drill!"

But the man was not for turning.

Indya Wynter had only just reached her cabin door when her husband caught up with her.

"Indy!" he called out, and she looked back with a pout.

"How could you let this happen?" she cried. "It's a honeymoon cruise. *Our* honeymoon. How can *your mother* possibly be here? And with her lawyer. They're not even a couple! How is it *allowed?*"

James reached for her hand and pulled her towards him. "I'm not sure, babe, and yes, it is a bit cheeky—"

"*Cheeky?* Can you both stop using that word like we've been pranked? This is unacceptable. She's ruined everything!"

"Babe, come on, let's not catastrophise it. It's not the end of the world."

His voice was tinged with sarcasm, and it enflamed her further.

"It's the end of our romantic holiday that's for sure! Why did you even mention it to her? I thought we agreed to keep the honeymoon secret."

"I don't keep secrets from my mother, you know that. Besides, she has every right to know where I'm going. She gets worried."

"But she has no right to *follow us.*" He seemed about to dispute that. "I thought you spoke to Boulder about this," she continued. "I thought he assured you he was going to pull your mother into line, not provide her with a *plus one.*" Indya took a deep breath, tried to calm her rage. "I know Elsbeth loves you, James. I know she misses you. I get that. But this... this is going too far. It is utterly unacceptable. She has to leave. They both do. Immediately!"

He looked amused again. "Shall we make them walk the plank? Get the captain to dump them off at the nearest atoll?" He grabbed Indya by the waist and pulled her closer, looking up into her fiery eyes. "Come now, sweetie, this really doesn't have to be a big deal. It's a very big boat."

"Not big enough for both of us."

"Babe—"

"Don't *babe* me, James. One day you're going to have

to choose, and I say that day has come!"

Then she wriggled free of him, wrenched the door open, and swept inside.

James growled below his breath, then followed her in, not noticing the handsome young butler lurking at the corner, a swan made of fresh towels in one hand, his phone in the other, the red button blinking as he recorded everything.

CHAPTER 3
Meanwhile Back at the Bar

The air in Nemo's Lounge was as stiff as the martini Pasha was now mixing.

No sooner had the young Wynters fled than Elsbeth Wynter had looked crestfallen—like her *joie de vivre* had fled with them—and she'd murmured something about powdering her nose and also vanished.

That left her plus one, Arne Boulder, smiling vacuously at the other guests as he strode down to join them.

"Bollinger?" Pasha all but yelped as she raced towards the bar.

"Make it a martini," he replied coolly, following her across while Claire shared a worried frown with Simon.

"That didn't look good," she said.

Simon nodded. "I'd better have a quiet word with Liz. See what the hell is going on."

Ten minutes later he was deep in conversation with the captain. They were standing just inside the entrance to the bar, whispering furtively, and Claire watched them keenly as she selected a fetta watermelon cube from the hors d'oeuvres on her table. Could it really be true that the media mogul's widow had gate-crashed her only son's honeymoon?

"Scandalous, isn't it?" came a man's voice beside her, and Claire looked up to find the muscle-bound, thirtysomething couple standing there, flutes in hand, looks of glee on their faces.

"I feel rather sorry for the poor thing," said Claire, dropping the cube back again.

"Indya? Oh, there's nothing *poor* about her," the man replied. "She's just married into the largest magazine publishing family in the country."

"I'm sure she knows that, Connor," said his wife. "We're not all complete morons."

"That's what happens when you marry into money," he continued, unperturbed. "Rumour has it, old Elsbeth has never approved of any of her son's relationships—always detonated them before they could get to third base. How young Indya survived to the altar I cannot say, but I have a hunch that's why the wicked witch is here now. Wants to blow up that relationship, too, if she can manage it."

"But they're *married*," said Claire.

"Yes, but for how long?" Connor wiggled his bushy eyebrows. "And if it came down to it, from what I hear, James would choose his mother over his wife any day of the week. Did you see how *delighted* he looked to see her?" He shuddered. "Bit creepy if you ask me. Far too close for comfort those two."

"You're pretty close to your mother, darling," murmured his wife.

"That may be," he shot back, "but I'd hardly bring her on our *honeymoon*. For starters, you'd throw me overboard."

"How do you know all this?" Claire enquired, half-interested, half-appalled.

"Oh, I read the gossip mags. Don't you?" Then, thrusting a large hand towards her, he said, "I'm Connor Dudley-Pine, by the way, and this is my better half, Cinnamon."

"Cindy please," said the woman, and Claire offered them her own hand to shake.

"I'm Claire Hargreaves, and over there is my husband—"

"Oh, we know all about your husband, darling,"

Connor said, giving Simon the once-over as he continued talking to the captain. "What we don't know is how you managed to snag Australia's most eligible bachelor. We all thought he was your classic George Clooney and would never say yes to anyone. Bit like James Wynter actually."

"Oh, George Clooney got married in the end, you nincompoop," said Cindy, eyes still on Claire. "But this woman's obviously not just *anyone*, is she?"

That left the book club member speechless. Claire loathed talking about her private life and certainly wasn't about to give these two perfect strangers more gossip, but she also wanted to be polite. She had a terrible tendency to clam up and come across as cold. Snobbish, even. It was something she would have to overcome, not just in her new role as the manager of Lyle's Rainforest Lodge but as Simon's new wife.

In the relatively short time she'd known him, Claire had quickly learned that Simon was a social butterfly, flitting from project to party and back again, all in the name of his beloved business. She tried to remember the tips Ronnie from book club had given her just before the wedding. It was one of many tips from the wealthy philanthropist, and this involved dealing with pushy strangers—smile, say something innocuous, then throw the spotlight back on them.

And so she mirrored the stewardess's smile and said, "Yes, I *am* a lucky woman, but tell me, how did *you two* meet?"

As the couple clapped hands and launched into a story about locking eyes over a set of barbells, Claire thought how clever Ronnie was. She was absolutely right. If there's one thing people liked more than gossiping about others, it was gossiping about themselves.

CHAPTER 4
Death Stares Under the Stars

"It's just like *Death on the Nile*," Claire whispered to Simon as they nibbled a delicious appetiser of pancetta-wrapped scallops on the gusty upper deck an hour later.

Cocktails had remained strained even after everyone returned and played nicely, allowing the captain, Liz, to make the formal introductions, then do the requisite muster drill before handing over to the serious young marine biologist, Roland. A strong, sinewy chap with a sun-scorched face and a bleached ponytail, he was also the resident dive instructor and gave a pre-dinner lecture on the reef they were heading to for their first stopover, then asked all those interested in diving to meet at the diving platform at nine the following morning.

No sooner had he finished, than Pasha announced that dinner was being served on the sun deck and asked them to follow her up using the elevator located beside the restrooms outside the bar. "Or, if you've got the ticker," she'd added with a wink, "feel free to use the exterior companionway; it's just a few flights up!"

Claire and Simon had chosen the stairs, but it was the view at the top that took their breath away. Five intimate tables for two had been set up on the open deck, each with flickering candles and bowls of fresh red roses. There were fairy lights strung between them and stars twinkling above, and it made for a stunning dining experience.

Yet Claire could not focus on any of that. She was still thinking of the warring parties.

"*Death on the Nile?*" repeated Simon as he reached for his wineglass. "Is that one of your Agatha Christie novels?"

"Yes," said Claire. *How did he not know that?* "It's the one where the honeymoon couple go to Egypt and are stalked by the groom's ex-fiancée. Except, in our case, it's the groom's mother who's doing the stalking, and the groom doesn't look at all concerned, like he invited her himself."

"James Wynter loves his mum. I guess we can't hold that against him."

She frowned, wondering if she should be relieved Simon's mother passed away before they had met. Then wondered if she was just jealous. Claire was distanced from her parents, her Anglo-Australian father long gone, her mother a Chinese Hong Kong national now living in Paris. She hadn't even bothered to fly over for Claire's wedding so was hardly going to gate-crash her honeymoon. There had been a lovely congratulations card, of course, with a sizeable cheque inside, but that had only left Claire resentful. She didn't want her mother's money, thanks very much. It was her *presence* she longed for, that feeling of being prioritised.

Claire wondered which was worse—a mother who suffocated you with love or one who barely remembered you were alive.

Simon misread her frown and said, "So how does that book end, dare I ask? Does the hubby cark it?"

She shook her glossy black hair, now set in victory rolls to match her original 1940s damask evening gown. "No, it's a double con—turns out the husband is in cahoots with the stalking ex-fiancée and it's the new wife who gets it."

"Goodness. Indya better watch her back then." He was joking of course, but the way Claire's frown firmed up made him grab her hand and laugh. "It's okay. Nobody is dying on this cruise. I forbid it! Besides, we're not living in the pages of a Christie novel."

Claire relaxed her brow and thought now of the new book resting beside her bed in their stateroom. "Not anymore we're not," she said. "As you know, I'm reading a modern-day writer called Ruth Ware."

"Oh yes. *The Woman in Cabin 10*. Sounds like a gripping travel yarn."

Actually, it was a gripping mystery, but he didn't need to know that. Nor the fact that it was the very book the Murder Mystery Book Club would be discussing tomorrow. She mightn't be part of the gang anymore, but that didn't mean she couldn't read along with them, even from a distance.

"Breaking the hex, hey?" said Simon. "Good." Then he dropped his head to one side. "You miss your book club friends terribly, don't you, Claire?"

She lowered her gaze. "It's *fine*. I mean… your business keeps me nice and busy."

In fact, she'd barely had time to read since he'd hired her to help renovate his lovely old holiday lodge up in the rainforest. It had taken longer than anticipated but was coming together now and soon she would settle in as the general manager.

Or would she?

Neither of them had discussed what would happen post-marriage. Would Simon move up with her? Would Claire do the job long-distance from his home in Sydney? Or would she be forced, as Ronnie did, to abandon her own career for the sake of her wealthy husband?

The very idea irked Claire. Despite once running her own vintage clothing store, she was a thoroughly modern woman. It was why she didn't take Simon's surname and why she hadn't yet broached the subject. Simon a good fifteen years older than Claire, and she was terrified of his answer, so she took Ronnie's advice and said, "So, scuba diving tomorrow. Have you ever tried?"

Then she smiled as he began to wax lyrical about his diving prowess.

"You know I can barely swim, Elsbeth. Why the blazes would you subject me to scuba diving?" said Arne Boulder, soaking the last of the appetiser up with some bread.

"No, I did not know that about you, and don't be such a baby," Elsbeth Wynter replied sternly. "You're missing two-thirds of the earth's surface when you stay above water. You simply must get a lesson with that hippie doctor, and we can splash about together."

"Roland? I thought he was a marine biologist."

"He is. He's also the dive instructor and expedition leader, a man of many talents. Didn't you listen to the lecture?"

"Of course I didn't. I was too busy trying to smile nicely at poor Indya, who looks frankly devastated. I think you've gone a step too far this time, Ellie."

"Nonsense. If the clothes hanger can't handle the heat, she should get out of the kitchen."

"I think that's what they call a mixed metaphor! And you're in no position to discuss kitchens—you've never stepped in one in your life." He frowned. "I'm with Indya on this one though. We should not have come. I really should have talked you out of it."

Elsbeth waved a dismissive hand in the air that saw her cream cardigan drop from her bony shoulders and onto the back of her seat as the butler-cum-waiter Freddy rushed over in anticipation. She shooed him away with a frown.

"Who cares what the latest scrap of a girl has to say? If I want to holiday with my baby boy, I'll holiday with my baby boy. There was no way you were going to talk me out of it, Boulder, so you had no choice but to tag along."

"I didn't have *time* to talk you out of it. You gave me twelve hours' notice! I'm not even sure I've packed properly."

"You have a sun hat and a tux? What more do you need?" Another dismissive gesture, followed by another aborted attempt to assist from Freddy. Again she shooed him away. "Besides, I would have convinced old Monty to come along. You're not the only bachelor I know."

"No, but I am the only one stupid enough to do as you ask."

"It's only because I pay you obscene amounts of money," she spat back, now waving a hand in the air for the waiter, who simply smiled and ignored her.

Boulder gave her a grim smile of his own but thought, No, it's because somebody has to keep you in line, you silly old girl.

As he watched the waiter ignore Elsbeth's waving hand, Arne Boulder thought of Jimmy and all the arguments over the wedding. Fortunately, young Indya was never privy to any of them. She would have been horrified to hear Elsbeth's view of the "vacuous clothes hanger" and James's limp defence of her. Even more horrified when he assured his mother that marriage was no longer forever and if Elsbeth really didn't warm to "pretty Indy", he could easily swap her for another. It was the only reason Elsbeth had finally given her consent, but Boulder had felt nauseated as he watched the pretty "clothes hanger" stride so joyfully down that aisle.

Little did Indya realise that blood was thicker than water and James would always take his mother's side.

No matter what.

Helping his wife into a seat at the other side of the deck, James tried not to grimace at Boulder. His mother had her back to them and had not seen them arrive for dinner, and he was glad of that. He couldn't bear another scene from Indy. They almost hadn't come, were going to order room service, but then he'd reminded her that Elsbeth would win if that happened.

"You mustn't let Mother ruin our holiday," he'd said. "She's here because she loves me. That's all this is. Pure maternal love and I really wish you'd understand that."

"It's weird is what it is, James. I can't believe you can't see that!" Indya had hissed back, and he'd given her a look he knew was glacial, but enough was enough.

She'd gone too far this time.

"I'm sorry you're not close to your family but I won't have you talk my mother down. I won't," he'd told her, and she had blinked at him, frustrated for many minutes, then finally relented.

And as they settled in now, he felt more hopeful. "See?" He waved at the candle and roses, the delicious course waiting for them. "It doesn't get more romantic than this. The stars are out, Mother's on the other side of the deck, and things will look a whole lot better in the morning. I promise."

Then he offered her his warmest smile, but he had a hunch things would never be better. Not unless his new wife was going to stop sulking and get with the program.

As she watched James Wynter swap eye rolls with his mother's consort, Boulder—*were they really expected to call him by his surname?*—Cinnamon's eyes were firmly locked on the elderly lady.

My God, what a coup! She never would've dreamed it!

It was exciting enough to be in such close proximity to James Wynter but now his mother? The indomitable publishing doyenne! Perhaps Cindy could snag her after dinner or maybe buddy up to her on the first dive tomorrow...

"What are you thinking about, dear?" Connor said, eyes narrowing because he knew her well and it was a rhetorical question.

"Don't you worry your pretty little head," she told him. "Nothing has changed. It's only upped the ante."

His eyes widened. "You're not worried?"

"Why would I be?"

"We had the perfect plan, Cindy, and now there's a fresh roadblock in our path."

"Elsbeth? Hardly! If anything, it's the moody supermodel we should be worried about. She's making everything unpleasant for everybody. If only she'd stop her sulking."

"Just as long as our investment pays off."

"*Our* investment?" she said, and his chiselled jaw stiffened further as his eyes slid away.

Cindy smirked, then snuck another look at the guests. Sure, her previous plan had been blown to smithereens, and the person responsible was snapping her bejewelled fingers as if the waiter was her own private concubine. But this was a good thing. It had to be! Their lives depended upon it.

Taking a fortifying sip of her wine, Cindy said, "Just stick to the script, Connor darling, and all will be fine. I will sort it like I always do. Until then, you should know that the frumpish Eurasian chick is watching us keenly, so look like you love me, why don't you?"

He did as instructed, smiling lasciviously, and she almost fell for it herself this time. They clinked glasses, then laughed heartily as she swept another look back at Claire Hargreaves. But she was no longer watching them. Claire's feline eyes were firmly on her husband, and the love she was showing was annoyingly—achingly—genuine.

Cindy sighed. She'd kill for a love like that. Wouldn't hesitate for one moment.

Pasha Patel stood to one side, black apron around her uniform, waiting to pounce. There were wineglasses to be kept filled and appetisers to be swept away and three more courses to be brought up via the service staircase at the side of the deck.

It was all about timing. Everything had to be just right. And it didn't help that the young Wynters had turned up so damn late. Now the diners were all out of sync and she could see the men fidgeting for more food while Indya had barely picked up her fork.

And why Freddy was ignoring Elsbeth's pleas for more wine was beyond her! Really, the lad was useless, should have been shown the gangplank after his first disastrous shift. She longed for their old butler, Gabriel...

Plastering her smile back on, Pasha snatched the bottle of sauvignon from Freddy and strode across to Elsbeth's table.

"More wine, madame?"

"Not yet," she said, scooping a silver clutch purse from the table. "I'd like to know where the ladies' room is first."

"Of course. It's downstairs, just outside Nemo's Lounge."

As Pasha pulled her chair out and pointed the way, she couldn't help thinking *But didn't you go there earlier, during welcome drinks?* And then, more importantly, bloody hell woman, now we'll have to delay the mains. Sergio will have a conniption!

Luckily, the old lady did not take long, and very soon she was striding back along the deck towards her table, so Pasha gave Freddy the nod to follow her down to the galley to fetch the next course, when something dreadful happened.

Elsbeth had stopped at the Dudley-Pines' table and was staring hard at Cindy.

"You look familiar to me," she said brusquely. "How do I know you?"

Cindy visibly blushed. "Oh, I don't believe we've met, Mrs Wynter." She leapt to her feet and thrust out a hand. "But it's such a delight. I'm Cinnamon Dudley—"

"Cinnamon? Yes..." Elsbeth ignored the hand. "That is familiar. Now how do I know that name?" Her beady eyes squinted through her glasses. "Something shifty, I'm sure of it..."

"I beg your pardon?" was Cindy's stunned reply.

"Hmmm, yes, definitely shifty..." Elsbeth's eyes were now narrow slits. "Never fear, it will come to me eventually."

Then she continued on like she hadn't just insulted a fellow passenger.

Pasha was aghast and watched as Cindy dropped to her chair, flabbergasted. And who could blame her? This was supposed to be a pleasant cruise! What was the old dragon thinking?

Shooing Freddy on, Pasha scooped up the sauvignon and returned to Cindy's table, filling her glass to the brim—she looked like she needed it—while Elsbeth began griping about the breeze.

"It's as cold as a witch's tit out here. Help me into my cardigan, Boulder."

He did as ordered, awkwardly pulling one skeletal arm through a sleeve and then the other, then Elsbeth finally sat down with a heavy "Hmf!", glanced at her empty wineglass, and said, "Who does a woman have to kill to get some attention around here?"

CHAPTER 5
Clownfish and Sharks

The coral was alive with a shimmering array of colours, shapes and textures, not to mention all the extraordinary slithery creatures, and Claire gasped over and over as she paddled above it, Simon by her side. She saw lurid parrotfish and red finger coral, green sea turtles and insanely large clams and, at intervals everywhere, the infamous clownfish bobbing in and out of the anemone, like she'd been transplanted into a Disney movie.

Despite their plans to scuba dive, Claire had chickened out at the last minute—having never tried it before—and opted for a snorkel instead. Now she wished she'd been braver as she watched the young Wynter couple and the Dudley-Pines decked out in scuba gear being taken through their paces by Roland.

The cruiser had sailed through the night and was now moored at a secluded reef, and it really was the ideal place to dip your toes, so to speak. There were numerous shallow pools just perfect for exploring the hard corals, and two floating pontoons, one much closer to the mooring than the other.

It was this pontoon that Roland insisted they stick to.

"That floating platform in the distance has quite a deep drop nearby, and I'd prefer if we stuck together today," he told them as they launched off the dive platform at the back of the yacht. "We can be adventurous tomorrow when we get to the mighty Osprey."

The Osprey Reef would be a whole different kettle of

fish, he added, oblivious to his pun. Located just beyond the continental shelf with no visible land mass nearby, it had a one-thousand-metre drop and would be "quite the feat", Roland told them.

"So I'd like us to perform a few shallow orientation dives first, just to make sure we're all fit to purpose."

That had elicited groans from several guests, but Claire could tell young Indya looked relieved, and the way she had to be shown how to use the breathing apparatus several times made Claire wonder if perhaps she was really a novice.

"The dive is planned for a maximum depth of fifteen to twenty metres with an estimated bottom time of 45 minutes," Roland told the divers, "so let's do a few test dives between the yacht and pontoon one and then finish up in time for midday lunch. After that we'll be sailing on to a lovely little lagoon for sunset cocktails, and you will have earned your 'sundowners' by then, I can assure you. And please, I know it's relatively shallow, but don't lose sight of your buddy at any time."

"I won't be taking my eyes off my buddy," said James as he sat on the edge of the platform, waiting to drop in.

His young wife looked happier this morning and giggled at that, then pulled out a chunky blue camera and snapped a selfie with him before they plunged awkwardly off the side.

Now as the others vanished deep below the water, then reappeared periodically, thumbs held high, Claire felt doubly bad about depriving Simon of a proper dive. Unlike her, he had explored reefs from here to the Greek Islands, but he seemed happy enough, paddling beside her. Even managed a smile when she held up the white flag a good half hour before lunchtime.

Claire was worried about sunburn. The sun this far north was as unforgiving as a wildfire, and she now wished she had pulled a summer wetsuit over her demure one-piece. Everybody else had opted for one, except for young Indya who, in her frightfully tiny bikini, was going to be even more fried than Claire.

Peeling her snorkelling gear off carefully, back on the dive deck, Claire suggested Simon buddy up with James for tomorrow's dive. "I think he'd appreciate it," she said, reaching for a pile of fluffy blue-and-white towels. "Indya looks as skittish as I do, so she might prefer to snorkel with me."

He took the towel she was offering and then dropped, dripping, into a lounge chair beside her. "If it's really okay with you, perhaps I should," Simon said. "I'd hate to miss out on the infamous Osprey drop."

"Pineapple cocktail?" came a voice behind them, and they glanced around to see Pasha leaning down with two icy glasses in her hands, her own bikini top poking out beneath her uniform. "Don't worry, it's really a mocktail. Just a refreshing shot of loveliness to keep you going."

They took the drinks and thanked her.

"You're diving too?" asked Claire, who had noticed the swimsuit.

"A girl can dream." Pasha sighed wistfully. "Lunch is up on the sun deck in thirty minutes, just FYI." Then she peeled her eyes outwards and began to frown.

"Everything all right?" Simon asked, following her gaze, and that's when he spotted someone in a full black wetsuit, splashing about. "Is that—?"

"Elsbeth Wynter, yes," said Pasha. "She slipped in on her own, not long ago. Mr Boulder is not a swimmer, so I'm keeping an eye out. Making sure she's okay."

"Shouldn't she have a buddy?" Simon asked.

Pasha shrugged flippantly. "Will you tell her or shall I?" Then she winked and walked away.

Claire frowned at that comment and began a monologue on how all passengers should be treated equally, but Simon didn't quite agree. The fact was Elsbeth Wynter was no mere *passenger*. He wished Claire could understand that; she'd have to learn the difference when they officially opened the luxury Rainforest Lodge she was managing. Mrs Wynter was one of the wealthiest women in the country, but more than that, she was one of the most powerful. He wasn't about to start ordering her around and getting in her bad books!

The situation with her daughter-in-law was tricky enough.

While speaking with Captain Flinders last night, they had discussed the obvious tension and whether it would be a problem, not just for Indya but for the other paying guests. Liz was both apologetic and mortified by the situation. It seems the older woman had fooled them all, signing up under Boulder's name and pretending to be newly married. If it were any other couple, they would have made them walk the plank by now, but this was Elsbeth Wynter. If she wanted to make a fuss, she certainly could.

And *would*, she told them when they'd gently approached her during Roland's lecture to suggest a graceful exit at Cooktown so as to give the young couple a few days on their own.

"I will do no such thing," she had informed them, plucking the olive from Boulder's martini. "If that ridiculous stick creature has a problem with me, she can be the one to make a graceful exit. Or disgraceful. I really don't care."

And so they had dropped the subject but not before Simon instructed the captain to do everything she could to keep the Wynter women apart. But it really wasn't good enough, he thought, as he watched her narrowing in on the group now. It wasn't just awkward for young Indya, the whole trip felt sullied somehow. Everyone seemed on tenterhooks.

Well, everyone except Elsbeth, who was now circling the newlyweds like a shark.

Below the water, Connor watched the monster-in-law splashing close to her son with about as much subtlety as Indya's gold string bikini and her matching gold flippers. James did not seem at all concerned, and he even gave his mother the thumbs-up at one point, then signalled downwards and they both dived deeper, leaving Indya floating alone like a spare tyre.

Even behind her mask, Connor could see the young bride's burgeoning frown. He wanted to frown, too, and not because he felt sorry for her. He felt sorry for himself and Cindy and all their grand ambitions.

The old battle-axe had clearly recognised Cindy last night, or was about to, and by dinner's end, his wife had gone from delight to despair. Now what were they going to do? If Elsbeth put it all together, the whole trip would be a gross waste of time.

Not to mention money…

~

First Officer Gary Andrews was leaning against the teak railing, his binoculars trained to the diving group, and did not notice the chef, Sergio Aloisio, approach.

"Are you checking out the string bikini or the old bag?" Sergio asked, making him jump and almost drop the glasses.

"Just enjoying the view," Gary spat back, and Sergio sniggered as he lit his cigarette.

"I bet you are, you dirty bastard. What will your lover say?"

Gary turned to look at him. "What lover?"

Sergio snorted. "I don't need binoculars to see what is what on this yacht. I may be a galley slave, but I have eyes and I have ears." He chuckled. "And you two have not been very discreet."

"We're not the only ones though, are we? Perhaps you should bring it up with the captain? Perhaps you should see what *she* has to say?"

That made the chef's smile falter briefly, and Gary offered his own snigger as he headed off towards his cabin. Sergio considered that for a moment, then picked up the binoculars and turned them back towards the divers. As he found the person he was looking for, his smile turned into a sneer.

CHAPTER 6
The Tardy Diners

The smorgasbord was almost as vivid as the coral, and Connor Dudley-Pine oohed and aahed as he helped himself to a plate. They had been diving for hours, and he was famished! He glanced at his watch. It was now 12:10 p.m.—they didn't go in for daylight savings this far north—and he could see the lovely Chinese Australian lady and her wealthy hubby already hooking into some oysters. He watched as Claire reached for her napkin and dabbed at Simon's lips, which appeared covered in cocktail sauce, laughing at him as she did so.

Those two didn't need oysters; they were clearly smitten. Which was a pity, really, because love could get you in so much trouble.

He sighed and looked around for Cindy, but apart from James Wynter who was just taking a seat at his table, the dining deck was empty. He wondered where Indya had got to, then thought about his own wife and her quick dash back to their cabin. Didn't know why she bothered. Sure, he was still dripping wet in his boardies, but this was a yacht, wasn't it? If you couldn't drip all over a yacht, where could you drip?

"Mango frappe, sir?" said the waiter, wielding a jug of something orange and frothy the moment Connor took his seat.

"Thanks, Freddy," he replied, moving his laden plate out of the way. "You might as well pour two. My wife will be here shortly."

Except would she? Cindy had a terrible tendency to be late. It was like she revelled in making him wait. One of the many ways she made him pay…

"The lobster looks good," said Cindy, panting as she dropped down into the seat across from him sometime later.

No apologies for her tardiness as there never was, and he went to say something when he noticed what she was wearing.

"I thought you were heading back to the cabin to change," he said.

"I did." She waved a hand down her glittering dress, which was cut low at the front and barely covered her muscular thighs. "If Indya can rock a string bikini all morning, I can't see why I can't don a designer kaftan!"

He frowned. That wasn't what he meant and she knew it. The kaftan was wet in spots, and he could make out her swimsuit underneath.

If she hadn't changed out of her cossie, what the hell had she been doing?

"Witch still on her broomstick. You can come out of hiding, babe!"

James added a love heart and sent the text on to his wife before realising there was no Wi-Fi reception, then dropped the phone to the table with a groan. He twiddled his fingers for another minute, then signalled for the waiter, who rushed over to refill his glass.

"Some wine or a beer, sir? To accompany your lunch?"

"Just get me a plate of food please. And one for my wife."

"Actually, sir, lunch is served buffet-style today, so you help your—"

"I know how a bloody buffet works, man! You think I'm an imbecile?"

"Oh, no, of course—"

"I want you to bring me a plate. I'm exhausted, and

when my wife gets here, she'll be exhausted too. Is that too much trouble?"

"No, no, no trouble at all," said Freddy, backing away from the table and towards the buffet.

"You sounded just like your mother then," came a voice behind him, and James looked around to see Boulder standing there, looking sweaty, his black linen shirt dripping wet.

"I'll take that as a compliment," James shot back, then glanced over his shoulder.

"Don't panic. Ellie's missing in action."

"That's *why* I'm panicking. So is Indy."

"If we're lucky, they'll be out there drowning each other." Boulder chuckled, then his expression turned sour. "I don't know why you chose to marry a woman who doesn't get on with your mother. I mean, really James, what were you thinking?"

The younger man scowled, and the older man held up a palm.

"I know, we all get led by lust, but lust can be very expensive, yes? It's a pity you didn't throw this one back like the others. She could take you for half of everything, and what would your mother have to say about that?"

James sneered up at him. "Who are you really worried about, Boulder? Me? My mother? Or yourself and your bank account?"

"I don't know what you're talking about," Boulder growled before turning away.

Growling some more as he strode towards the smorgasbord, Boulder thought what a fool young Jimmy was. So, too, Elsbeth. The lawyer wasn't blind. Had seen how she'd wriggled her way between the newlyweds out there on the reef, like they needed any more tension between them.

He scooped up an oyster, sniffed it, then dropped it back again. *Oh Ellie*, he thought again, *you silly, doddering fool.*

It wasn't the first time she'd overstepped, and it wouldn't be the last. Despite his pleas, she was refusing to give the young ones their space, certainly refusing to be choppered off, and there was nothing he could do about that. The captain seemed equally as hamstrung, so too that Simon Barrier fellow who was obviously part of management the way he swanned about.

Boulder leaned over what looked like grilled swordfish and scowled.

"Were you after anything in particular, sir?" asked the waiter, now cramming two plates with food, and the older man shook his head.

"Has Elsbeth returned yet? I don't see her at our table."

"I am not sure, sir. Would you like me to check her room for you?"

"No, no, you've got your hands full, and Ellie loves her diving. I'm sure she won't die of starvation if she misses one meal."

But he did wonder why she was taking so long. Perhaps she'd finally given up her quest and was enjoying herself instead, although he doubted it. Elsbeth knew how to have fun, but it was always at someone else's expense. He'd learned that the hard way.

Young Indya would be learning that for the rest of her marriage, if indeed she survived it.

~

Captain Flinders was dragging a finger down the digital logbook Gary had left, her hair slicked back beneath her black-and-white cap, when the chief stewardess appeared at the bridge door. She had a slightly harried look about her.

"Sorry to disturb, Liz," Pasha said. "But you did want to finish up early today and get moving to Sunset Lagoon."

"It's *Captain Flinders* now, remember?" said Liz,

pointing to her cap. "And what of it?"

"Well, we're still waiting on Mrs Wynter. Roland says she's still diving, so he's heading out now on the zodiac to lure her back. Usually our delicious buffet does the trick, but... well..."

"Oh, that is annoying," said the captain. "Which Mrs Wynter are we talking about?"

"Sorry?"

Liz sighed. "We have two Mrs Wynters on board in case you haven't noticed, Pasha. Is it the young one who's still diving or the older one?"

"Oh, I'm not sure. I just assumed..." Pasha stopped and smudged her lips downwards. "Does it matter?"

Liz stared at her for a moment, then mirrored her smudge. "I guess not." She glanced at her watch. "Okay, we can put it off another hour; that's no big deal. We should still be able to make the lagoon in time for sunset." Then she turned to the screen and began studying it before glancing back at Pasha, who was lingering in the doorway. "Was that it?"

Pasha hesitated, drew in some breath. "It's about Freddy."

Liz frowned. "What about him?"

"I thought we were getting rid of him after the last cruise and getting Gabriel back."

"Gabriel has returned to the Philippines, so I'm afraid you're stuck with Freddy."

"But he's hopeless!"

Liz closed her eyes as though bracing herself as Pasha continued. "I know you... well, I know you have a soft spot for the young lad, but he's utterly useless. He was supposed to help me with cocktails last night but didn't even show until halfway through it."

"He was probably busy turning down the beds."

"There are *six* beds, Liz. I mean *Captain*. How long does that take? I really could have done with his help in the lounge, what with all the drama coming from the new arrivals. As for his silver-service skills? I'm not convinced he has any! He spilt asparagus spears in Claire Hargreaves's lap last night. Thank goodness it was Claire. Anyone else would have made quite a fuss."

"What do you suggest I do about it now, Pasha?" Liz flung a hand in the air. "Dump him out here on a pontoon and see if there's a spare butler floating about?"

Pasha frowned. "No, of course not. It's just... Where did you *find* him?"

The captain closed her eyes briefly, took in a deep breath. "I really don't have time for this. Work around him, do your best, handle it. Will you please?"

Pasha shrugged. "Fine."

"Good," said Liz, exhaling heavily as she returned to studying the log.

~

As he steered the light dinghy across the tranquil water towards the outer pontoon, his eyes scanning the horizon, Roland wondered if Mrs Wynter had got lost out here and felt a moment of joy before his stomach dropped. He recalled a fellow instructor who lost a handful of divers not far from here some years ago. They were all found eventually, severely sunburned and dehydrated, clinging onto the reef. He could think of nothing worse than losing someone on his watch. It had taken a lot of nifty sidestepping to clinch this job and a lot of hours sucking up to Liz Flinders, whom he first met while giving a talk about the reef at a black-tie dinner back in Cairns. Marine conservation was his first love, diving just a side hobby, but there were not a lot of jobs to go around on yachts like this, and so he'd agreed to lead the expeditions in exchange for all this glorious time on the water pursuing his research.

And his mission, his *real* mission, but he couldn't think about that now...

Roland surveyed the sea again, and it did not look so tranquil suddenly. A growing wind was causing surface ripples, and the water was getting darker, which meant it was also getting deeper. And that was ominous. Surely she hadn't dived this far?

He felt a trickle of annoyance more than anything. He had clearly instructed them all to stay between the yacht and the first pontoon. Was assured that they would. This wasn't Osprey, but the reef dropped away here quite dramatically, and he hoped he didn't have to jump in and swim after her. He was still in his wetsuit but had only a face mask with him, and he wasn't in the mood now, had had quite enough of entitled rich brats for one day.

Stalling the engine, he reached for his mask and then leaned over the side of the dinghy, immersing his face in the water, looking this way and that. And finally he saw her, about ten metres down, just above a rock on an outer reef. Exactly where she shouldn't be.

Furious, he revved the engine and raced across to her, telling himself to calm down, he had to play this sensibly. These rich brats held all the cards; he could not afford to lose his temper.

Not if he wanted to fulfil his mission.

As he got closer, Roland cut the engine so as not to startle the woman, but she did not surface, which surprised him. He looked down again and noticed there were no air bubbles anywhere near her, and his heart suddenly felt as though it was trapped in a vice, as a spike of adrenaline rushed through him.

It was in that moment that Roland realised there *was* something worse than misplacing a guest out here on the reef.

Something much, much worse.

CHAPTER 7
But Which Mrs Wynter?

Claire was polishing off a cup of Earl Grey tea when she noticed the chief stewardess dash in from the stairwell, her expression, well, *odd*. Pasha's eyes were too wide, her smile too stiff, her hands clutching onto each other as though for dear life as she strode across to Freddy. He was calmly rearranging some platters, but his calm dropped away as she began to whisper in his ear, and now Claire's interest was piqued. She continued watching as Freddy's eyes also widened, then swept across to James Wynter, who was still alone at his table, sucking on a lobster claw and staring out to sea.

Pasha said something more, then took a deep breath and marched across the deck towards him.

"Something's happened," Claire whispered to Simon, who was working his way through half a pineapple that had been packed with every other kind of fruit. "Ms Perky is looking peaky."

Simon held the spoon up and glanced towards Pasha. "I think that's just her look, darling. She's one of those worrier types. Perhaps they've run out of dessert? Hope not. This fruit salad's delicious. You really should get one."

"Something's going down, I'm telling you."

Simon chuckled. "We're not with your book club now, Claire. The only mystery here is how the chef gets his hands on fresh raspberries this close to the equator."

Claire went to object, then thought better of it. He was

probably right. She was clearly turning into Alicia from book club, seeing danger at every turn. Still, she wasn't the only one. Boulder and Cindy were also watching Pasha intensely as she squatted down beside James and began whispering something into his ear.

Whatever she said, James wasn't at all alarmed. Just put out.

"For Pete's sake, can't a man eat his lunch in peace?" He tossed the claw over the side of the yacht. "And what's she still doing on the dive deck?"

Not waiting for an answer, he pushed his chair back, dumped his serviette on the table, and marched off, Pasha close behind.

"Back in a jiffy," said Claire, discarding her own serviette.

"Everything okay?" Simon spluttered, mid-mouthful.

Offering him a breezy smile, she followed fast behind Pasha. But instead of heading portside as they had done, Claire took the starboard stairs and dashed down that side of the boat, towards the lower deck.

She knew something was up. There was no denying it. And yet Claire wasn't prepared for what she was about to see when she got to the dive platform.

A woman's body was lying prone across the deck, and a man was leaning over her, smashing away at her chest like he wanted to kill her. No, Claire realised, Dr Roland was doing the opposite, trying to bring the poor woman to life while the captain watched, knuckles gripping onto her cap, horrified.

Roland was counting aloud as he performed CPR— "Twenty-eight… twenty-nine… thirty!"—then Liz threw herself on the woman's lips, puffing air in awkwardly.

"You have to pinch the nose!" cried Gary, who was just reaching the deck himself. "Here, let me."

He pushed Liz aside and took over the breathing, then sat back as Roland began another round of chest compressions.

"What's going on?" came James's booming voice as he too finally reached the platform. Then, shakier, more strangled: "My God! Is that... *Mother*?"

Still clad in her full wetsuit, her dive gear discarded beside her, Elsbeth Wynter had lost her cheeky spark. She seemed almost doll-like as the crew worked hard around her.

"Mother?" James repeated, rushing across the deck only to be stopped midway by the captain.

"Just let them do their thing, James. Please. Let them *try*."

While Roland kept right on counting: "Twenty-eight... twenty-nine... thirty!"

Now it was Gary's turn again, and he leaned forward, bringing his mouth down tightly over Elsbeth's lips, one hand clinching shut her nose. Two heavy puffs of air.

All to no avail.

But that didn't stop Roland, who resumed chest compressions once again as the deck quickly filled with passengers—first Simon, who'd followed Claire and was now standing behind her, then Boulder, who was just behind James, one hand grasping his shoulder, Pasha grasping the other, like they were holding him in place. Behind them were the Dudley-Pines and Freddy, all three staring, aghast. Disbelieving. Shocked.

The only person missing was Indya, but Claire wasn't sure anyone noticed. All eyes were on Elsbeth and her lips, waiting for the watery splutter that never came.

Eventually, after a final effort, Roland gave up and dropped back on the deck, exhausted, while James finally wrenched free of his captors and fell down towards his mother.

As he did so, he screamed, "No!" while Pasha cried out, "Keep going!" But it was pointless. There would be no bringing Elsbeth back.

And so Captain Flinders offered her condolences as

James clutched onto the cold, limp body of his mother.

There was a period of stunned silence as they watched him gently brush the hair from Elsbeth's face, slowly release a gold chain that was caught behind her ears, softly stroke her crepey cheeks, before dropping his head into her neck and sobbing. Then it must have hit him, finally, and he looked up, his features contorted as he turned to Roland.

"What did you do to her?" he croaked.

"What? No, sir, I didn't—"

"Mr Wynter, we're so sorry," Captain Flinders said again, stepping in and nudging the instructor backwards. "Roland discovered your mother out past the second pontoon. We performed CPR, tried everything we could, but it was too late."

"Too late?" James cried, eyes still on the dive instructor. "But... how could this happen?"

"I... I don't know," Roland spluttered. "She was gone when I found her. I don't know if she had a medical episode or..."

"My mother was as strong as on ox!"

"Yes, but she was out there for some time."

"What was she *doing* out there by herself?"

Roland flinched at that, and Liz stepped forward again. "It will all be investigated, sir, we—"

"You bet your arse it'll be investigated!" came a booming voice behind her, and Liz swung around to look at Boulder, and that's when she finally realised she needed to bring the spectacle to a close.

She flashed Pasha a disappointed look, then held two hands up and addressed the group. "Please, everyone, I know it's very distressing, but James deserves some privacy. You need to vacate the platform."

Yet no one seemed to hear her, including Pasha, who was dumbstruck for a moment longer before finally snapping out of it.

"Yes, come on, please, people!" she called out.

"Let's go back inside."

The Dudley-Pines didn't look like they wanted to go anywhere, but they did turn away, as did Claire, until Simon grabbed her by the elbow.

"No, stay. Please."

Captain Flinders looked ready to object, but Boulder was now pushing past her and reaching down towards Elsbeth, huffing a little as he went. He seemed to be checking for life, as if no one had thought to do that, then he patted James gently on the back and used the railing to pull himself up.

"I'm going to need to know exactly what happened here," he said, his voice now eerily calm. "But not right now. Let's give Jimmy a moment with his mother, hey?"

James's back stiffened then, but it clearly wasn't his mother he was thinking of. "Oh God, Indy. I have to tell Indy."

Then he finally let go of Elsbeth and stumbled to his feet.

"We can do that for you," said Simon, but James was shaking his head, rushing past them all now and making a beeline for the carriageway.

Once again, Claire was hot on his trail.

Indya Wynter had finally made it to lunch and was seated at her table, seemingly oblivious to all the commotion at the lower end of the yacht. Or to the fact that everybody had vanished and she was the only one eating. Not that she was doing a lot of that, just picking at a plate of green salad in front of her and casually scrolling through her iPhone, an almost bored look on her perfect tanned face, her white hair scooped high in a messy, wet ponytail, a bright sundress on.

Nor did she look up as her husband approached, and it was only as he dropped to the ground beside her and began to speak that she pulled her eyes from her device and towards him. Claire was watching from the buffet table, wondering if she should step forward if things got emotional, which was how she managed to see the tiniest flicker of relief sweep across the young woman's face just before it morphed into shock and concern.

Claire wasn't sure if James had clocked it, but she had a pretty good idea that Boulder had.

He was standing just behind Claire, and when she turned to look at him, he said, "Oh well, at least there's one silver lining, I suppose."

CHAPTER 8
Bring Up the Body Bag!

Unexpected deaths were a ship captain's worst nightmare and not just because it was deeply unpleasant for everyone involved. There was also the minor matter of what to do with a decomposing body in the middle of nowhere.

While large cruise ships usually had cold rooms for such a purpose, smaller vessels like the *Living Large* have no such convenience, but they did carry body bags, thankfully, and it was into one of those that the elderly lady was now being gently manoeuvred by Roland and Gary.

"Where will you put her?" Simon asked Liz, still watching from the dive deck.

"There are several empty staff cabins on the lower deck. We'll place her in one of those until I work out what to do next."

The captain looked flummoxed, and Simon didn't blame her. "Have you ever—?"

"No." She gave him an apologetic smile. "I haven't been captain long, as you know, but even as first officer before that, nothing like this ever happened on my watch. Of course, there were deaths when I worked the larger cruise ships, but I was never senior enough to deal with it directly."

He squeezed her shoulder. "We'll work it out." Then a quick glance at his Rolex watch. "Boulder wants to meet with us in your quarters soon. We'd better make tracks."

Liz nodded but her eyes were now locked to the body

bag, her brow deeply furrowed, like it was only just occurring to her the enormity of the situation.

"Liz?" Simon said. "Are you okay?"

"What?" She shook herself out. "Of course, yes. Let's get going."

She gave the men some final instructions, then led the way up to the bridge deck where the captain's quarters were located. It was actually two separate spaces—one a private stateroom so she could sleep close to all the action; the other a compact office, complete with its own kitchenette, sofa set, and a desk with two chairs in front of it, and it was here they met up with Boulder.

He had changed into a fresh shirt but had the same steely expression in his eyes, so Liz headed for a small cabinet and pulled out a bottle of bourbon whisky, holding it aloft.

The lawyer nodded and said, "I hope there's something stiff for James back in his cabin. He's there with Indya now. Both in complete shock. I've asked Pasha to look in on them. I don't know what I'm going to say to the rest of the family, to the company, to the shareholders..." He shook himself a little. "For starters, let's just get the facts."

Simon tried not to scowl at what felt like insensitivity, and yet he understood the man's concerns. His own mind was wafting to his company, his shareholders, and his stomach began to tighten.

Boulder took the tumbler Liz was now handing him and turned his watery green eyes upon him. "I've only just had it confirmed that you're the owner of this vessel."

His tone was almost accusatory, and Simon tried not to bristle as he also accepted a tumbler. "Co-owner and, yes, I didn't want to advertise the fact. I'm not here on business. I'm on my honeymoon." *Unlike you* he could have added, but diplomacy was needed now and lots of it.

Boulder slugged his whisky down in one gulp just as Roland appeared still in his diving gear.

"Everything sorted?" Liz asked.

He nodded. "Cabin B6."

She returned the nod, then waved a hand. "Come in, Roland. I believe Mr Boulder has some questions. Please let's all take a seat."

The older men settled into the sofas while Roland perched uneasily on the edge of a chair, like he was worried about wetting the furnishings. Or perhaps he was hoping to slip away at the first opportunity.

"So what happened? Do you know? Did she have a heart attack?" demanded Boulder.

Liz held a hand up. "I'm not sure Roland can answer that at this stage, Mr Boulder, but let's get the basics first, shall we?" She was sitting on the edge of her desk, her hands clasped in her lap as she stared at the instructor. "Have you had a chance to inspect the equipment yet?"

He shook his head, and she looked disappointed.

Roland blushed at that. "I… I thought you needed me here quickly."

"Well, do that after this. But first, if I remember procedure correctly, we have to alert the Maritime Authority and prepare an incident report, and I can't do that without the facts, so let's get a precise breakdown of exactly what happened and when. From the beginning please. When did you all start diving?"

She reached for a leather-bound notepad on her desk and an elegant-looking biro, then took the spare desk chair and nodded for Roland to begin.

He cleared his throat. "Right… So the diving excursion was scheduled for just after breakfast, as it always is. We all met at the platform at around nine. I got everyone fitted up with gear, and we went through the usual safety procedures."

"Fat lot of good that did," murmured Boulder, and Roland winced.

Liz ignored the comment and said, "Who was there? Exactly."

"Um, just two couples at that stage. James and Indya Wynter and the Dudley-Pines." He glanced at Simon. "You and Claire were also there, but you were about to go snorkelling."

Simon nodded. "And Elsbeth Wynter?"

"She was not with us initially," he explained. "I gave my usual instructions to both couples, who assured me they had some diving experience, a quick run-through of the equipment, checked everyone's gear was working and then led them to the nearest pontoon for an initial shallow dive. We really could have done it with snorkels, it was that shallow, but it was a test run, an orientation dive we call it, to make sure everyone's up to speed and also in preparation for the big dive tomorrow at Osprey. People often exaggerate their skills, you see."

"What do you mean by that?" Boulder demanded.

He looked embarrassed again. "Ms Wynter—Indya—was not as experienced as she claimed. Nor was Connor for that matter. I was glad to have the chance to run them through their paces, but I was going to recommend they avoid the Drop tomorrow."

"So where does Elsbeth Wynter fit in?" asked Liz, confused.

"Mrs Wynter joined us soon after we'd set off for our second dive. We always do an initial short dive, just to dip the toes, then have a quick break back at the yacht, then a longer dive after that. We were on that longer dive when I noticed Mrs Wynter waving from the yacht. The others were all diving happily enough around the pontoon at that stage, so I signalled for them to stay close and swam back to get her hooked up."

"Did you check her gear?" demanded Boulder.

He nodded furiously. "It was all in working order. Top shape. She had a full tank of air. I turned it all the way on myself, and then we both swam back to the group. She insisted she didn't need lessons, but I did watch her for a bit, just in case." His jaw tightened. "She appeared to be very proficient. Swam off like a seal she did! I... I had no concerns..."

Boulder glared at him, and Liz reached for the whisky and poured him another shot, then asked Roland, "What time did you notice she was missing?"

"I didn't, Captain. Not initially." He scraped shaky fingers through his damp hair, releasing it from its ponytail. "At 11:50 a.m. we were starting to run low on air again, and so I signalled for the guests to return to the boat for lunch. The dive was over."

"And where was Mrs Wynter at that point?" asked Simon, sitting forward.

Roland blinked. "Um... that's right, she was on the other side of the pontoon—the first pontoon—so I swam across and gave her the same signal as the others, but she..." He smiled awkwardly. "She made it clear she wanted me to go away." Another uncomfortable look. "I made her surface and reminded her that she probably had just ten minutes or so left in her tank. She said she would swim back to the yacht when she was good and ready, or words to that effect..." He paused again, still looking embarrassed, and Boulder held up a hand.

"Hang on. How long had she been out there? How long does the air last?"

"As I said, usually about forty-five minutes, sir, which is why we do several dives over the morning. But it does depend on the diver's experience. A good diver can make it last a full hour, a novice tends to breathe heavier and often only gets half that."

"And Mrs Wynter?" asked Simon.

"She was an excellent diver!" said Boulder, his tone fierce.

Roland nodded. "That's what I deduced. That's why I wasn't concerned. Also, as I said, she started later than everyone else and hadn't been diving deep. Not deep enough to get into any kind of trouble. If she did run out of air, she'd be back at the surface in seconds, could just swim back like the others."

Boulder verbally growled at that but said nothing.

"So what happened after you left Mrs Wynter?" asked Liz.

"I swam back to the yacht."

"Where were the others at that stage?" asked Simon.

He paused for just a moment, then shrugged. "They'd all returned, as you had. I mean, I saw Connor on the dive platform, and he told me his wife had gone to their cabin to change. I assumed the others had done the same. Connor needed help getting out of his wetsuit—he was struggling a little." Then a look of apology at Boulder as he added, "He's a very bulky man; he should have chosen a larger size. After that I wished him a pleasant lunch and made my way to the galley to get myself a sandwich."

"So when did you work out Mrs Wynter was missing?" asked Liz, frowning.

"Freddy came down to tell the chef to go easy on the food as half the women were missing. That got me worried."

"Finally!" said Boulder, throwing his arms in the air.

Liz looked up from her notes. "What time was this exactly?"

Roland shook his head. "I got back to the yacht just after twelve. I guess Freddy came down about twelve thirty?" He rubbed a hand over his mouth. "I didn't think too much of it to be honest." A wary glance at Boulder. "They often miss meals, the women. There's a lot of food wastage on this yacht. It's almost criminal." A frown flickered across his brow. "Anyway, I went to the dive platform to check the gear, just to be sure, and that's when I noticed all sets were back except one. Mrs Wynter's. So I told Pasha I was heading back out to find her."

He took a long breath, and when he spoke again, he seemed calmer, more assured, like he was presenting his case to a coroner. "I circled the first pontoon and could not see her, so I headed to the one further out. I located Mrs Wynter just after 12:40. She was just above a shallow rock, about ten metres to the northeast of the second pontoon. I manoeuvred the dinghy closer and saw that she did not appear to be breathing. I dived straight in, released her heavy weight belt, and somehow got her onto the dinghy, tank and all. Don't know how I did it; the adrenaline must have kicked in. I performed preliminary CPR, then gunned it back here for help. But… well, I believe she was deceased when I found her." Another quick glance at Boulder. "There was nobody else present. She was completely alone."

"Well, there's your first mistake," Boulder growled. "Isn't there supposed to be a buddy system… or, er, something?"

Roland glanced at Liz and then back. "It is protocol to have a dive partner. But she refused one."

"So? You should have demanded it! Or is it also protocol to let guests do exactly what they please even if it kills them?"

His words were like a slap across Roland's face, and his cheeks lit up again, but Liz was having none of it.

"Mr Boulder," she said, her tone authoritative, albeit a little wobbly. "It's not normal, you are correct, but when the guest is as stubborn as I think we can all agree Mrs Wynter was *and* when that guest's so-called husband demands we keep her as far away from her daughter-in-law as possible, these things can happen."

She gave the lawyer a defiant look, and he stared at her, outraged for a moment, then exhaled like he'd just been pricked.

Roland said, "I'm so sorry about all this." He was addressing the captain, not Boulder. "She assured me she'd been diving for decades; she said she'd be okay. I'd never normally—"

"We'll discuss all that later, Roland," Liz said, her tone flat. "Please check the dive gear now, make sure everything is in order, and report back to me directly when you're done. Just me, got it?"

He nodded and stood up, went to say something to Boulder, who was staring glassy-eyed at the carpet, but Liz shook her head, so he simply turned and left the office. She filled a jug with water, then poured them each a glass.

"Once Roland's checked the equipment," she said, "I'll email in my report."

Boulder looked up. "But what will you say? I'm no clearer than I was before. Was it her heart? Did she drown?"

"I can't tell you that. None of us can. Judging by her age, it was most likely a medical episode. These things do happen, I'm afraid. We will remove Mrs Wynter's body at the earliest opportunity, and an autopsy will need to be performed. There's not much more we can do at this stage, but I would like to get the yacht moving if that's okay with you both." She glanced between Simon and Boulder. "We're miles from Cooktown, so we'll need to get cracking. We'll head straight there. It's the closest port town. Mrs Wynter will probably be transported by ambulance down to Cairns after that."

Simon nodded but Boulder seemed ready to object, then just exhaled again and pulled himself up.

"Do what you have to do," he said. "I need to look in on Jimmy."

"Of course," Liz said. "Please let us know if there's anything we can do."

"I think you've done enough, don't you?"

His tone was bitter, and now she looked like she'd been slapped.

Simon said, "Mr Boulder—"

The man held a hand up. "My apologies, Captain. It's been…" He let that drop.

Simon shepherded him to the door lest the man's fury flare up again.

As he went to leave, Boulder stopped and turned back.

"So this is all just a terrible accident, is that what you're saying?"

Simon looked at him astonished. "Of course. What else?"

Boulder looked visibly relieved as he turned away.

CHAPTER 9
Blaming the Equipment

"*Of course* it's a terrible accident," said Simon, standing just outside the bridge, repeating Boulder's words to Claire as they watched the yacht slowly manoeuvre away from the fatal reef and perform a U-turn. The infamous Osprey drop was now off the itinerary, and they were heading southwest, straight for the mainland. "It's just a terrible, tragic accident, that's all it is."

Claire had intercepted Simon as he left the captain's office, offering him a cup of black coffee and a comforting hug.

"I should be comforting you," he said. "This is all such a debacle. God knows how I'm going to explain it to Tommo."

Claire tried not to frown. Surely Simon's business partner, Tommo, wasn't a priority? There was definitely something whiffy about Mrs Wynter's demise. And it didn't help that the daughter-in-law looked far too relieved when James broke the news. But that's not what fuelled Claire's suspicion. Hell, who wouldn't be ever-so-slightly relieved to see the back end of their nemesis? No, Claire thought, as she felt the engine surge and pick up pace, there were worse expressions than relief.

Like, say, unadulterated delight.

And she had seen *that* expression on several faces down there on that gusty diving platform as Roland pumped away at the old lady's heart, trying in vain to bring her back to life. She had seen it on Cindy's face. And Pasha's.

And, most shockingly of all, the lawyer's.

"Will Boulder accompany the body?" Claire asked Simon. "Along with James? Do you think?"

"I assume so. And Indya of course. I mean, they're hardly going to continue holidaying now."

Claire nodded sadly, thinking how ironic it was that Elsbeth's mission to disrupt her son's honeymoon had been such a spectacular success. Then she swatted the ungracious thought away. "And the Dudley-Pines? Do you think they'll stay?"

"I believe Pasha is consulting with them now. We're offering a full refund should they wish to disembark in Cooktown. Can arrange complimentary flights home from there. We understand this can be distressing. We've also reached out to the fifth couple, a Mr and Mrs Tanner, who were due to join us in a few days."

"Oh goodness, I forgot all about them. You think they'll want to cancel?"

"It does rather put a pall over the whole thing." Then he met her eyes. "I'm so, so sorry."

"It wasn't your fault, Simon."

"Yes, but I promised you there would be no deaths and look what's happened. Everything's ruined."

Claire went to object—he really had so much still to learn about her—when she saw Roland approach, the stricken look still etched in his sun-scorched face. Her heart reached out to him as he gave her a quick nod and then looked at Simon.

"I have news about the dive equipment, and it's not good."

"Oh dear," said Simon just as the captain swung her office door wide.

He repeated the words to Liz, and she looked a little startled.

"You better come inside," she squeaked, glancing up and down the deck.

"I'll join you," said Simon, turning back to Claire.

"Could you do me a favour and see how the other guests are faring?"

"Of course," said Claire, trying to hide the disappointment in her voice. She'd rather stay and hear the startling news.

"The valve was turned off," were the first words out of Roland's mouth the moment the door closed behind them.

Liz blinked at him mutely for a moment, then waved them into chairs and hovered over them, hands on her hips. "That can't be right, Roland. You mean it was turned *on*? As normal? Yes?"

Roland shook his head, sadly. "No, Captain. When I found Elsbeth Wynter out on the water, her valve was off. And I didn't do it."

"No, of course you didn't," she said quickly, "but are you *sure* you're not confused? I mean, it's easy to get muddled with all the drama. Did you double-check the valve again, like I asked you to?" He nodded with certainty as she paled before their eyes.

"It was off, Liz. There's no sugar-coating this one."

The captain drew two hands to her face. "But... don't you see what this means? How this will look... especially for *you*, Roland? You were the instructor; you might never work again."

Simon held a hand up. "Easy there, I'm not sure it will come to that."

He glanced at Roland, but he had paled too.

"I know what this means," the instructor said. "I know it's horrific, but I have to tell the truth. And the truth is the valve was off."

"Damn it," said Liz, collapsing into a chair.

"I'm confused," said Simon. "Does it matter at this stage? Really?"

Now Liz was shaking her head and Roland sat forward.

"It does matter, Simon, it makes all the difference in the world. There's very little chance Mrs Wynter could have done it herself, so if the valve was off, it means she was likely murdered."

Then Simon's tan also drained away.

CHAPTER 10
Oxygen Thief

Sergio looked murderous as he stared down Pasha in the galley, but she wasn't budging.

"I know a woman has just died, Chef, you don't need to tell me that, but it doesn't mean our good service has to die with her. *Of course* we stick to the itinerary, and that means afternoon tea needs to get out to the sun deck in the next hour. And I expect the usual assortment of light sandwiches and cakes."

"But what is the point? They barely ate the lunch."

"That's not your concern. The guests have paid for afternoon tea, so we present it as usual."

"And if it goes to waste like half the seafood? I just binned two dozen oysters!"

"So? Nobody's going to dock it from your salary."

He made a *pft* sound. "What salary? I barely earn a pittance."

"Take it up with the captain," she slapped back. "But not before you get cooking. And make sure there's plenty of herbal tea today please. They're going to want something soothing after what they've just been through."

"Forget the tea, I should brew some of my famous rum punch after all this mayhem and murder."

"Murder?" Pasha took a step back. "Who said anything about murder? Mrs Wynter just drowned… didn't she?"

He looked flustered again and yelled, "Get out, woman! I have cakes to bake!"

~

Back in the captain's office, Liz was grasping two hands at her mouth, like she was trying to swallow that word down even though it had come from Roland.

"Murder?" Simon repeated, making her blanch further.

"Yes," said the divemaster, his voice now barely audible. "When I first reached Mrs Wynter out there on the water, I was in a bit of a panic. I just assumed she'd run out of air. I mean, why else would she drown? On the way back to the yacht, I checked the valve on her tank and saw that it had been turned to the Off position, which is weird."

"But…" Simon was confused. "Could she have turned it off herself?"

Roland lifted one sinewy shoulder. "No way. I mean, I doubt it. She'd have to be extremely flexible. The knob that closes the valve is behind her, attached to her back. But even if she did, even if she could have, even if she'd decided her dive was over and was going to swim back to the yacht, she would not turn off the air. It makes no sense."

Simon nodded. "No. Right, stupid suggestion." He turned to Liz, who was now slumped in her chair, chewing on her nails.

"Oh my God," she began wailing. "My second captaincy! I'm never going to live this down. I'll lose my license. I'll never get another posting…"

Simon leaned across and grabbed her hand, gave it a gentle squeeze.

"Let's just take a deep breath here." Then a wince at his appalling pun. "There has to be another explanation. Could the equipment be faulty? Could it have turned itself off? Roland?"

He knew it was another stupid question, and Roland's expression confirmed it.

"I checked and rechecked the gear myself before the

dive. I always do. It's the best equipment. Virtually unused. There would not be a fault, but even if there was, it would not involve the air valve." He shook his head. "The fact is it's possibly the safest apparatus on the planet. They've fool-proofed the hell out of it, sir. It's a mechanical dial, can't be bumped or turn itself off. If she didn't turn it off—and I honestly can't imagine her doing it—then…"

"Someone else turned it off," said Simon. "Okay I get that, but could it have been innocent? Maybe they thought they were turning it on, giving her more air, not less."

Again Roland did not look convinced. "That's not how it works, sir. It can only be on or off. If someone turned it off, Mrs Wynter would have known and signalled for them to correct it."

Now Simon paled. "And if they refused?"

"Depends how deep she was. I found her out past that second pontoon. There is a significant drop there. She might have panicked, hyperventilated, struggled to reach the surface in time and passed away from lack of air, or…"

"Or?"

Roland swapped a look with Liz, who had her shoulders up around her ears. "Or she might have been deliberately held under. Like I said, she was elderly. It would not have been hard."

"Bloody hell," said Simon, as he finally accepted the obvious and dropped back into his chair.

There were many minutes of stunned silence as all three swapped worried frowns. Then Simon sat forward and cleared his throat.

"Okay, let's try to see this through to its logical conclusion, shall we? Who was diving with Mrs Wynter? Who was in the vicinity? Who could have done this thing?"

Roland looked perplexed. "No one, Simon. Everyone else had returned to lunch, and I found her completely alone."

"Well, you can't have it both ways, man! Either she turned it off herself or somebody else did it!" He was yelling and he knew it. Took his own deep breath, tried to calm himself. "Sorry, it's just… well, it's very perplexing."

"It's a bloody disaster is what it is!" said Liz. "This changes everything. We're past just reporting this. Now I need to radio it in and confirm a suspicious death." She glanced at Roland, worriedly. "That sparks off a whole different set of maritime procedures. We'll need to bring someone on board to properly investigate. That's the protocol. We need to get statements from everyone, images of all the equipment… And we haven't even said anything yet to James or Boulder. Oh God, they're going to explode."

"They don't know? About the valve?"

Another glance at Roland as he shook his head. "I came straight to you, like you asked, Captain. You're the only ones who know."

"I think Claire has probably guessed," said Simon, then, noticing Liz's panicked expression, he quickly said, "Don't worry, she's discreet."

"I think Gary's guessed too," said Roland. "He had a suspicious look when I passed him at the bridge earlier."

Liz closed her eyes briefly. "He's going to love this." She sighed heavily and opened her eyes. "But I can't worry about that now. I'm concerned for the guests, Simon. This is not going to be pretty. They are going to have to be detained in Cooktown for questioning, and who knows how long that will take. And we haven't even considered the press…"

"Shouldn't we just push on straight to Cairns?" said Simon.

"That's another two days of sailing, and I'd rather unload the body if it's all right with you."

He nodded. "Yes, of course."

How had a happy honeymoon cruise come to this? thought Simon now as they swapped frowns again. One minute they were frolicking in the sea, the next they were discussing a murder investigation. He couldn't wrap his head around it, none of them could, least of all Liz, who was back to ranting mode.

"It's going to be such a *scandal*. An absolute bloody circus! The guests are going to sue us, the police are going to be all over us—"

"The police?" said Roland. "You're bringing in the police?"

"Yes, Roland! What did you think? It's a murder inquiry now. Who else do we bring in? Santa Claus?"

"I know someone," said Simon, leaping to his feet.

"Sorry?" she said.

He held up a palm, scratched at his cheek, gave it some more thought. Then he said, "I need to get Claire in here."

"I don't think that's appropriate—"

He cut her off. "You also think this is murder, and if that's true, it will be more than a bloody circus. It could mark the end of your job and everyone else's. This yacht will be seized and impounded; they'll crawl through all our lives. Believe me, I've been through this before and it's traumatic." He turned to Roland. "There's a slim chance she could have turned it off herself. You said that, yes?"

Roland looked uncertain. Held a hand up and reached it back behind his neck. "Very, very slim."

"But a chance nonetheless," said Simon. "Perhaps she got disoriented out there and did it in a moment of panic. I don't know, but I do know I'm not willing to risk everything until we know for absolute certain."

They both stared at him frowning as he added, "I have a solution, and it involves my wife's book club."

The captain's scowl deepened as he bolted for the door.

CHAPTER 11
A Cry for Help

The book club were just finishing their lively analysis of *The Woman in Cabin 10* when Alicia got the call. Followed quickly by another. She was congratulating Queenie on an exceptional range of questions—their best yet perhaps, although she kept that from Missy, who was looking uncharacteristically sullen—and let the calls go to voice mail, not recognising the number, assuming it was spam. A few minutes later she ignored a call from Jackson.

"You're popular today," said Ronnie.

"Well, it's book club day, so they can all just wait."

"Actually, I've also got a call to return," said Queenie, holding up her phone although no one had heard it ringing. "I'm sorry to bail so quickly, but I'll need to go to the office for this one. It sounds urgent."

"But it's Sunday," said Lynette. "And your boss is miles away—on a cruise with Claire."

Queenie also happened to be Simon Barrier's executive assistant at Living Large Enterprises—that's how she'd discovered the book club—but she didn't reply to that, just smiled mysteriously and left them to it.

It was sometime later, once the books were firmly shut and fresh wine bottles opened, that Alicia got a third call from that strange number. Once again she let it go to voice mail, but Ronnie was not happy.

"You young people are hopeless at picking up. It could be urgent."

"It is, Ronnie," said Perry Gordon, stroking his goatee nefariously. "Someone urgently needs Alicia to put ten thousand dollars into a phoney bank account."

Missy fell into a fit of giggles as Alicia reached for her mobile.

"Fine," she said. "I'll check it out, just for you, Ronnie. But first I'll see what Jackson wants."

Her detective boyfriend knew better than to call her on Book Club Sunday, and she was about to tell him exactly that when his own phone went straight to voice mail.

Okay, *that* was odd.

"He always picks up," she murmured, imagining Jackson tangled under a bus or hanging from a power line, no longer able to reach out...

"Everything okay?" This was Lynette, and Alicia shook the typically dark thoughts away and then listened to the first saved message. It was from Claire.

"It's not her usual number," Alicia told them as she began to listen. "She must have used the ship's phone."

"Aww, she's missing us already," said Missy.

"That doesn't bode well for her marriage," was Ronnie's comment. "She should be focusing on her new husband, Simon."

Lynette nearly choked on her merlot. "It's not the fifties anymore, Ronnie!"

"I don't care what year it is," Ronnie replied. "Good manners are perennial. So too is romance. They're on their honeymoon for goodness' sake! Something's not kosher."

Alicia stared at her phone. Scratched her blond pixie hairdo. "Mmm, she did sound weird. Just said hello and said she needed to speak to Jackson urgently."

"Jackson? That's even weirder," said Perry. "Why would Claire need to speak to *your* boyfriend while she's on *her* honeymoon?"

"I'm telling you," said Ronnie. "It does not bode well."

"Maybe the woman in cabin ten has gone missing?" suggested Missy, eyes glinting behind her thick red spectacles as she pointed to the book they'd been discussing.

"Or maybe someone's fallen overboard, like the cruise where Jackson and I met," said Alicia, and now Lynette was tsking again.

"Don't let your imaginations run wild, peeps. I'm sure it's nothing."

Alicia placed the phone to her ear to listen to the second message Claire had left, except it wasn't from Claire this time, it was from Simon, and it was a lot longer than the first.

As she listened, the others began to chat amongst themselves until something in Alicia's expression had them staring at her again.

"You've got to be kidding me," said Lynette.

"No way!" squealed Missy.

"What?" demanded Ronnie, who hadn't been in the group long enough to recognise the signs writ large across Alicia's face.

"There's been another murder," whispered Perry, a finger to his lips.

When Alicia finished listening to the message, however, even Perry was confused. Oddly, Alicia looked both exhilarated and deeply disappointed.

"What?" screamed Perry now. "What is it?"

"There's good news and bad," she replied. "The good news is, there *has* been another murder, on Simon's superyacht."

"That's the *good* news?" said Ronnie, appalled.

"You'll get used to us," said Perry, waving her off. "So what's the bad news?"

Alicia dumped the phone back onto the couch. "The bad news is, it's not us Simon wants."

CHAPTER 12
Dusting off the Helipad

The last time Detective Inspector Liam Jackson was in a chopper he was hovering over the grimy inner-city streets of Sydney in pursuit of a suspected drug trafficker, and as he caught sight of the white superyacht shining like a pearl on the glimmering sea below, he thought, boy, aren't I moving up in the world? In fact, he was moving backwards because Jackson's first job before he joined the police force was running security for cruise ships. That had segued into his career as a detective, which in turn had resulted in him being assigned an undercover job on the *SS Orient*, tracking down a jewel thief. And that's where he'd met Alicia and her meddling book club.

Jackson thought of his girlfriend now as the chopper closed in on the *Living Large* and how dejected she'd be that she was not alongside him. He knew Alicia was an excellent amateur detective in her own right, had proven it multiple times, but he also knew this was the real world and they needed a professional for this job and one with undercover experience.

That had been a stroke of genius on Simon Barrier's part. Simon knew of Jackson's background and was eager to keep Mrs Wynter's murder as hush-hush as possible until it could be investigated. Substantiated.

"We might have it all wrong," he'd told Jackson soon after he'd reached him on his mobile phone at home. "But if we're right, there's a killer on board and they may escape at the next port. We need to act fast. I've already arranged for our company jet to start refuelling, and you can be in the air in an hour."

"Hold your horses," Jackson had spluttered. "Isn't there a detective you can winch in from Cairns or Brisbane? They're so much closer."

"Yes, but we'd appreciate some discretion. For the family's sake."

Jackson figured it had more to do with his company's sake but wasn't going to knock back a complimentary cruise if he could wangle one. "That may be so, but I'm not a free agent," he'd told Simon. "I'm required to call my superiors and get their permission, and I don't like your chances. I suspect we'll get kickback."

Except what he got was a massive kick-along. It turns out his superiors were as desperate for discretion as Simon and waved the irregular request through. The deceased woman had very powerful friends in very high places, and within ten minutes, the police commissioner himself was on the phone to Jackson ordering him to board the *Living Large* at the first opportunity. And not just for Elsbeth's sake.

"Let's keep any mention of homicide under wraps for now," the commissioner had barked down the phone. "It's my wife's sixtieth birthday party tomorrow, and she'll never forgive me if we have the bloody media on our doorstep. Not until we know for certain. Get in, investigate quietly, and report back to me before this breaks."

Jackson had assured him he'd do just that and then called Alicia at book club to let her know, but of course she did not pick up. Next, he'd hurriedly packed, then jumped aboard the four-hour chartered flight straight to Lizard Island from Sydney, the tab picked up by LLE. There, a helicopter lay in waiting, and no sooner had Jackson touched down than he was up again, soaring out across the cerulean sea and towards the *Living Large*.

The yacht had been backtracking to Lizard Island

where it would anchor offshore for his arrival, then continue on to Cooktown.

Jackson was officially undercover again, this time playing the part of the coroner's assistant. Just there to tick the requisite boxes, and that's how he would explain it to the passengers and crew.

"I'm just here to tick boxes and make sure the paperwork is in order," Jackson told Gary as he was chaperoned from the gusty helipad to the captain's quarters. He was testing out his story, and the look of scepticism on the first officer's face was not reassuring.

"I thought we could do all that in Cooktown," Gary said. "If it's just an accident, why the urgency? We'd be there in half the time if we hadn't detoured here."

"Yeah, mate, usually you can," Jackson said quickly, then lowered his voice and added, "But you know how it goes. Different set of rules for the rich and famous."

Gary smirked, like that made sense, then knocked firmly on the office door. "Head on in. Captain's waiting for you. I need to get back to the bridge."

Jackson thanked him and let himself in, closing the door behind him.

Liz was at her desk, Simon and Claire in the chairs in front of her, and the latter jumped up when she saw Jackson and ran to hug him.

"I feel so much better with you here," she said, and he smiled.

"Thank you for coming," said Simon, taking his hand and giving it a good pump. Then he turned and waved it at Liz. "This is Captain Liz Flinders."

"Flinders?" said Jackson. "Like the famous British navigator?"

"No relation," she said almost wearily, like she'd heard that too many times, then waved him into the third chair that had been placed at the desk.

She then asked, "How was your flight, Jackson? Can we

get you anything? A beverage perhaps?"

"No, thanks. I'm just keen to get cracking before we hit Cooktown and everyone flees. Which just gives me this evening, is that correct?"

"And a few hours tomorrow," she replied. "We should be in Cooktown by midmorning."

Or at least that's what Liz hoped.

She glanced at her watch. It was now six forty-five p.m. on Sunday evening. The yacht would stay anchored until the dinner shift was over, then they would fire up the engines and continue on to Cooktown. It was Simon's idea to dawdle. He wanted to buy Jackson more time, but Liz couldn't get there fast enough.

"Pre-dinner drinks have been pushed back an hour," she told him, "so you'll have a bit of time between now and then too." Also Simon's idea. "Otherwise you can interview the guests straight after dinner."

There was a sudden grimace from the captain.

She added, "That is if anyone shows up for any of it. It feels so terribly frivolous now, but we must still push on."

"That's important," said Jackson, "especially if we're to convince them it's not suspicious."

Captain Liz nodded. "I understand you've done this kind of thing before, but how exactly is this going to work?"

"It's very simple," Jackson replied. "As far as everyone is concerned, I'm a stranger to you all, just here to prepare a report for the coroner. So no more hugs from you, Ms Hargreaves." He lightened that with a wink. "I'm *officially* here to ascertain details regarding the death— time, place, manner and cause. I won't be making accusations or any suggestions of guilt or homicide."

"Good," said Simon. "No unsettling the horses. Because the official story that Mrs Wynter died by misadventure seems to have stuck, and I don't believe anyone suspects it's murder."

"Apart from the murderer that is," said Claire, causing Simon to look like a very startled stallion indeed.

CHAPTER 13
Sorting Through Suspects

While Simon tried hard to look brave in front of his new wife, Jackson decided to throw him a lifeline. "Any chance this could be suicide?"

Logically, Elsbeth Wynter's death appeared to be murder, but suicide was one hypothesis that needed exploring. "From what you told me over the blower, Simon, I think I understand the situation with the air valve, but I do have to ask if she showed any signs of depression. Suicidal ideation?"

"Oh, that would be good," he said, then promptly apologised, adding, "I mean… surely that's preferable to murder?"

But Claire was having none of it. "Sorry, honey, but the only person depressed on this yacht was her daughter-in-law, Indya. I'll explain it all later, Jackson, but suffice to say Elsbeth Wynter gate-crashed her son's honeymoon and the young bride was not happy. As for Elsbeth? She seemed to be enjoying herself."

"*Enjoying* herself?" said Liz. "She was revelling in all the trouble she was causing. I know, it's awful to speak ill of the dead, but Elsbeth Wynter was a mischief-maker. And not just with Indya. According to my staff, Mrs Wynter had words with another passenger during dinner last night—called her shifty or something equally egregious. I had to have a quiet word with her afterwards. Asked her to pull her head in."

"How did that go down?" asked Simon.

"Not well." A troubled look now. "You don't suppose... I mean, could my words have forced her hand?"

"It was *not* suicide," said Claire, more firmly this time. "There was something else that happened at dinner, Jackson, that I think's very telling. It got chilly out on the open deck, and Elsbeth asked her lawyer friend, Boulder, to help her into her cardigan. I don't believe she had the flexibility to twist her own arm up and behind her back to turn off the air valve, which I hear is the key to all of this. She wasn't limber, and it wasn't suicide."

Jackson nodded firmly. He liked her certainty. Trusted it. Said, "Then I'll work on the premise it was murder. Besides, even in a suicide, we assume murder and work back from there, and frankly I haven't got time to consider anything else." Eyes back on the captain he said, "What about your crew? How much do they know?"

"The only other person who knows about the sabotaged gas cylinder is our dive instructor Dr Roland Brown, and I have sworn him to secrecy."

"And your first officer? He doesn't suspect?" Because Jackson had definitely caught a whiff of suspicion in Gary's demeanour.

"Gary knows nothing." A slight frown flicked across Liz's forehead again.

"Problem?"

"Not at all. I just don't like keeping secrets from my crew, and you can't possibly think one of them was responsible? They barely knew the woman."

"How do you know that?" said Jackson. "Have you checked their backgrounds? Have you asked them?"

She sat back, frown in full flight.

"The chances are it *was* one of the guests," Jackson told her, trying to sound reassuring. "It was most likely someone in her family group; that's the usual pattern with homicides. But we make no assumptions and take nothing for granted in an investigation. And in this early stage, we have to keep an open mind. Everyone is a suspect, including you I'm afraid, and even my two friends here."

He smiled towards Claire and Simon, who did not look nearly as offended as the captain.

Her voice was a little squeaky as she said, "So where do you want to start?"

"I need a list of everyone on board, including your crew. I need full names and addresses, any references, that kind of thing, and also copies of the guests' reservation information, passports, whatever you have on file. I'll need to get up to speed and then question each of them separately—starting with the dive instructor who found her, then the two family members who are most likely to depart tomorrow."

Liz nodded and began rifling through files on her desk. "You can set yourself up in here," she said, finding what she was looking for and handing it over. "This will give you something to start with. I'll see what else I've got."

"Perfect." He was referring to both the office and the passenger manifest he was now scanning.

"I'm afraid mobile coverage is virtually non-existent out here," Liz told him as she caressed a wireless phone that sat on a cradle on her desk. "This is a satellite phone; we used it to call you earlier. Your mobile will begin to receive calls the closer we get to the mainland."

Jackson tapped a hand at the list he'd just been inspecting. "I understood there were four couples on the yacht, yet I'm seeing five lots of names here."

Liz swapped a look with Simon. "Yes. The Tanners. They were due to join us in Cooktown but…"

"But?" said Jackson.

"But…" Liz shot another glance at Simon, who was now staring at Claire.

Claire looked like a deer caught in the headlights and Jackson's senses went on alert.

"What's going on, Claire?"

She grimaced slightly. "I'm not sure how you're going

to feel about this…" She darted her eyes back to Simon, who urged her on. "It wasn't my idea, I mean, not at first—"

"What's going on, Claire?" Jackson repeated, his voice low and gravelly.

"The book club…"

"What about the book club?"

"I'm sorry, don't scream at me, but some of them will be joining us tomorrow."

Then she ducked behind Simon as though waiting for impact.

CHAPTER 14
Back in Cattle Class

Alicia could not be more excited. Earlier that afternoon she had been lamenting the fact that her boyfriend got to enjoy a Great Barrier Reef cruise—a honeymoon one with a mystery to boot!—and now she was winging her way to join him.

Well, sort of.

As she glanced out of the Virgin Airlines window at the darkening horizon, she felt a slight dip in her mood. Yes, she was heading off to join a honeymoon cruise, but Jackson had never actually popped the question and the man she was sharing the honeymoon suite with was someone else entirely.

"We should have pet names for each other," said Perry in the seat beside her. "I'm thinking, coochie-coo for you and stud-muffin for me."

She glanced back from the window and rolled her eyes.

Yep, there was nothing romantic about this voyage. She was "honeymooning" with her good friend and fellow book clubber Perry.

Claire wasn't lying when she said it wasn't her idea. It was her new husband's. Simon was mortified that he'd "ruined" Claire's honeymoon, and so, when the Cooktown couple, the Tanners, had chickened out of the cruise and demanded their money back (which Simon immediately offered with an added bonus in exchange for their discretion), he'd suggested two of her friends take their place. He was doing it purely for moral support, but Claire had loved the idea and run with it.

Not only could two book club friends come along, she told Alicia when she rang her later that day while Jackson was making his way north, but they could pretend to *be* the Tanners. They could be faux newlyweds—just as Elsbeth and Boulder had been—and could also help investigate undercover.

Alicia had loved the idea, of course, as did the rest of the group, who had hung around long after book club to discuss the case. The only question: Who would play the fake bride? Because Perry was the obvious choice for groom, being the only male member of the club.

Ronnie had opted out first. "I'm far too old to play a blushing bride," she told them. "Besides, I know the Wynter family through my charity work, so I'd fail the first hurdle."

Missy had no affiliation with the family but couldn't get time off from her library job so quickly, and Queenie was otherwise occupied, back at Simon's office.

So it came down to the Finlays.

"You do it," Alicia told Lynette, knowing how much she loathed playing second fiddle to her sister.

Then a fresh idea was hatched and it was decided that both women could go. Alicia would play Perry's new bride, and Lynette would act as a sous chef, there to assist the crew.

Of course, none of this was what Simon had in mind when he suggested the idea to Claire, but now it was like a runaway train and he seemed incapable of stopping it. And so he had spent significant time convincing an equally sceptical Captain Flinders, who eventually had to concede that, yes, there was a spare staff cabin in which to house Lynette, and sure, her beleaguered crew could do with the extra help now that he mentioned it.

And so, as Alicia, Perry and Lynette scrambled to start packing back in Sydney, Queenie showed just why she was such a highly paid executive assistant. They'd barely dragged their suitcases from below their beds when she rang with booking details of their last-minute flights to Cairns, then on to Cooktown, where they would overnight before joining the yacht when it docked the following day to remove Mrs Wynter's body. They were not able to access the company jet as it was still refuelling at Lizard Island, so it would be a slower journey, but Alicia relished it nonetheless.

The only hitch in the plan was the fact that half the passengers—aka the suspects—were likely to jump ship in Cooktown just as they were boarding. But that didn't deter the club members. No siree! They all agreed it was better to be on board, exploring the evidence, questioning the crew, than miles away back in Sydney. A lot more fun too. Not that they mentioned *that* to Ronnie, who seemed positively perplexed by their obvious excitement.

And so it was that Alicia found herself rolling her eyes at her faux husband on a commercial flight to Cairns.

"Stud-muffin? Are you serious?" she asked. "You're married to me now, so you'll need to play it straight. And that canary-yellow jacket isn't exactly helping. What were you thinking?"

"It's Alexander McQueen, and it's *citrus*," he said, pouting.

"Doesn't make it look any straighter."

Alicia locked eyes with Lynette, who was seated on Perry's other side, chuckling. But she wasn't feeling so carefree suddenly. She loved Perry, but pretending to be married to him was going to require an Oscar-worthy performance. And then there was the small matter of Jackson. He'd been out of range when the idea was hatched so couldn't be consulted.

Which was probably just as well because Alicia had a hunch he would not be so happy to see her.

~

James Wynter watched glumly as the brawny newcomer studied his mother's body down in Cabin B6. He didn't like the look of the sandy-haired coroner's assistant one bit. Seemed a bit shifty, like he was trying to find evidence against him. Not of anything malicious, he didn't think that. But of associated guilt. It was the same look everyone had been giving him since they'd discovered his poor mother's body, checking to see if he really was sorry. Like James had brought all this upon them.

And perhaps he had. Perhaps his wife was right. He should not have mentioned the cruise to Elsbeth. Should have known she would sneak on because she snuck into everything he ever did—from his first school dance to his orientation week at university. He smiled now, remembering how outraged his friends had been on his behalf, how sorry they had sounded for him, and yet he despised their pity. He was the lucky one, surely? How could they pity him a mother who adored him so completely?

Adored him more than any woman ever would.

His mind wandered to his wife and how quiet she'd been since it had happened. And he remembered the missing half hour when she hadn't shown for lunch, before they found his mother and his whole world imploded. Later, after Boulder had ushered them to their cabin, he'd noticed Indy's bikini dumped in a wet puddle in the bathtub along with her matching flippers, like they had been removed in a hurry.

She didn't go back out there, did she?

"Mr Wynter?" This was the coroner fellow, staring at him blankly.

"Sorry," James replied. "It's been a very traumatic day."

Liam Jackson nodded. "I was asking about your mother's health. Did she have any pre-existing conditions that—"

"No. My mother was in supreme shape for a woman her age. Walked every day, loved to swim, adored her diving. I can't wrap my head around any of this." He stared hard at Jackson. "Was it a heart attack do you think? That's what Boulder says."

"None of us can say for sure at this stage. That's what an autopsy will ascertain. So when you saw your mum this morning, she appeared fine?"

"Yes! I mean, initially I didn't think she was joining us, she wasn't at the dive platform, but then she suddenly appeared, like a mirage. I was thrilled because I'd spotted a stingray and wanted to show her. She is such a massive fan…" He gulped. *"Was."* Gulped again. "We dived for a bit together, and then I signalled that I was heading back to Indy and she signalled that she wanted to continue, so…" His face clouded over. He looked suddenly shattered. "That was the last I saw her."

"What happened after that?"

"Happened?" Now James just looked confused. "Nothing. That's about the time we got the signal from the divemaster to head back to lunch, so we all swam back together."

"All?"

"Yes! All! Well, apart from Mother of course. But yes, my wife and I swam back together. We were just behind that other couple, the muscley chaps."

"The Dudley-Pines."

"That's them."

James tried to hold the blow-in's gaze, but he had a deadpan expression in his eyes. Inscrutable. It gave James the willies.

Eventually the coroner's assistant said, "And you'll be accompanying your mother's body off the yacht tomorrow when we arrive in Cooktown?"

"Why would I do that?"

That got the guy's expression moving, crow's-feet appearing around his blue eyes. "I just assumed."

"Well, you assumed incorrectly. Boulder brought her onto the yacht. Boulder can jolly well take her off it."

Then, his voice gentler, James said, "My wife has asked if we can finish our honeymoon. She thinks if we let..." He caught himself, gobbled his next words down. "She thinks we should continue on as best we can."

"Even after what's happened to your mother?"

James was scowling now. He knew what the man was insinuating. "It's tragic what's happened to my mother, but at least she died doing what she loved, with the people she loved around her. Now it's our turn to keep the spirit of the holiday alive, to see it to its conclusion. I owe my mother that. I also owe Indy."

Jackson nodded slowly. "Okay, I guess that makes sense."

As Jackson watched the victim's son fold his arms defiantly, he thought it made no sense to him at all. If it was *his* mum, he'd be shepherding her every inch of the way (not that she'd ever do anything as intrusive as gate-crash his wedding!). Still, he'd been told James adored his mother, was thrilled when she arrived. It must have taken Indya some doing to convince him to plough on with the voyage.

Perhaps she wasn't as helpless as the others had made out.

"Tell me about Arne Boulder," Jackson said. "He and your mother were not actually partners, is that correct?"

James looked surprised. "So you heard? Yes, well, they weren't strictly partners, more like partners in crime."

He smiled fleetingly. "It was rather cheeky of him to bring Mother aboard. But then that was Mother for you. She couldn't help herself. She just wanted to be part of all my special moments."

Another wistful smile. "The night I proposed to Indy, Mother had snuck into the restaurant and was at a table nearby. I didn't realise, but Indy spotted her and thought it was hilarious at the time. Really she did! That's why I knew she'd make the perfect wife. Indy didn't mind Mother being part of my life; she understood how important it was to me."

That's not what Jackson had heard, nor was he buying it. Indya was already at the top of his suspect list. He wasn't sure there was a woman alive who would tolerate such an interfering in-law.

Speaking of interfering... Jackson's thoughts flitted to another woman then, a much younger one. He'd been shocked to hear Alicia was on her way, although he shouldn't have been. His girlfriend was incapable of staying downwind of a mystery once she got a whiff of one, and at first he'd been furious. It wasn't just the interfering—one day her meddling would see a viable case get thrown out of court—it was the danger. She was willingly jumping onto a ship with a killer. He'd almost lost Alicia last time. Could he keep her safe now?

Because that was the thing that everyone was keenly downplaying. If this really was murder, then someone on the ship was culpable. And if it was Indya, or James for that matter, they were now staying on board and would be rubbing shoulders with his girlfriend. He knew Alicia was as tough as nails, but that didn't mean she was bulletproof.

Jackson had already interviewed Dr Roland before he met up with James, and the dive instructor had seemed pretty tough, too, considering what he'd just been through. He'd answered all of Jackson's questions carefully, methodically, but he hadn't really shed any new light on the meticulous notes that the captain had given him.

"But what has any of this got to do with her death?" James was saying, dragging him from his reverie. "It was all just a terrible accident, wasn't it?"

Jackson swiftly replied, "When there's death by misadventure, part of my job is to explain discrepancies, and the fact that your widowed mother was on a honeymoon cruise with a man who was not her husband... well, that is a rather large discrepancy."

"Oh... okay. I know what's going on here." James's

eyes were now narrow slats. "I know what you're really doing on this boat. I'm not a fool."

Jackson's stomach tightened, but he kept his expression neutral.

"This is about the insurance, isn't it?" said James. "You're trying to stop me from suing the boat because Mother was here under false pretences."

"I don't work for the boat, sir," Jackson replied, feeling a rush of relief that his cover hadn't been blown. "That's a matter between you and the company. Now, if you don't mind, I need to finish up here, then I'd like you to ask your wife to meet me at the captain's office, which is located near the bridge. I'll be there in ten."

Now it was James who was trying to seem unfazed. "Indy? I can't see why you'd need to talk to her. Besides, we have sundowners coming up."

"I will be speaking to everyone on board," said Jackson. "It's just protocol. Don't worry, I won't keep your wife away from her piña colada for long."

~

As she stared at her reflection in the full-length mirror in her cabin, Cinnamon was also banging on about protocol to Connor, who did not like the sound of this intruder one bit.

"Who exactly *is* he, and must we really answer his questions?" he asked as her expression turned pensive.

"Pasha told me the chief coroner sent him," she said, swivelling back. "What's missing? Earrings?"

He looked her up and down, then grabbed some pearl beads from the vanity table. "Try these."

She snatched them from him and turned back to the mirror. "He's just here to do the paperwork apparently. He's questioning everybody. It's not personal."

"What paperwork?" asked Connor.

"Honey. When there's an unforeseen *incident* on a yacht,

it can't be swept under the carpet. Even though that's exactly how it feels right now. I was sure they'd cancel dinner, or at least sundowners. Feels a little disrespectful or something."

"We can't huddle in our cabins forever. Bring on the free booze I say. And nobody wants to sweep anything under anywhere, but I really don't see how we can help."

Cindy groaned. "Just play nicely, answer his questions politely, and it will all be over before we know it. In fact, I think I know a way to turn this to our advantage." Her eyes glinted mischievously at Connor, then she stared back at her reflection and said, "Now, which watch? The Cartier or the Tag Heuer?"

CHAPTER 15
Legs Eleven

The leggy bombshell gave Jackson an uncertain smile as she stood at the door to the captain's office and said, "You wanted to see me?"

He looked up from his notes. "Indya Wynter?" She nodded. "Please come in and close the door behind you."

Indya looked worried suddenly. "Should I bring my husband in for this? Or better yet, Boulder?"

He smiled. "Do you need a lawyer?"

She blinked, then closed the door and took the seat across from him. "Is everything okay?"

"Of course, Mrs Wynter—" he began before she cut him off with a subtle snort, flicking her long white hair from her face.

"Sorry, it's just… I'm not, like, used to that name yet. I prefer Indya."

He nodded. "Indya it is. So, as your husband has hopefully explained, I'm here on behalf of the coroner, just preparing a report about what happened to your mother-in-law." He glanced at his notes and back. "I'll try to make this as painless as possible."

"Thank you. It has been… well, yeah, *painful*, I guess."

"You were close to your mother-in-law?"

She blinked. Flicked her hair again. "We got along fine. Like a house on fire, in fact."

That must be the official family line, Jackson thought, letting it go. "You were diving with your husband this morning. What time would you say you returned to the yacht?"

She shifted in her seat. "Time? Gee, um, I'm not sure I noticed. What did James tell you?"

Jackson remained silent.

With another flick of her hair, Indya said, "I wanna say… twelvish? Whatever time James said."

Jackson glanced at his notes again. "So, just before midday, is that correct? You all returned together? You, James, and the Dudley-Pines."

She lifted one painfully thin shoulder. "I don't know about them, but I guess so."

"It *was* just this morning, Indya."

"I know! It's… well, it's been, like, really traumatic. You must get that?"

He waited a beat. "Can you remember when and where you last saw Mrs Wynter? She didn't return to the yacht when you did, is that correct?"

"No, I mean yes. The last I saw her she was heading out to the second floating thing. I think."

"You saw her swim towards the farthest pontoon?"

She blinked. "Not just me! Like, everyone did. We were all so relieved… I mean, not *relieved* relieved. Just…" She was now blushing. "She was a live wire, old Elsbeth. Liked to make an entrance. Lots of splashing even though we were supposed to be diving. She… Well, it was freaking out the fish, that's all. I'm not saying she meant anything by it, but I could tell Roland—that's the divemaster— he wasn't happy. He was trying to show us some stuff. Anyway, then she finally swam away and we all kept diving and then… headed back to the yacht."

"And that was the last you saw of her?"

Her perfect brow crinkled ever so quickly, then was as smooth as glass again. "Yep."

He smiled. He'd spotted the crinkle. "Is there anything you'd like to add?"

There was another shake of the hair, another blink.

"That will be all for now," he told her. "If you think of anything else, anything that might assist with my enquiries, just drop back in. Any time."

She nodded but couldn't get those long legs moving fast enough.

~

"He thinks I had something to do with it," Indya hissed as she joined her husband at the steps to Nemo's Lounge.

James swept a hand across his dinner jacket and glanced back towards her. "The coroner's assistant? Why would he think that? It was just an accident."

"I can tell. He asked some really bizarre questions."

"Did you stick to the story? Like I told you to?"

"Yes, of course, but he still blames me. I could feel it." Her eyes turned to the guests who were already sipping drinks, some staring up at them. "They all do."

"Don't be neurotic. Nobody blames you."

"You do."

He turned and clutched her wrist. "What are you saying? Of course I don't blame you."

She wrenched free. "Why don't you ask me then?"

"Ask you what?"

Her stare was scathing. "You know exactly what I'm talking about."

"Welcome, guys!" said Pasha, who had crept up on them as they stood hissing together at the entrance. They both jumped, and she quickly reached out a hand. "So sorry. I didn't mean to startle you. Please come in, take a seat and I'll fetch you both a drink."

"Make it a strong one," growled James as he strode down the stairs, leaving his new bride alone at the top.

"Trouble in paradise?" whispered Freddy as Pasha approached the bar and told him to mix two cocktails.

She gave him a withering look. Not unlike the one

Indya had just given her husband. "They've just lost a loved one, show some respect please."

"Sheesh, no need to be testy."

But Pasha was feeling testy. In fact, she was feeling *tested*, like everything she did over the next few days would determine her future. And she wasn't just talking about the yacht. "At least you're here on time, unlike last night. Where were you by the way? You know I prefer to play the piano while you mix the drinks."

Freddy shrugged as he reached for two tall glasses. "Was just prepping the beds like I'm supposed to do."

"Well, you took your sweet time about— No! Not the *depressant!*"

She was glaring at the gin bottle in Freddy's hand. "They'll be blubbering before entrées," Pasha added. "Make margaritas. We need to lift the spirits, not leave them sobbing. I can't believe I have to do this job for you as well."

"Sorry if I don't know what drink to give someone who's just lost their mother," he snapped back, and she snarled at him but let it go.

More arguing was not what the cruise needed.

Pasha had caught the couple's argument though, or the tail end of it, and she wondered what to make of it.

Did James really blame his wife for his mother's drowning?

Was that why the captain had whooshed the coroner's assistant on board so quickly? Was she doing Mr Wynter's bidding? Or was there something else going on?

Pasha had witnessed accidental deaths on ships before, and this was quite irregular.

As she handed the surly couple their cocktails and took her seat at the piano again, she couldn't help feeling a little surly too. The captain was going off script; could have filled in the paperwork herself, so why winch someone in so quickly? So dramatically?

Did they suspect something?

Five minutes later, as a sulky-looking Indya sucked the lime slice from her cocktail, James pretended to be engrossed in Pasha's abysmal and, frankly, inappropriately jaunty playing, and Claire pretended not to be watching. Just as she pretended not to know the handsome man who was just entering the lounge. It was DI Liam Jackson, and he was not dressed for dinner. Instead, he had his work suit on and a clipboard in his hand and was glancing about. He spotted Pasha and headed straight for her, stopping her mid-tune.

Oh the relief!

As they spoke quietly below their breaths, shooting glances around the group, Claire turned back to her husband.

"It's going to be hard pretending not to know lovely Liam."

"It'll be even harder pretending not to know your book club friends when they get here in the morning," Simon whispered back. "I'm not sure we've been very smart there. Jackson didn't look happy."

"Oh, he's just concerned for their safety."

"As am I. I can't believe I even suggested it. And I'm worried about you too. If we're right, there is a killer on this vessel. What I should do is have us all disembarking in Cooktown."

"But where's the fun in that?" she shot back, chuckling at his wary expression.

"What are you two laughing about?" Connor called out from a distant table.

Being a honeymoon cruise, the furniture had been arranged in intimate sets of two, and while that suited Claire that first evening, it wasn't going to cut it now. She wanted to notch up some clues before the duo jumped aboard tomorrow.

So she smiled and called back, "Connor, Cindy, why don't you join us?"

Connor looked delighted by the offer and scooped up his glass while Cindy seemed hesitant for just a moment before following him over. Simon also hesitated, looking disappointed, but jumped up nonetheless and helped Connor move their chairs across. Then he turned to the Wynters, wanting to invite them too, but they were deep in conversation again, their faces close together, so he left them to it.

As they settled in, Claire said, "I really shouldn't be laughing, Connor. It's all been very tragic."

"That's one word for it," he replied. "Debacle is another. I'm not sure I'll recommend this cruise to my friends." Then he must have caught the frown on Simon's forehead and said, "Sorry, mate. I hear from the grapevine that you might be the yacht's owner?"

Simon gave him a curt nod.

"Has our stowaway given you a grilling yet?" Connor was referring to Jackson, who was now talking to Boulder at the foot of the bar-room stairs. The lawyer had only just arrived and was shaking his head, rumbling about something. "Or do you get off scot-free?"

"I have spoken to him, yes," Simon said. "From what I can see, he seems very efficient. Just here to go through the motions. Apparently."

"Just here to muck for mud," said Connor, leaning in closer. "I don't like the look of him one bit."

"Really?" said Claire. "He looks quite sweet to me."

"Careful, Claire. You'll make your new hubby jealous!" Connor had mischief in his voice, but his gaze was still on Simon. "Is it also true that this incident hasn't scared our fifth couple off? I heard they were joining us early when we get to Cooktown tomorrow."

"That's right," said Simon. "The Tanners. They get an extra day of cruising, so they're not too concerned."

"Plus you don't have to reimburse them, so that will please your business partners," said Cindy making Simon frown again.

He went to object when Jackson appeared at their table.

"Good evening, everyone," he said, giving them each the once-over. "My name's Jackson and I'm here to prepare a preliminary report for the coroner."

Claire tried to smile as benignly as she could as the others turned varying expressions upon the detective. Connor's was the most aggressive, and Jackson must have noticed.

"Cinnamon and Connor Dudley-Pine I presume?" he said, glancing between the two of them and causing Connor to frown further. "Don't worry, I won't interrupt the festivities for too long, but I would appreciate a word after dinner. Perhaps I could start with you, Mrs Dudley-Pine."

His eyes now rested on Cindy, who looked as cool as a cucumber. She could have taught her husband a thing or two.

"Why do you need to speak to my wife?" Connor demanded.

"Darling," she said, "it's *fine*."

"I'm speaking with everyone, sir," said Jackson. "Including you." He turned back to Cindy. "If you could find your way to the captain's office, near the bridge, when you've finished eating. Say, about nine thirty? Then your husband could join me at ten."

She shrugged nonchalantly, then swept her eyes to Claire and Simon expectantly. For one worrying moment, Claire thought the detective was going to turn away, but then he said:

"I have, of course, already spoken with you, Mr Barrier, but I would like to have a word with your wife too. Mrs Barrier?" He stared casually at Claire. "Is ten thirty too late?"

"Not at all," she replied, then added, "But it's Ms Hargreaves. I didn't take my husband's name."

"Oh, my apologies, Ms Hargreaves."

Jackson bowed and walked away, and she smiled to herself and thought, *Like he didn't know!*

The guy was one smooth operator.

CHAPTER 16
Dinner Conversations

After thoroughly inspecting the cold club sandwiches that had just been delivered to their Cooktown hotel room, Lynette was unimpressed, but Alicia didn't care what was on the tray, she was starving. By the time they'd arrived, the hotel restaurant was closed, but they had managed to rustle up some room service, and that was certainly preferable to raiding the mini-bar, which contained little more than peanuts and booze.

The trio had spent all evening travelling—first the long flight to Cairns, then a connecting flight to Cooktown, and then the bus to the hotel, a drab-looking place with a ridiculous price tag. Thank goodness Simon's company was paying.

The plan was to order food first, then Perry would join them to do a little google sleuthing before they hit the sack, but they already had some background, thanks to wealthy book club member Ronnie.

"I knew Elsbeth socially," she'd told them before they departed. "But we weren't close. She was too much of a diva for me. Had quite the reputation. Worked hard, gave generously, as she should, but she expected a lot in return and was a hard taskmaster, according to the rumours, ruthless even. I heard she used to swan into her office, and if she found her employees eating lunch at their desks, she'd sack them on the spot."

"What for?" gasped Perry, who often ate at his desk to save time running out.

"She felt they shouldn't be relaxing at her expense."

"They were eating their well-earned lunch!"

"Couldn't agree more. I told you she was ruthless. Someone would always pop in soon after and smooth the waters, but still."

"She made enemies by the sound of it," said Alicia. "We should see if she made an enemy of someone on that yacht, and I'm not just talking about her daughter-in-law."

Because Claire had given them the full rundown over a crackly satellite phone and they already knew of the tension in the Wynter family.

"Or *before* she got on the yacht," said Perry. "Maybe she had history with someone and they took the opportunity to exact revenge."

But now, as she trawled the internet from their hotel room, Alicia found herself distracted by the *Living Large* website. The yacht looked shockingly luxurious.

"Check out our cabin, Perry," she declared when he popped in to join them. "It's called a stateroom, don't you know? And look at the size of that bed. I bags the right side."

Perry blinked back at her. "You're sharing the bed with me?"

"What did you think? I'd shove you on the couch?"

"It's large enough," he said, zooming in on the image.

Alicia laughed. "We've been through more than your average married couple, so I'm hardly going to treat you like a stranger now. Although if you hog all that lovely, luscious duvet, I will kick you out."

"At least *we* get a bed." Perry grinned at Lynette. "You're crew, Lynny, so you're probably sleeping in a hammock beside the engine."

Lynette winced while Alicia whacked Perry lightly on the shoulder.

"I'm sure it won't be that bad," she said. "Surely that room's reserved for the pesky coroner's assistant."

~

In fact, the pesky assistant was going to be accommodated in a plush stateroom of his own. Jackson just had to trawl through it first with a fine-tooth comb. It was cabin number A5, the deceased's suite for just one night, but who knew what secrets it might contain.

So, as the guests finished their cocktails and made their way to the top deck for dinner, he pulled on rubber gloves and began a thorough inspection.

"What exactly are you looking for?" Captain Flinders enquired as she watched from the doorway, not permitted any further. Jackson had asked for the stateroom to be secured soon after he got the call-up and just hoped she'd done it before anyone got in and messed with potential evidence.

Elsbeth might have died at sea, but her cabin could still provide clues.

"Won't know until I see it," he told her as he glanced about, then rubbed a hand through his tussled hair. "So let me get this straight. Mrs Wynter and Boulder booked separate suites. Wasn't that your first hint that they were faking it?"

"Not necessarily. Lots of married couples sleep separately."

"Even on their honeymoons? It's not a promising start."

"Oh, you'd be surprised what amounts to a marriage these days." Liz's eyes clouded over, but she blinked it away. "How long do you need before I send Freddy in to pack Elsbeth's things and freshen up the room?"

He checked his watch. "I shouldn't be more than an hour. I'll try to get it done before my nine-thirty interview. Where is everything going? To the son?"

"Eventually I suppose. At this point into storage below deck. There is quite a lot of stuff."

It was an understatement. The cabin might be extra

spacious for a yacht, but Elsbeth had brought enough things to fill a McMansion. Every available surface was crammed with cosmetics, clothes and accessories, and Jackson began to rifle through them when the first officer appeared, tray in hand, frown on his face.

"Oh, Gary, I thought Freddy was bringing dinner up for Jackson," said Liz.

"Freddy's missing in action. I didn't want this to go cold. I'll just pop it in—"

"I'll take it, thank you," said Jackson, stepping forward to stop him crossing the threshold.

Liz frowned. "Where's Freddy?"

Gary's eyes squinted. "I thought you'd know. *Captain.*"

The way he emphasised that word made Jackson look twice, but Liz did not appear to notice.

"Thanks, Gary," she said breezily, but he lingered and she frowned. "Was there something else?"

He shoved his hands into his pockets. "I've just had Sergio whingeing to me. He's confused why we're bringing in a sous chef tomorrow."

He was referring to Lynette, and Liz shot a quick look at Jackson and back. "You'd think he'd be happy to have the extra set of hands."

"It's a good question though, isn't it?" Gary persisted. "I mean, we never normally—" His eyes were on Jackson now, like he could explain it.

Liz put her body between them. "The company and I feel that in light of the recent tragedy, we're all a little shaken and it won't hurt to have an extra set of hands on deck to help out. It will also free you up for any questions that Mr Jackson might have."

Gary nodded like he wasn't convinced and then took the hint and headed off down the corridor. As he did so, Liz turned to Jackson and said, "God that man can be trying."

Jackson wondered if she was referring to Gary or the chef. Before he got a chance to enquire, there was another crew member at the doorway. This time it was Pasha, a bottle of red wine in one hand, a large wineglass in the other.

"You look like you might appreciate a good vintage," the stewardess said to Jackson as she held the bottle aloft. "I've taken the liberty of selecting the perfect drop to accompany the rack of lamb's tasty blueberry *jus*."

"Thanks," he replied, surprised. Jackson didn't normally get offered alcohol on assignment, let alone *blueberry jus*, but then this wasn't strictly a police case, or at least that's what she thought.

"I'll take that, thank you," said Liz, now looking oddly put out.

"Oh, no trouble at all!" Pasha ignored her boss as she tried to move past her and into the cabin.

Watching them now, Jackson swallowed his smile. They all seemed very keen to ingratiate themselves to him, or was it the cabin they were trying to access? He grabbed the wine and the glass and said, "Thanks, ladies, but I can take it from here."

Liz looked slightly offended, but Pasha just winked and said, "Call me if you need anything. Anything at all. Very happy to help."

"Oh, I'll be calling you," said Jackson, reaching for the door. "You can be assured of that."

Then he closed the door firmly on both of them.

After they had left and he'd had a chance to swallow a few mouthfuls—Sergio might be a whinge, but boy he could cook—Jackson returned to searching the room, and there was a lot to search. Elsbeth Wynter had certainly settled in and not just across the surface. All the cabin drawers and cupboards were full, and he went through them carefully, then the papers on her desk, the book by her bed, the pockets of her bags and clothes, and found nothing of any interest, apart from an old ticket stub for the opera, a few loose fifty-dollar bills, and the beginning of a letter addressed to someone called Darling Monty.

None of it raised any flags, so he returned to her desk where a slim laptop had been set up. He clicked and found it was password protected. Damn it. Then he noticed a silver clutch purse pushed deep underneath the desk. Deliberately hidden? Or just clumsily discarded?

He pulled it out and opened it wide. There was very little in it, apart from a brassy Chanel lipstick, some wadded tissues, a slim silver pen, and a tiny notepad. He reached for that and began flicking through, seeing nothing of any interest, just a scribbled note to check the alarm clock was working and a brief list of ingredients.

Hang on a minute…

Jackson turned back to that page and read from it aloud: "Cinnamon & Spice." A question mark had been scrawled beside it, but Jackson was now grinning. He had a hunch these were not random ingredients, and he knew the answer to Elsbeth's hurriedly scribbled question.

CHAPTER 17
A Spicy Interview

Cindy gave her husband a quick peck on the cheek and said, "Wish me luck," as she placed her serviette on their dining table, then made her way down the external stairway and onto the bridge deck. Glancing at her watch, she saw that it was right on nine thirty p.m., so she returned to the stairwell and continued down to her cabin.

Might as well reapply some lippie and show the ring-in who was boss.

When she finally reached the captain's office, she found the coroner's assistant sipping a cup of something black and staring out the window at the dark, swirling sea below. He had propped the door open for her, and so she stepped in and made for the desk chair, but he turned and waved her onto the couch.

"Let's try to keep it informal, Mrs Dudley-Pine," he said, sitting across from her.

"In that case," she said, "you'd better call me Cindy." She crossed one leg over the other, and her silk dress slipped back so he could see her muscular thighs. "I don't know why you need to speak to me though. I'm not sure I'll be much use."

"Just ticking boxes," he said, using the mantra that they all needed to hear. "So tell me about this morning. When did you last see Mrs Wynter? Mrs Elsbeth Wynter."

"Oh, I guess the same time as everyone else." She smiled. "You couldn't really miss her. We were having our second dive, and she suddenly appeared, swimming in between us all like a shark. Or a dolphin, really. Lots of splashing about. Being a complete nuisance."

She smiled sweetly, like she hadn't just insulted the deceased.

Jackson said, "But then the splashing stopped."

Her smile slipped. "Yes, I guess it did. To be honest, Jackson—it is Jackson, yes? I wasn't really watching Elsbeth. There was a lot of competition in those waters. Lots of exotic fish, and I haven't even got started on Indya and her ridiculous swimsuit!" Another innocuous smile.

"How long have you known Mrs Wynter?"

"*Known* her? Just twenty-four hours. I mean, we all knew *of* her, of course, but I don't know why you think I knew her."

"She had your business name listed amongst her possessions."

Cindy's eyes widened along with her lips, but she quickly shrugged him off with a casual lift of one brawny shoulder and said nothing.

Jackson had now rechecked the passenger file and seen that his instincts were spot-on. The Dudley-Pines' stateroom had been paid for by a company called Cinnamon & Spice. But that was as far as his research could go without decent internet reception.

"What sort of business are you in, Cindy?"

"I own a boutique investment company."

"Was Elsbeth Wynter a client?"

Cindy's smile widened. "I wish! No, I can assure you, that was not the case."

"So why was your business listed in her notepad?"

"I couldn't say," she replied smoothly. "Perhaps one of my many satisfied customers recommended me to her, which is just lovely of them. In any case, I'm not here on business, Jackson. This is supposed to be my honeymoon."

Jackson tried not to snort at that. He knew Cindy's type. Everything was about business. He could tell she was a player, from her brassy, fake tan to her flashy, diamond-encrusted watch, which she was now twiddling idly.

"There was some altercation between you and the deceased last night," he said, surprising her with the subject change. "Care to tell me what that was about?"

Her plucked eyebrows arched. "I wouldn't call it an altercation. Like I said, we'd never met before. I think she mistook me for somebody else. She was getting old, you know? Perhaps a little batty." And there was her benign smile again—like she was just commenting on the weather. After another moment, she said, "Is this important? To how she died?"

Now Jackson was mirroring her smile. "It goes to her state of mind."

"Are you suggesting she might have done this deliberately?"

"What time did you return to the yacht after diving?"

Another subject change. Another arch of the eyebrows. "Same as everyone else."

It was a common answer. Like they were all in it together but hadn't quite decided their alibi. "I do need specifics."

"Oh, goodness, I'm not sure I noticed the time, but let me see if I can work it out for you. I guess I swam back just before lunch at noon, like we were asked to do. Again, does it matter?"

He ignored the question. "And you swam back as a group?"

She stared at him for a moment. Nodded.

"So all four of you swam back together just before noon."

She didn't hesitate this time. "That's correct."

"When did you first notice that Mrs Wynter was missing?"

"I didn't. Not at first. I was a bit late to lunch myself." Her expression lightened. "It's a bad habit, I'm afraid. Drives Connor bananas. After we'd hoiked ourselves back on board, I stopped at my cabin to change, so when I did get to the buffet, I was famished. Not really wondering about an old lady, even one as demanding of attention as Elsbeth was."

That too was followed by a smile so serene you'd think she'd just paid her a compliment.

Ten minutes later, Connor was parroting his wife. Yes, he told Jackson, they had all practise dived together since nine that morning. Yes, all four of them had returned together for lunch, and no, he had not given Elsbeth Wynter a second thought once he'd clapped eyes on that smorgasbord.

"Wasn't really our job to keep tabs on the old duck," he said lest he come into any criticism.

Jackson nodded. "I'm still trying to sort out the timeline, and I'm a bit confused. I have it on good authority that only the men were at lunch, so I'm wondering where the women had got to."

"I have no idea where Indya was, probably in her room sulking, but Claire was there and Cindy wasn't far behind me. She... she had stopped first to take a shower."

"And why would Indya be sulking in her room?" Jackson asked, catching the throwaway line.

Connor's eyes twinkled, and he leaned forward conspiratorially. "Oh you *must* have heard how unwelcome old Elsbeth was? Muscling her way into her son's honeymoon! Darling Indya was distraught, you could tell. She was not a happy camper. And who would be? It's their *honeymoon.*"

He stared at Jackson pointedly like that was the worst thing that had happened on this fateful cruise.

"Did you witness a fight between the two women?" Jackson asked.

"Well..." Connor rolled his tongue over his lips. "Who knows what happened after we all finished dinner last night. Cindy and I just scuttled back to our cabin—

we're early-to-bed types. Up with the sparrows. But there was certainly some argy-bargy during the dive this morning."

"What do you mean?"

He blinked. "One doesn't like to gossip, but let's just say James spent a bit too much time with his mother and not quite enough time with the missus. I did see Indya splash him at one point, and it wasn't a friendly gesture, I can tell you that." He winked slowly, then quickly added, "But I'm sure it was nothing. Nothing at all." Then, his voice a few octaves higher, "You're not suggesting the young lady had anything to do with this, are you?"

Now it was Jackson's turn to sound nonchalant. "Of course not, sir. It was an accidental drowning. Or do you have information to indicate otherwise?"

"Christ no!" But there was a glint of mischief in Connor's eyes again.

Jackson's final interview for the night was with Claire, and this was really just a ruse. The detective had almost forgotten to invite her during sundowners earlier and only realised his error when he spotted the alarm in her eyes. If he needed to chat to the others, why not Claire? And so he'd quickly arranged this meeting and deliberately fudged her surname in the process, and now, as he showed Connor to the door and waved Claire through, he maintained the ruse while Connor was still in earshot.

"Thanks for your time, Mrs... er, I mean, Ms Hargreaves was it?"

"That's correct," she said, her tone flat as she made her way in.

Once the door was shut, Claire's face lit up. "How's it all going?" she whispered.

He smiled back. "No need to whisper, Claire, these doors are soundproof. I've already tested them out." He offered her the wine he'd brought up, and she shook her head, so he continued. "I'm still a little foggy on the time everyone returned from the dive. Perhaps you can help me with that."

Claire's feline eyes narrowed. "I don't know about the dive—we were already back and getting dressed for lunch when they all returned—but they certainly arrived in spits and spurts to the lunch deck."

"Okay, give me each spit and spurt as they happened. Including the crew if you can."

She beamed. "Right. Well, Simon and I finished snorkelling about half an hour before lunch, and they were all still out diving. Well, all except for Boulder, who doesn't dive. We then dressed and sat down for lunch at exactly midday and were the first to arrive. Freddy was serving drinks, and I did see Pasha come and go. She was bringing platters out to the buffet. About ten minutes later James got there, and then Connor strode in soon after that."

"What about their wives?"

"Both late." She tried to think. "Indya didn't show up until well after the body was discovered, which is very telling if you ask me." She gave him a loaded look. "And Cindy was pretty tardy too. She turned up to lunch at about 12:20, 12:30 maybe, looking a bit puffed, it has to be said. She got there just before Boulder."

"Hang on," said Jackson. "So Elsbeth's lawyer was also late to lunch? I thought you said he doesn't dive. So where was he?"

"No idea. The first I saw him after breakfast was at lunch. He had a few words with James, which seemed to get him hot under the collar, before he helped himself to the buffet. Indya still hadn't arrived at that point, and to be honest, I assumed she was avoiding the mother-in-law who, as you know, had not shown. Everything was relatively quiet for a bit. I noticed Freddy disappear for a few minutes, then return with some tea, but it wasn't until Pasha returned that I knew something was up. She looked alarmed, must have known about Elsbeth then."

Jackson nodded. "What time was that?"

She shrugged. "Twelve forty-five maybe? We were onto dessert, but I didn't check the clock, sorry. I do know Indya was still AWOL at that stage."

"Interesting. Did Boulder or James mention anything? Ask why the elderly lady wasn't back? Or Indya for that matter? Was the alarm raised by either of them?"

"Not that I noticed. Pasha mustn't have said too much because James wasn't alarmed. He just looked annoyed and followed her to the dive deck. But I could tell something was up, so I raced ahead of them and... well, that's when I saw that Elsbeth was in trouble. Roland and the captain were performing CPR, then Gary took over from Liz. After that everyone else appeared and all hell broke loose. As you can imagine."

Jackson gulped his wine and gave it some thought. "I'm speaking with the staff tomorrow after we dock at Cooktown. They can't leave the vessel like the others, plus Liz needs all hands on deck until then. It also gives me a viable excuse to remain on the yacht, although it will still look suspicious, me not escorting Mrs Wynter off. Hopefully they won't twig. As for Boulder? He's refusing to be interviewed. Bloody lawyers."

"Is he *allowed* to refuse?"

"He is when he thinks I'm just the coroner's lackey."

"I would've thought he'd want to be helpful."

"He's a lawyer, Claire. It's the last thing he wants."

She smiled. "And what about James and his wife? Have you spoken to them?"

"Just briefly before dinner." Jackson scratched his stubble. "But I need to question them again. They're lying about Indya's relationship with her mother-in-law. Have glossed over any problems; say the two women got along like a house on fire."

"Yes, a roaring inferno. Doesn't take Miss Marple to see they loathed each other."

"Okay, so why lie about it? And, more importantly,

what else are they lying about?"

Claire raised her eyebrows. "And, more *interestingly*, where was Indya for the forty-five minutes we were all eating lunch? The first I saw her was when James went to tell her the grim news about Elsbeth. And here's another titbit I haven't mentioned." Claire's eyes narrowed again. "Young Indya looked positively relieved for a second before she began commiserating with her husband."

That didn't surprise Jackson. "Okay, so I definitely need to nab them before they jump ship tomorrow. Because he might be surly now, but I can't imagine James is going to continue his honeymoon."

"You haven't heard?" said Claire. "They're definitely staying on board until the end of the cruise. At least that's what they told us over dinner."

"James is leaving the task to Boulder, hey?"

"Oh, no, Boulder's staying put too. Apparently no one feels any need to accompany poor Elsbeth back to Sydney. They want to continue the cruise."

"What about procedure? I'm trying to remember my maritime law, but shouldn't somebody escort the body? I don't want to do it. I really need to remain here investigating."

"Don't worry, Boulder's arranged for his law firm to fly someone up to do the honours. Told Simon it's a 'gross waste' of his time. Said he'd be more useful on board, helping James and Indya recover from the trauma." She rolled her eyes at that, and then they lit up again. "At least the book club will be happy. All the suspects will still be here when they join us tomorrow."

She sounded exhilarated by that, even a little relieved, and Jackson wondered why.

Had it not occurred to Claire that if all the suspects remained, so too did the killer?

CHAPTER 18
Land Ahoy!

As she slowly manoeuvred the *Living Large* into Cooktown Harbour, Captain Flinders couldn't help feeling a deep sense of shame and disappointment. Elsbeth Wynter's drowning did not reflect well on her captaincy, and she knew the sharks would be circling.

They were supposed to be docking out on Osprey Reef today, the passengers enjoying the sparkling marine life. Instead, they were dispensing of a corpse, her passengers and crew rattled. Worse, they were opening their arms to more intruders.

Liz didn't like Simon's plan one bit. It was hard enough convincing everyone that Jackson was not a detective, but now she had to pretend to welcome in a fresh "couple" and an undercover cook. Little wonder Sergio was so confused.

She should have refused outright, would have, too, if it wasn't for the fact that Simon owned the yacht and held her future in his hands. It was a tenuous future now, and she would do everything she could to win Simon over and get her career back on track.

Softly stroking the golden epaulet on her uniform, Liz thought how long and hard she'd worked to earn those four stripes and how quickly it could all be ripped from her.

~

Watching as the port of Cooktown slowly came into focus, Gary slurped on a strong coffee and leaned against the safety rail, thinking of his next step. And how weary he felt. They'd got to Cooktown in record time. He'd been on night duty as always and had gunned it after dinner as hard as he could, the image of the *Titanic* bursting open on an iceberg keeping him from overdoing it. He wondered if all sailors thought of this as they navigated in a hurry. Then he thought of Captain Flinders and knew she'd be the type to go down with the ship.

Not Gary though. He was going to get through this, cling on to a floating iceberg and come out the other end. He was nobody's martyr. Not even the poorly named Captain bloody Flinders!

"Got five?" came a voice behind him, and he swung around to find the coroner's assistant standing there, also clutching a hot drink. Gary tried to conceal his frown. He nodded. No point putting it off any longer.

"Where do you want to do this?"

"Here will do," said Jackson. His eyes turned to the view. "Not a bad life you guys have."

"Yeah, when the guests aren't getting themselves drowned." His tone was droll, and Jackson turned back to look at him.

"Ever had this kind of thing happen before?"

He shrugged. "Once or twice."

Jackson's look intensified. "Care to elaborate?"

"Don't get excited. It's only because I once worked the major cruise liners. They lose passengers on a regular basis, usually just the elderly who should've been back in aged care. And the odd drunken lout who falls over the side of the ship." His jaw visibly tensed at that. "Never would have expected it on a boutique honeymoon cruise though. But then she was elderly and it wasn't really her honeymoon."

"So you knew about Mrs Wynter's subterfuge?"

He scoffed. "It's a small vessel, mate. Everybody knew

about that. And how miserable it made the young wife."

"What do you think happened?" Jackson peeled his eyes back to the approaching wharf. "Out there that day?"

Gary whipped his eyes to Jackson. "She drowned. Didn't she?"

Jackson didn't answer that. "Where were you when it happened?"

"Where I should be now, head down, snoring in my cabin. I'd done the night shift as always. I do the toughest shift, but for some reason the captain gets twice my salary, a swankier cabin, and all the glory. Go figure."

"So how did you happen to be on the deck, helping with the CPR?"

Gary's expression shifted. "My cabin's close to the dive platform. I heard the footsteps, the running. That's unusual on a yacht. Most people are pretty wobbly on the water; they walk with care—except the aforementioned drunks of course." His jaw tensed again. "Anyway, it woke me up. I got to the stern as fast as I could, and that's when I saw Roland performing CPR. Liz was trying to help, but she was fudging it, so I took over the breathing from her. Really, she should know how to do CPR. She is our commander, apparently. Anyway, the old lady was dead before I even touched her lips. Didn't stop me from having a crack. Sometimes you do that more for the sake of the spectators than any real expectation that you'll get them gasping again. That woman was gone long before she got back to the yacht."

"You sound as though you speak from experience," Jackson said, and Gary's frown returned.

"Like I said, I've seen enough death to know what's what." Then he pushed himself back and said, "Is that it? I should really get to the bridge. Make sure Liz doesn't crash into the marina and lose more passengers."

As he strode away, the first officer hoped Jackson wasn't as thorough as he looked and kicked himself internally for even mentioning the major cruise liner.

Gary had buried that nightmare three years ago; didn't need it dug up and resuscitated now.

~

Lynette grabbed Alicia's hand and tried not to sound too much like Missy as she squealed, "Oh my God! She's *gorgeous!*"

The gleaming white superyacht was now gliding slowly towards the Cooktown marina, dwarfing every yacht it passed and leaving most of them looking frumpy.

Alicia entirely agreed but shook Lynette off.

"We're supposed to be strangers, remember? No more sisterly contact."

"Oh, *I see*," said Lynette, waving a hand down the chef's uniform she'd dragged on for the role. "Too posh to talk to the hired help now you're a wealthy honeymooner, hmm?"

"Absolutely. If we start acting like nice, normal people, we'll give the game away. Now back off, oh servant girl."

Lynette rolled her eyes as she took a step backwards.

Fortunately, the yacht was still some distance away, and as they watched it close in, Alicia peeled her eyes for Jackson and thought she saw him at the bow but could not be sure.

"Do you think he'll be happy to see you?" said Perry, also locking on to the lonely figure at the front.

"Hope not," she replied. "He's also a 'stranger', so he'd better act very nonchalant."

"And you'd better keep your hands off," whispered Lynette. "No getting busted hooking up under a deck chair."

"Stop talking to us," Alicia hissed through tight lips.

They were standing at one end of the dock and began to make their way across just as they noticed an ambulance pull up and two paramedics jump out. At the same time, a young man in a Hawaiian shirt stepped out of a dusty four-wheel drive. He spoke to the paramedics briefly, then made his way to Alicia and Perry.

"Are you the Tanners?" he asked, his tone hopeful.

"Yes, we are," said Perry, who then cleared his throat and dropped his voice a few octaves. "Can't bloody wait to get on the ship with my missus."

Perry flung his hand out to shake as a soft snort could be heard behind them. It was Lynette, but Alicia didn't turn, she simply extended her own hand to shake.

"Good-oh," said the man. "I'm Glenn Lawson, the *Living*'s booking agent. Good of you to bring your trip forward a day."

"An extra day to enjoy the reef? It was a no-brainer," said Alicia, smiling. She noticed his glance back at the ambulance and said, "They're here for the body we presume?"

Glenn's smile froze, and she held out a hand again.

"It's okay, we were informed. It makes no difference to us. We won't be doing any diving. Just safely snorkelling, hey darling?"

"Yep, can't bloody wait, love."

"Good-oh," the man said again, then turned his eyes to Lynette. He stared down at her black-and-white-checked trousers and then at his clipboard and back again. "I'm sorry... Are you also waiting for the *Living Large*?"

"Captain Flinders arranged for me to come aboard," she said quickly. "I'm Lynette, the new sous chef. Here to help out in the kitchen."

"Really?" He looked confused. "Right." He turned back to Alicia and Perry. "The yacht's just docking now, as you can see."

"Yep, she's a bloody beauty," said Perry, and he smiled.

"I believe the chief steward will greet you when they're secure and get you settled in. I'll make sure your luggage follows you safely." He glanced warily at Lynette, then added, "Bon voyage, folks."

The booking agent then strode back to the paramedics

while Alicia turned to Perry.

"You don't have to sound like Crocodile Dundee to be married to me you know? And you *do* need to come up with some better adjectives than *bloody*."

"I'm trying to sound like Jackson."

There was another snort from Lynette, and he turned to scowl at her but she was now staring at the yacht, which suddenly loomed like an enormous white spacecraft above them.

After it had securely docked, a large brunette appeared at the gangway, clad in a white uniform, a stiff smile on her lips.

"Must be the chief steward," whispered Lynette. "Pasha I think her name is."

"I hope she doesn't ask us for ID," said Alicia, "or we'll be doomed. Maybe she already knows the Tanners? Maybe she has their pictures on file? What if she doesn't let us on board?"

"Stop stressing, woman," said Perry. "She's not worried about us, she's worried about that corpse, because that smile's fooling nobody. Come on, let's get this show on the road."

He began to make his way up the gangway while Pasha descended towards them.

"Mr Tanner?" she called out. "Robert Tanner?"

He did a little salute. "Bob please, and my wife, Marie."

Alicia smiled brightly as the introductions were made, and it seemed Perry was right. Pasha barely gave them a second glance and was already waving them upwards.

"Welcome to the *Living Large*. If you'd like to head on board, your butler will greet you and see you to your cabin. Help you settle in. My apologies, but I have to…" She glanced down towards the ambulance and back. "I'll see you a bit later. Morning tea is being served on the sun deck at the top, so once you've settled in, do make your way there for some light refreshments."

"Sounds lovely," said Alicia as Pasha offered another

stiff smile and continued down the plank.

Lynette was still waiting on shore, and Alicia noticed Pasha hold her hand up like a stop sign before gliding straight past her towards the ambulance.

~

Captain Flinders watched the interaction from the bridge, fuming.

"What's going on?" she asked Gary when he stepped inside. "I thought we arranged to have the paramedics here first to remove the body discreetly before the new guests arrived?"

"Don't blame me. I think Pasha organised it."

Deliberately botched it more likely, Liz thought, although it didn't really matter. The so-called Tanners already knew the truth, but *Pasha* didn't know that and it seemed insensitive of her to have them all show up at the same time. She knew Gary had it in for her but wondered if Pasha was also baying for blood.

~

Freddy was not nearly as distracted as the stewardess. He greeted the faux couple warmly and handed them each a glass of icy coconut water, then casually walked them through the yacht and towards their stateroom, giving them a tour of the facilities as he went. There was classical music coming from somewhere and the pleasant smell of bergamot, vanilla, and timber varnish.

"You are going to love my killer cocktails," he said after briefly stopping at Nemo's Lounge. "Sundowners start at six every evening, but you can drop in any time of the day or night; all the drinks here are complimentary. Oh, and if you are hungry, we do room service until ten pm, but if you head up to the top deck now, you will see morning tea is currently being served. There is also a jacuzzi up there and lots of deck chairs for lounging."

No mention of murder or corpses, but Alicia wasn't surprised. His job was to settle them in, and he was doing a good job. For just a few minutes, Alicia forgot their grim purpose, but then she got a rather wet wake-up call.

They were heading down a narrow, windowless corridor, halfway to their cabin, when Perry suddenly turned and pulled Alicia towards him, smashing his lips onto hers. Shocked at first, she didn't know how to respond, then from the corner of her eye she spotted another couple sweeping past them, the man offering her a lascivious wink.

"Couldn't even wait until you got to the honeymoon suite hey?" he said, then turned to his wife and added, "Why do you never kiss me like that, Cindy?"

"You know why, darling," she mumbled as they vanished around the corner.

Only then did Perry release his grasp.

"Goodness! That was amorous, sweetie," Alicia said, wiping a hand across her mouth.

Freddy was further ahead, waiting by their open door now, and Perry glanced at him and then back to Alicia and whispered, "Sorry, but we're not the only ones faking it."

"Huh?"

"That couple who just passed. I know that man. And it's little wonder his wife doesn't kiss him passionately. He's as gay as an Enid Blyton novel."

CHAPTER 19
Hiding in Plain Sight

Back at the marina, Lynette tapped her foot impatiently, waiting for someone to acknowledge her existence. The cranky-looking stewardess was still talking with the paramedics and the guy in the Hawaiian shirt. They had now been joined by a man in a stiff-looking suit, who'd driven up in a shiny hire car, and Jackson, who had completely ignored Lynette as he made his way down the gangplank and towards them.

Eventually, after several more minutes, the woman returned to Lynette, frown on her face.

"Lynette Finlay?" she asked.

Lynette held her hand out to shake, but the woman had already turned away.

"I'm Pasha Patel, chief steward," she called out as she marched back up the platform. At the top she looked around, sighing heavily. "What's taking that stupid boy so long?" An irritable glance at her watch. "The butler's supposed to be back here to escort you to the galley. I've got paying guests to attend to."

"I can find my own way," Lynette said.

Pasha looked relieved. "Good. Follow that handrail all the way down until you get to a door marked AUTHORISED CREW ONLY. You'll find your way to the kitchen from there. Do not enter the lounge area at any point, and keep well away from the passengers. There's to be no interacting with them whatsoever."

Will they turn into pumpkins? Lynette wanted to ask but

simply smiled and swung her bag to her shoulder. "What about my cabin? Can I pop this in first?"

Now Pasha looked irritable again. "Let's get our priorities straight, yes? It's morning teatime, and Sergio will also be prepping for lunch. Chop chop!"

Lynette's smile stiffened as she headed off, finding her way to the staff entrance and then into a long, shadowy corridor. If Pasha's cold welcome hadn't yet put her in her place, the corridor sure did. Lynette was now in a very different class to the others. There was no gentle music piping through here, and the hallway was narrower, the ceiling lower, the air more stifling, although there was a delicious smell of rose and pistachio coming from somewhere.

She followed it, along with a growing chorus of expletives, and found her way to the galley, where her mood dramatically lifted. The kitchen was not at all as she expected with its expansive benchtops and generous portholes and gleaming, state-of-the-art appliances. The head chef was a squat Italian man dressed head to toe in white, and he looked up at her, surprised, when she stepped through the open doorway. He had a pot above his head and another swear word tipping from his tongue.

He quickly swallowed it back and called out, "The dining area is upstairs, ma'am!"

"Oh, I'm not…" Lynette waved a hand at her checked trousers. "I'm Lynette. Reporting for duty, Chef."

He stared at her confused for a moment, then his whole demeanour changed and he dropped the pan with a loud thunk.

"Hurry up then," he growled. "Wash your hands, get that apron on and start slicing my *cacen ffenest*. It won't plate itself, you know!"

And down tumbled her mood again.

~

Despite offering to show them through the suite and help them unpack, butler Freddy was quickly given the brush-off by Perry, who closed the door firmly and turned back to Alicia, delirium in his eyes.

"We're not the only frauds aboard this yacht! I know that man who just passed us. It's Mr Pecs from my local gym."

"Mr Who?" Alicia reached for her phone and started scrolling, looking for the email Claire had sent her with the guest list. "I don't remember any..."

"Don't know his real name. We call him Mr Pecs, for obvious reasons. You could see his guns bursting through his shirt just now. It's him. I'm sure of it."

"Okay, take a deep breath. I believe you." She tapped the screen. "That must be Connor Dudley-Pine and his wife Cinnamon. Damn, this is very worrying."

"I know," he said, misunderstanding her. "I wonder if the poor woman has any idea she just married the gayest man in Sydney."

"Who cares about his wife? If you know him, then he must know you. We've come all this way, and already our cover is blown. And you can't keep snogging me every time he walks past."

"You wish!" he said, winking. "Don't worry, Mr Pecs wouldn't know me from a barbell. We've never actually met. He owns the gym so doesn't work out with us plebs, and from what I'm told, I'm not his type. He likes them young and exotic. And male! Or at least he used to."

"Cinnamon could be his beard, of course," said Alicia.

"His pay cheque more likely. Last I heard his gym was struggling, and that was pre-COVID. Maybe he married this Cinnamon woman for her money. What do we know about her?"

Alicia was scanning through the files she'd downloaded to her phone at the hotel last night. She held up a finger, reading. "Okay, from what I can gather, she does have a lot of cash or at least access to other people's. She runs her own investment company. Cinnamon and Spice."

"Catchy," said Perry.

"And thriving, if her fancy website is anything to go by. So why would she agree to marry a gay guy? It's not the 1920s. Gay men don't need beards anymore. Maybe she's clueless?"

"Or maybe she just likes the idea of having a bit of brawn on her arms," said Perry. "Speaking of which, did you see the size of *her* biceps? Looks like she benches more than he does. And… *hello!* Will you get a load of this room!"

Because, in all the excitement, they had barely noticed the stunning suite that was now their home, and they took a moment to gape at the breathless luxury around them. The plush king-sized bed, the shiny timber cabinetry, and an en suite bathroom embellished with gold and marble and every conceivable toiletry.

"Such a pity we won't have time to enjoy all this," Alicia said, staring wistfully at the enormous spa bath.

"Always time for Dom," said Perry, snatching up a chilled bottle of Dom Perignon that had been placed beside a bowl of chocolate-dipped strawberries near the bed.

"Don't even think about it," she said. "It's tea and scone time I'm afraid. Besides, we need to test your theory and see just how old and forgettable you really are."

He pretended to pout as he returned the bottle, and they made their way up to the sun deck. And it was not easy going. The yacht was setting sail again, and there was a worrying pitching motion.

"No need to rush," said Alicia, clinging on to a guardrail. "If we get there late, they may not even notice us."

"Here they are at last!" came a loud voice the moment Alicia and Perry stepped onto the top deck, and the former recoiled as every eye turned towards them.

So much for going unnoticed.

Pasha was smiling widely, a jug of iced tea in one hand. She used the other to wave them forward. "Welcome, newcomers, come on over and I'll make the introductions."

Alicia took a deep breath and smiled back as they stepped towards the group.

She spotted Claire and Simon first, sharing a daybed under the shade near the jacuzzi, and gave them the ghost of a smile before glancing at the couple several deck chairs away, basking in the full sunshine. It was the Dudley-Pines. Connor was giving her another wink; Cindy was giving her the once-over. Then Alicia's eyes drifted to a large, older gentleman who was leaning on a railing, watching them curiously, before she finally spotted the young Wynters seated right on the other side of the bubbling jacuzzi, both looking bored.

"Everyone, just a quick moment, if you will!" Pasha called out. "I'd like to introduce our newest guests, Marie and Bob Tanner. They'll be joining us for the voyage to Cairns."

James's expression darkened considerably, as did Boulder's, Alicia noticed, but the Dudley-Pines seemed delighted, and Connor was already striding across to introduce himself. Alicia stiffened and glanced at Perry, who looked positively blasé.

"Welcome aboard," said Connor. "Good to see you two could tear yourselves away from each other to join us."

"Thanks, mate," said Perry. "But with a woman like this"—he nudged a thumb at Alicia—"you can't blame a bloke, hey?"

Alicia smiled stiffly. Perry was still using his ocker accent, and she wondered how long he could keep that up and whether anyone would buy it. Connor appeared to be. He was already waving his wife over.

"This is my better half, Cindy, and I'm Connor."

They all shook hands, and for a moment Alicia felt herself relax. But then it happened. Connor squinted and said, "Gee, you look familiar."

She turned her eyes to Perry, waiting for him to talk himself out of this one until she realised that Connor was referring to *her*.

"Me?" said Alicia. "I look familiar?"

"Mmmm. I'm sure I've seen your face before…" His eyes squinted further. "Are you on TV? In the media perhaps?"

Alicia's stomach dropped, and she didn't know what to say. Yes, she did write for a group of magazines, but it was her byline she used, not her face. Then she remembered all the press they'd received after the last adventure, not to mention the follow-up book that had been written by one of the survivors. Connor must have recognised her from that.

"Oh, no, no, no," she said, "I'm just a boring housewife."

"Not *just a boring housewife*, honey," said Perry. "You keep the home fires burning." Then he grabbed her by the elbow and said, "Let's get some tucker, hey? I'm starving!"

And they walked away as casually as they could muster, considering their ruse was fast going up in smoke.

Claire could not believe it. She had been so excited to see her book club friends and was just approaching them when she heard the words "familiar" and "media" and saw Connor grilling Alicia. She stopped, gasped, then pivoted to the buffet table. Within seconds, Alicia and Perry were following, so she snatched up two slices of a gaudy-looking pink-and-green cake and returned to Simon.

Dropping back onto the lounge, she wondered how soon it would be before Connor put two and two together. He'd clearly recognised Alicia from all the press they'd received after the fire at Lyle's Rainforest Lodge.

Thank goodness they were now sailing away from Cooktown, away from internet reception.

"What's going on?" Simon asked. "You look like you've seen a ghost."

"I'll explain later," she whispered. "Until then, if you see Connor reach for his phone, smack it into the sea." Simon blinked at her, confused. "Trust me," she added, "we do not want that man anywhere near Google."

~

Lynette could have smacked Sergio across the head several times in the first hour, but she kept her cool as he ordered her about—"Get those dishes out of the way and that cake tin cleaned up!"

"No worries, Chef," she told him. Because he might be channelling Gordon Ramsay but Sergio might also have seen or overheard something useful to the case, so she needed to become his best friend and confidant, fast.

"I can cook, you know," she added, but he just made a *pft!* sound as he vanished into the cold room.

After reappearing a few minutes later, hands full of plump tomatoes, coriander and spinach, Lynette asked, "Who normally does dish-pig duty?"

"Me! I do it all. And when I am super busy, sometimes the butler helps, but not this one. He is useless. And don't look so grumpy. You will get a break once the lunch buffet is out. Until then, it is chaos! Not like my last job. That was so easy. This. *Pft!* Hard, hard work."

"Last job? What was that?"

"No time for chatter!" he yelled as he scuttled back into the cold room.

~

Pasha coughed discreetly as she stood at the entrance to the bridge. Gary and Liz were pointing at a high-tech screen with a detailed map of the coastline on it, and the latter did not look happy. Her frown firmed up when she spotted Pasha.

"What is it, Pasha? We're busy here."

"Sorry to disturb, Liz, but I've had some rumblings from the guests."

"It's Captain Flinders, Pasha, how many times must I say it? What kind of rumblings?"

"Mr Boulder wants to know why we're not heading northwards." Then she smiled stiffly and added, "*Captain.*"

Liz frowned. "Because we're en route to Cairns, of course. Does he know how a compass works?"

Pasha's smile was at rigor mortis stage. "I'm just the messenger, *Captain*. He's in his stateroom now and would like a chat."

"Oh for goodness' sake, like I don't have enough on my plate." Liz sighed heavily. "Fine. Tell him I'll be there in ten."

She turned back to the map while Pasha caught Gary's eye. They shared a conspiratorial eye roll, then Pasha smiled, and this time it was genuine.

~

Indya Wynter was sobbing. Or at least, that's what Perry had deduced.

He and Alicia had remained on the sun deck as long as they could, getting little more than small talk from the other couples before they all departed. Pretty soon only the Barriers were left, and so they'd stumbled across to say a proper hello to Claire and Simon.

"I'd give you lovebirds a decent hug, but I'd probably fall overboard with all this listing and rolling," Perry had said. "Besides, the butler's still lurking."

Freddy was indeed lurking, standing to one side of the buffet table, watching them keenly.

"Yes, best to play it straight," said Simon, then he

blinked at Perry and blushed at his *faux pas*.

Perry laughed at his discomfort. "Which is exactly what someone else is doing on this boat."

"What do you mean?" asked Claire just as Freddy made his way over, as wobbly on his feet as they were.

"Please can I get you anything else?" he asked.

"No, we're fine," said Perry.

"Actually, folks," said Simon, "I think that's our cue to let Freddy prepare the tables for lunch. Let's head down to the promenade deck."

And that's when a sobbing Indya nearly bowled them over.

The glamorous supermodel had changed into a pair of tiny, lightweight shorts, runners and a ripped designer T-shirt that probably cost more than all their outfits combined and was racing along the deck, buds in her ears, tears streaming down her face.

"Soz!" she cried out, pulling up short and looking startled, then embarrassed.

"Oh, Indya, are you okay?" asked Claire, reaching a hand towards her.

Indya ripped the buds from her ears and said, "What? Oh, this?" She wiped at her tears furiously. "It's just the wind! Always makes my eyes water."

Then she plunged the buds back in and continued past them.

"Where does she think she's going?" asked Alicia. "This yacht's hardly big enough for a decent run, and if she's not careful, she could fall overboard with all the swaying."

"She'll probably do a few circuits," said Claire. "Not a bad idea considering the cakes we've just eaten and lunch fast approaching."

Perry was more interested in her sobbing.

"Those were proper tears," he told them as he held the heavy, gangway door open. "We know Indya's not crying because she misses the monster-in-law, so what's she feeling so bad about I wonder?"

CHAPTER 20
The Band's Back Together!

Morning tea rolled into lunch for Lynette, too, but not in a good way, and she didn't have a spare second to interrogate the chef. Let alone catch her breath. It was not until mid-afternoon that Sergio finally called time on the shift.

"Good work today," he told her, "but it's not over yet. I need you back here at five to help prep for dinner. But now you can go, find your digs, relax while you get a chance."

He nodded towards the backpack she'd discarded in the corner.

Lynette could think of nothing she wanted more, but she had a second job to do, and so far she'd made no progress. So she asked if she could make a cuppa first and then slowly prepared some tea.

As the water boiled, she said, "How long have you been on the yacht?"

He looked up from the barramundi he was filleting. "Since its maiden voyage. Two years ago."

"You like it?" Because he certainly didn't act like he did.

He shrugged. "Is okay. Not as easy as my last gig."

"Yeah, you mentioned that. Easy is not a word that usually goes with cheffing."

"It is when you work corporate. That is the best. You just feed the rich publishers at lunchtime and cater for the odd cocktail party. Otherwise, good hours, big kitchens, even bigger salary package."

"That does sound ideal. And you get free books too, I guess."

He stared at her confused, then said, "You want a break or not? Because I've got plenty of jobs if you want to hang around."

"No, I was just—"

"Then go, get some rest. Come back at five. And don't be a second late!"

Lynette didn't get a chance to rest. After wandering the corridors confused for many minutes, she ran into Freddy, whose big brown eyes boggled at the sight of her, then directed her downwards.

"Crew are in the dungeon," he said, grinning. "Cabin B7 is spare and should be open. If it is not made up, please come back and I will give you sheets. Happy to make your bed for you if you like."

I'm sure you are, thought Lynette as she thanked him and made her way downwards, noting that things got even dingier and more claustrophobic in the crew section. Still, at least she had a cabin all to herself, albeit a tiny one, and she was just checking the bed for sheets when she noticed a note on her pillow. It was from Jackson, asking her to join him in Cabin A5 at three p.m. She checked her phone watch, sighed, then headed back up to the whiter, shinier section.

~

Jackson opened the stateroom door a smidgin and peeked out.

"Just lil' ole me," said Lynette.

He double-checked the corridor anyway, then pulled her in and secured the door firmly, applying the chain lock.

Inside, the rest of the book club were assembled, or half of them at least, and were busily catching up as old friends do. The moment Claire saw Lynette, she leapt from her chair and enveloped her in a hug so tight, it almost took her breath away.

"I'm so, so happy you came," Claire said. "Thank you!"

"Happy to be here," said Lynette, also sharing a quick hug with Simon. "So how's married life suiting you?"

"You mean pre-corpse?" Claire swapped a worried smile with Simon. "It was lovely. Now…"

"Now you're enjoying it even more, don't lie to us, Claire," said Perry, and she mock gasped.

"I *do not* wish people dead, Perry. But I must confess, a good mystery does add an extra spark to any holiday."

"Really?" said Simon, and now the others were laughing.

"You have so much to learn about your new wife," said Alicia, and Claire flashed her a stern look.

"And we still have so much to learn about this case, so can we cut the small talk and focus?" said Jackson, who always thought trying to control this lot was like corralling cats.

It was mid-afternoon and the yacht would soon be putting anchor near a shallow lagoon so the guests could have a refreshing swim. This meant he had a small window to interrogate the remaining crew, Freddy, Pasha and Sergio.

But first Jackson needed to have a stern chat with these cats…

"How many lives do you people think you get?" he asked, shaking his head. "It's a risky game you're playing, stowing aboard the *Death Star*."

"Steady on," said Simon.

Alicia looked delighted. "So it was definitely murder?"

"I'd put money on it," said Jackson. "Listen, I'm not going to reprimand you for coming because you never listen to me anyway, but since you're here, you might as well be useful. The priority is to find a link between Elsbeth Wynter and the others—both guests and crew—

and I've already made a good start."

He produced the note he'd found in Elsbeth's handbag. "This is the name of Cindy's investment company. She insists she'd never met Elsbeth before this cruise and can't explain why her name would be amongst the deceased's belongings."

"Obviously lying," said Perry.

"I'm not so sure," countered Claire. "Cindy looked genuinely surprised when Elsbeth approached her during our first dinner."

Claire went on to describe the altercation between Elsbeth and Cindy to the others. "But Elsbeth clearly knew her, or at least she thought she did, just couldn't remember the details. But here's the thing. She said Cindy was shifty. Called her that twice. And it clearly hurt. I wonder whether there's a story there and Elsbeth had to be silenced before her memory kicked in."

"What kind of story?" asked Simon, looking rattled. "What could possibly be so bad it leads you to murder?"

Jackson picked up his phone and glowered. "I'd look into Cindy's background if I could get a blasted connection."

"There is that satellite phone in the captain's office," said Simon. "You're welcome to use it if you need to, Jackson. I'm sorry if that wasn't made clear. There's another phone on the bridge. You can also use our satellite data connection to send emails through the desktop that's connected up in the office."

Jackson looked relieved and thanked him while Alicia said, "Can I use it too? I'd like to jump on and do some background research of my own."

Simon baulked at that. "Well... if you really *must*, Alicia. It's just that there's very limited data. We're not a large ship, so we can't afford to have our own satellite for at-sea connections. We rent some bandwidth from a private maritime communication company, but it's only for business use, not for the guests, and it does run out fast."

"Which is in our favour," said Claire soothingly. "Otherwise, we might all have been outed by now. It only takes one Google search."

"I'll be sure to use it sparingly," said Jackson. "Perhaps, Alicia, we can send one email to Missy and Ronnie later this evening with a full list of what we want researched. That way they can use their unlimited data and we won't use up all the yacht's. Does that sound fair?"

Simon nodded, looking relieved.

"Good," said Jackson. "Now can we get back to the case please?"

"I have another theory why Cindy might have wanted to kill Elsbeth," burst out Perry, like he'd been waiting for the opportunity. His eyes twinkled as he turned to Jackson. "Her marriage to Connor is a con. In every sense of the word. He's as camp as a row of tents. Maybe that's what Elsbeth was referring to."

He grinned as he filled the others in on Mr Pecs from the gym and his penchant for young men. It still didn't add up to murder, at least not in Jackson's book. But Perry would not be dissuaded.

"The secret Cindy might have been hiding could be her gay husband. They had to kill Elsbeth to protect their business interests."

There were several scoffs in the group, loudest from Lynette. "Who cares which way your husband swings? That's so old-school. These days, anything goes."

"Sure, in the creative world of cooking, Lynny. But maybe things are more conservative in a respectable business like investments?"

All eyes now switched to Simon, who looked both amused and bemused by the group.

"I do not believe anyone, in any world, would kill on such a flimsy basis," he replied, and Perry visibly deflated.

"I agree," said Alicia. "They're probably just one of those quirky couples. Maybe they want kids. I could look into it further? Shall we do as Missy always suggests and split up and each investigate a different suspect?"

"That won't work," said Lynette. "I'm the only crew member. Won't it be suspicious if one of you starts showing an interest in, say, Freddy?"

Alicia frowned. "Why? Are you interested in him?"

"Don't be ridiculous. He's too young and poor for Lynny," said Perry, grinning.

"Leave the crew to me for now," said Jackson. "I haven't had a chance to interview them properly yet. I've got Pasha scheduled in at four, then Freddy. I'll get to Sergio after that."

"Get to him fast," said Lynette. "He starts dinner shift at five, so he'll be flat-chat. As will I! Which is why we need to speed this up. If I'm to do any investigating, I have to get my skates on before I report back to duty."

"What's he like?" asked Jackson. "This Sergio fellow?"

"You mean, is he a killer?" she responded. "I'm not sure he'd have the chance. It's bloody hard work alone in the galley. Barely time to scratch your nose. No wonder he wants to get back to publishing."

"Oh schnookems," said Perry, but Jackson had a hand up.

"Hang on, what's this about publishing?"

"Not publishing, exactly," said Lynette. "He told me he'd previously cooked for a publisher and it was easier and more lucrative."

"Books or magazines?" Jackson persisted.

Now she was frowning. "Does it matter?"

"Yes!" said Jackson and Alicia together and then the latter explained:

"The Wynters own the largest magazine publishing company in the country, Lynny." Alicia glanced at Jackson now. "That could be our link?"

Lynette's eyes widened. "Sorry, I just assumed he meant books. No wonder he looked at me strangely."

"Did he say why he left this publisher?" Jackson was asking.

"No, but I get the feeling it wasn't by choice. I mean he was really raving about the gig, like he'd much rather be there. And he's right. It might sound glamorous working on a yacht, but when you're stuck in a hot, sweaty kitchen while everyone else is swanning about, it's no fun at all."

"Oh *schnookems*," said Perry again, but that, too, was ignored.

"See if you can get a little more out of him on that score," said Jackson. "Be subtle about it; we don't want to give the game away. But if he did work for the Wynters, we need to know why he left their employ, especially if he loved it so much. What happened to drive him away? Maybe there was some bad blood."

"And maybe some of it spilled over on this yacht," added Alicia, locking wide eyes with her boyfriend.

There was a sudden loud knock on the door, and they all jumped, then glanced between themselves worriedly. Jackson held a finger to his lips and strode across to reopen the door a fraction. A second later he was letting the captain in.

Liz looked warily at the group but quickly introduced herself, then rested her eyes on Jackson. "Can I have a quiet word please? There's mutiny afoot."

CHAPTER 21
Calming the Troops

As the others headed off to fetch their swimmers, eyes darting curiously as they went, Simon remained behind with Jackson to discuss the trouble that was brewing.

"Mr Boulder and the Dudley-Pines are insisting we finish the cruise," said Captain Flinders. "They want to head back to Osprey."

Jackson scowled. "I thought we'd agreed we're heading straight to Cairns."

She glanced at Simon. "Look, this is a very expensive cruise, and if we bail out now, we lose everything. Boulder is saying that Osprey is the jewel in the crown and he wants a full refund if he doesn't get to see it."

"But he doesn't even scuba dive!" said Simon. "Unbelievable. Okay, well, we can't have him suing us."

"We're not going to Osprey," said Jackson, tone resolute. "It's in the middle of nowhere. I don't care about lawsuits, Simon. I care about lives, and I won't allow it."

"But surely the target was Elsbeth," he replied almost flippantly.

"Doesn't change the fact there's a killer on this boat," Jackson shot back. "We'd be better off sticking close to the mainland. In fact, the smart thing would have been to get everybody off in Cooktown and interrogate them officially. But since that's not happening, I suggest we head straight for Cairns and do it there. I really don't want to delay that. It's bad enough we're making this swim stop. It's risky."

"I can't very well tell the passengers that now can I?" said Liz. "They think it was a terrible accident. Telling them we have to race for Cairns because their lives are at risk will give the game away. But I'm not keen on heading north to Osprey either. It will put the schedule right out and get the guests back a day late. That will play havoc with connecting flights and could very well delay the next cruise, which is scheduled straight after."

"Good point," said Simon. "We don't want to be refunding yet more disgruntled passengers."

Jackson shook his head at him. He didn't care about connecting flights and future cruises and disgruntled passengers. "We're not extending the journey, Simon, and we're not going out to Osprey. That's not up for discussion."

Liz cleared her throat. "I have a solution."

Retrieving a map from her jacket, she opened it and pointed to a cluster of dark shadows on the outer edge of the Great Barrier Reef, southeast of Cooktown. "We could meet the guests halfway on this. Move the dives to Escape Reef. It's truly lovely—more touristy than we'd advertised—but it's almost halfway to Cairns. So at least we're heading in the right direction, and the guests get more of a dive holiday without becoming suspicious."

Simon studied the map and considered it, but Jackson was shaking his head.

"If we detour to this Escape place, that'll delay our return. I want it on record: I don't like it."

"Oh, it'll be fine!" said Simon, eyes on Liz. "Will the guests buy that?"

"If we promise to dock on the outer eastern rim, far from any other vessels, then maybe." Then, in response to Jackson's growl, she added, "Privacy was the key selling point for this cruise. If we tell them we need to be safely near others, that will cause more suspicion. Besides, we have to pretend to give this new couple a bit of an adventure or it'll be far too obvious."

"Okay, so it's agreed," said Simon, not noticing the loaded look she was now giving him. "After dinner tonight we'll head south, stop at Escape Reef for a day and night, then we'll up anchor and sail on to Cairns. That will get us back right on time and might just halt all talk of lawsuits and any further chaos."

Liz was nodding, but Jackson felt a lump in his gut, and it had little to do with the idea of being stuck on board an extra day with a killer. Simon seemed more concerned with covering his losses than protecting the lives of his passengers.

He wondered if Claire had any inkling how ruthless her husband could be.

~

For a group who believed that Elsbeth's death was an accidental drowning, they were all watching each other a little too closely when the yacht came to a rolling halt and they got a chance to swim that afternoon. Everyone, that is, except Simon, who was still conferring with the captain.

The *Living Large* was now anchored off Osterlund Reef, just south of Cooktown, and the diving equipment had not been produced, nor was anyone complaining. They simply helped themselves to the snorkelling gear and paddle boards that Roland was offering, along with a cheerful smile that no one was buying.

By the time Alicia, Perry and Claire reached the dive platform, the Wynters and the Dudley-Pines were already paddling about, and nobody commented on their tardiness as they stripped down to their swimsuits and reached for snorkels and goggles.

"Sunscreen, honey?" Claire said to Alicia, sounding a little too familiar, and Alicia noticed Boulder look up from his perch on the edge of the platform.

Once again he wasn't hitting the water, just dangling his pale, chubby legs over the side, also watching them all as though playing lifeguard.

Was he worried there'd be a repeat of Elsbeth?

"Thank you, that's very kind," said Alicia, trying to sound more formal.

"If you're entering the water, might I suggest this sunscreen," said Roland, holding out his own tube of SPF. "It's made from natural ingredients and doesn't harm the marine life like that brand does."

Claire said, "Goodness, I didn't realise. Sorry!"

"No harm done," began Roland, but Boulder was now scoffing.

"I'm tired of all this woke nonsense," he grunted. "So what does she do now, hmm? Throw away a perfectly good sunscreen to protect a few fish? How is that good for the environment?"

"Well, sir, it's about *not* buying it in the future," explained Roland. "It's about sending a message to the company. If they stop making profit from a bad product, they'll start producing a good one."

"Bollocks," said Boulder below his breath.

"Just trying to protect our World Heritage-listed marine park," Roland said politely, swapping a subtle eye roll with the two women as they finished lathering up.

By the time they hit the water, it was easy to forget all about murder, let alone environmental doom because Roland was quite right. Large swathes of the famous reef were now in crisis. Here, however, the coral was not yet bleached, and the fish life was still abundant. Alicia noticed a strange-looking sea creature and pushed her mask and snorkel set off to ask Roland about it, when she heard a familiar laugh and a splash coming from the other side of the yacht. She paddled around to find Lynette and Freddy were also swimming and spraying water at each other.

"Is she flirting intel out of him," asked Perry, who'd followed her over and was spluttering through his snorkel, "or is she just hard up for romance these days?"

"Knowing Lynette, all of the above," Alicia replied,

turning back to see Connor Dudley-Pine treading water nearby.

He had his mask off too and was watching the young crew members closely.

~

Jackson was rushing to make his four p.m. interview with Pasha, which had been organised in Nemo's Lounge. There she was busily preparing the bar for sundowners.

"I won't be a second!" she called out as he strode in. "Grab a seat and I'll finish up and join you."

He chose a side table and watched as she stacked champagne flutes, then dropped fresh coasters on every table. Occasionally she looked up at him with a flirty smile, and when she eventually joined him, she had two tall glasses of lemon squash and a bowl of mixed nuts in hand. Like they were on a date or something.

"So, how long have you been working for the coroner?" she asked as she took the seat closest to him.

"I'll ask the questions, if you don't mind, Pasha. I'm on a tight schedule."

"Sorry, small talk is an occupational habit." She chuckled. "And I know we have to leg it to Cairns, so time is of the essence."

She clearly hadn't been informed of the captain's decision yet, and he let it go.

"Thanks for your time," he launched in. "I know the guests keep you busy."

"Oh, they're not so bad. I've worked much busier ships than this."

"Ever worked with any of the crew before?"

Her smile slipped slightly. "Now who's making small talk! This is important I assume?"

"Just getting the lay of the land."

"Sure." She took a good sip from her glass. "Most of us have worked together on this yacht since it first launched two years ago, although this is only Liz's second official cruise as captain. She was just one of us plebs before that."

He studied her. Was there bitterness in her tone?

"Freddy's relatively new though," she added. "More's the pity. We had a terrific butler before him, an older Filipino guy called Gabriel, with actual cruise experience. I'm not sure Freddy's ever worked ships before. I had to teach him towel origami! Really, how can you call yourself a butler if you can't fashion a swan from a hand towel?" She was being facetious and offered a flirty smile above her glass. "Still he is very pretty, young Freddy. Perhaps that's why Liz brought him on—for eye candy."

There was another smile, this one more loaded, and he didn't take the bait. It felt like a distraction. "Where were you when Elsbeth drowned?" he asked instead.

"Do I *need* an alibi?"

Jackson went to drag out his trusty box-ticking line, but she was already responding.

"I was busily overseeing Sergio's stunning lunch spread up on the deck, then making sure it all stayed lovely and fresh for the tardy guests, of which there were a few."

"Such as?" He knew the answer, but he wanted to see how observant she was.

"Oh, let me think." She took a handful of nuts. "Um, the men were all starving; they're usually the first in. But I did see Cindy come in late and Indya got there eventually but not before we'd dragged poor Elsbeth back to the yacht."

"So you were on the lunch deck full time between twelve and twelve forty-five?"

She chewed, shrugged, said, "On and off."

"What does that mean exactly?"

A frown now. "It means I was traipsing up and down the stairwell like a galley slave to keep the fabulous food coming."

"Was Sergio there the whole time? In the kitchen, I mean."

"As far as I recall. We don't really interact. He leaves the platters on a heated counter, and I just whisk them up to the hungry hordes, why?"

"I believe you were the one who raised the alarm about the missing woman. Can you walk me through that?"

Her nose crinkled. "Actually it was Freddy who first sounded the alarm. About the only useful thing he's done! He must have mentioned the tardy diners while down in the galley, and I gather Roland overheard and that's when he went into a panic. At least that's when he first grabbed me, said he was heading out to look for Mrs Wynter."

"What happened then?"

"Roland jumped in the zodiac to look for her, and I alerted Liz. Then I ran and checked the cabins in case she was there. I… Well, I wasn't sure exactly which woman was missing at that point, but neither of the Wynter women were in their rooms."

He sat forward. "Neither of them?"

"If they were, they weren't answering. Indya could have been in the shower I guess. By the time I got back to the deck, I could see Roland returning, and I felt a moment of relief before…" Her crinkle was back. She gulped. "It was all such a shock."

He nodded. "Did you have a swim that day? Did you see anything?"

"Me? No, I didn't get a chance to swim in the end, but even if I did, I wouldn't be much of a witness. The crew are instructed to swim on the opposite side from the passengers. We try to give the guests their space. No fraternising with the enemy!" She smiled, her voice playful. "There's a retractable ladder we can use. It's midship, not far from the galley, but I can assure you I never found a moment to enjoy myself that day. Not that I don't enjoy my work normally, of course."

"Of course," he said, wondering about that. Wondering

if she could have snuck off during lunch and done the deed, wasn't convinced the times worked.

"Do you have a relationship with the deceased? Anything I need to know?"

She looked at him bewildered. "Why would you assume that?"

Now he was smiling casually. "I'm not assuming anything. I'm just ticking boxes, and you still haven't answered my question."

"I'd never met the woman before in my life."

"Okay, thank you, Pasha. I appreciate your time."

Jackson got up and left the lounge, but he noticed she didn't say goodbye nor was she as flirty as before. She was chewing on the nuts, a million miles away.

~

Now it was Freddy who was running late for his interview. He'd had far too much fun flirting with the new cook. Man, she was *fine*. And she didn't look down on him like the others did. Turns out, there's a pecking order on ships, and butler was the lowest of the low.

Ha! If only they knew.

Still, hierarchy didn't seem to matter to the fit newcomer, or perhaps she didn't know how things worked on the water. She seemed even more sketch than him, and he was sure he saw her wandering the guest corridor earlier. That was taboo.

Freddy was just reaching the captain's office when he noticed Liz leaving, and his smile lit up. "Anything I should be worried about, Cap'n?"

The captain stared at him hard for a moment, then glanced at the closed door and back.

"Just try not to say anything stupid. If you can manage it."

She shook her head at him, like he was twelve, then strode off, and he wondered what bug had got up her—

"Freddy Cruz?" came a voice behind him, and he turned to see Jackson standing in the doorway. "Come in. I've only just got here myself. Take a seat and I'll be with you in a sec."

By the time Jackson had got his act together and they were seated across from each other at the desk, Freddy's good mood had fallen away, reality rushing in.

"Okay, where am I?" Jackson said, scanning his notepad. "Ah, yes, still trying to sort out the timeline around Mrs Wynter's death." He tapped the pad, then met Freddy's gaze. "I hear you're the hero of the day. You were the first to notice she was missing, is that correct?"

Freddy felt his mood lift again. "Yes, hundred percent. They were all too busy eating, eating, eating... but I could tell something was suspicious."

"Good on you," said Jackson. "Tell me how it all went down."

As Freddy began to recount the story, Jackson didn't hear anything he hadn't heard before. Well, apart from Freddy's heavy rhotic accent, that is. While he spoke impeccable English, the butler couldn't disguise his Philippines origins.

He'd been tending lunch on the sun deck, he told Jackson now, when he noticed several of the guests were missing so had mentioned it to Sergio in the kitchen, and that's when Roland overheard and "went super crazy", rushing for the zodiac.

Jackson frowned. "It sounds like almost everybody was in the water that day. Did you also have a swim?"

"Me? No way, man. I was too busy cleaning the rooms while everyone was diving. That is my 'window'." He added the quote marks himself. "After this I had to race to the deck to set up for lunch before Pasha got on my case again. Then I did the lunch shift. I do not get time for swimming."

"So that wasn't you I saw in the water just now?

Swimming with the new cook?"

Freddy blinked then smiled, giddily. "Not gonna lie, that was me. But it was *her* idea. She asked me to show her where the crew swim and then made me jump in. Sheesh, I think she wants me baaaad." He giggled suddenly.

You're not nearly old enough or rich enough for Lynette, Jackson wanted to respond, instead he asked, "Did you have any dealings with Mrs Wynter or her family before her death?"

The giggling stopped. "Dealings? Like, before this trip?"

Jackson shrugged and the butler's smile was back.

"No, no. I am just an ordinary citizen, trying to earn an honest living. People like the Wynters, they do not let me near them."

Except you are near them, thought Jackson. You're making their beds in the morning and turning down their sheets at night. As for being an honest citizen? "I thought you were a foreign worker. Didn't I read in your file that you're from Manila?"

His face tightened. "No way, man! I am Aussie. True-blue! I come up from Sydney."

"Duly noted," said Jackson, wondering why the young lad had turned so defensive so fast.

CHAPTER 22
A Pre-dinner Announcement

It was just after six o'clock and the guests were seated in the lounge, nursing cocktails, champagne or, in James's case, a tall frothy glass of lager. The crew were also in attendance, although the only thing they were nursing were frowns as they stood as a group in the at-ease position at the back, quietly waiting for the captain to arrive.

Simon was also missing. Claire hadn't seen her husband all afternoon, and when he walked in with the captain and Jackson, she could tell something was up.

He looked worried but not panicked. The captain soon explained why.

"Ladies and gentleman," she called out, bringing them all to attention. "Hello and thank you so much for your time. I'll try not to take too much of it. I know some of you have to get back to your stations"—a quick, apologetic look at Sergio who was standing, looking grumpy beside Lynette—"and some of you have Freddy's delectable cocktails to enjoy."

"Hear! Hear!" said Connor, chuckling as he raised something red and frothy.

"I do appreciate it's been a very trying few days, and I know it hasn't been easy with Mr Jackson here asking questions on behalf of the coroner, but I do appreciate your cooperation and candour."

Claire heard a soft snort at the back, but when she glanced around, she couldn't work out who it had come from. She locked eyes with Lynette, who then darted hers in the direction of Gary and Pasha.

"Having said that," continued Liz, "Jackson assures me he has now managed to speak to most of you. I think there's just one crew member to go?" She glanced at Jackson, who nodded.

"I may still need to check a few things, so please don't be alarmed if I speak to you again. I'm just—"

"Ticking boxes?" someone yelled out. Alicia noted it was Gary and he had a smirk on his face.

Jackson stared hard at him. "But other than that, my work is complete and I'll leave you all in peace."

"With that in mind," continued Liz, "I would like to clarify our itinerary for those who are not in the loop." Her eyes slid to Gary, then back to the guests. "I have heard from you each individually, and I appreciate your concerns. I have also spoken with the ship's owner, and we have agreed to extend the cruise. Or, should I say, continue the cruise as best we can."

"Good to hear," said Boulder, raising his martini glass now.

Liz had a hand up. "Unfortunately, that does not mean we can return to Osprey."

"What?" Boulder's martini was back on the table.

"I'm terribly sorry, folks, but it's just not feasible. We've lost valuable time and that will get us back to Cairns too late; some of you will miss your connecting flights. However, Roland assures me there are lots of wonderful sights to behold on our way back down to Cairns, and that's why we've decided to up anchor after dinner tonight and make our way to a lovely little spot called Escape Reef for another day of diving. Roland will tell you a little about Escape in a moment"—a quick glance at Roland, who was now cueing something on the TV screen, looking flustered—"but suffice to say, we'll have you all safely disembarking in Cairns on Thursday morning as scheduled. I think this should make you all happy?"

As she glanced from face to face, Claire saw that they

did, indeed, seem happier. The Wynters were now holding hands, Boulder was smudging his lips into the semblance of a smile, and the Dudley-Pines were clinking glasses. Even the crew looked lighter, all except for Gary, who was glaring towards the captain.

"Great," said Liz, not noticing. "I'll get back to the bridge and leave you to it."

As she left, Claire heard Gary say, "Is she *serious*?" before marching across the carpet and following the captain out.

Once the crew got back to work, Alicia noticed Claire give her the eye, and so she nudged Perry and they wandered over to her table, leaning in casually, like they were simply making small talk.

Claire said, "Listen, if Roland drones on like he did the other night, we won't get much time before dinner. I just wondered what you thought of Gary. He seemed positively riled up."

"And why would Jackson say he was finished?" said Perry.

"He's just trying to disarm everyone," explained Alicia. "He wants them all relaxed so they start to make mistakes."

"Kudos to him, because it's working," said Perry, nodding his head towards the Wynters, who did, indeed, look like a weight had lifted from their shoulders.

They were now standing at the bar, smiling at something Cindy was saying, Connor just beside her. It was the first time Alicia had seen them engage with anyone else, and she was just considering joining them when Connor caught her eye and strode across.

"Shoot me now," he said. "My wife has just started banging on about her business, boring the poor Wynters senseless." Then he chuckled. "But one mustn't moan. It does allow us to splurge on fabulous cruises."

Alicia could feel Perry twitch beside her.

"You're not part of the business?" she asked, drawing Connor away.

"Hell no. I'd be bored senseless. No, no, I run a fitness centre. A very successful one right in the heart of Sydney."

"Really?" said Alicia. That's not what she'd heard from Perry. She smiled blithely and said, "That's lucky after COVID shut down so many gyms around the country."

"Oh, we got through it, no sweat. Well, a little bit of sweating. It is a gym after all." Then he winked and said, "I'd better rescue the Wynters before they scuttle back into their shell."

He chortled as he left her, but Alicia had a feeling he was rescuing himself from more of her questions. Or was it his wife he was rescuing? Because she could see the Wynters were now staring hard at Cindy and no longer smiling.

~

Liz had just reached the bridge when Gary came flying in, a scowl across his brow.

"So that's it? You're pretending nothing's happened?"

Liz gulped. "I'm sorry?"

Gary exhaled loudly and closed the bridge door firmly. "You're going back into holiday mode and pretending a woman wasn't just murdered on your watch."

Now Liz was scowling. "What are you talking about?" Because he wasn't supposed to know about that.

He shook his head at her, contempt in his eyes. "You think I'm a complete idiot, don't you?"

"Gary—"

"You really think I don't know why you brought that knob on board? Coroner's assistant my arse. He's a cop. I can tell from his stupid questions and 'ticking boxes' bullshit. He's here to investigate Mrs Wynter's murder."

Liz blinked rapidly, unsure how to respond. "No, that's not right, Gary. You've misunderstood."

"So there was no murder. Is that the story you're sticking with?" She folded her arms, unable to find her voice now and he scoffed again. "That's a pity, *Liz*, because I saw the murderer. I saw them with my own eyes."

CHAPTER 23
A Sight to Behold

Sergio did not look happy when Jackson strolled into the galley kitchen and introduced himself. Nor did Lynette for that matter. She glanced at the clock on one wall that read 6:50 p.m. and offered Jackson a pointed glare, but she let her new boss do the barking.

"I do not have time for this!" he bellowed. "I have dishes to plate, hungry beasts to feed. I am on a tight schedule. You come back later."

"No can do, mate," said Jackson, completely unfazed. "I'm on a tight schedule too, and I've put this off long enough. Your sidekick looks pretty competent. I'm sure she can hold the fort while we talk. It will only take five minutes."

Lynette produced a relaxed smile and said, "I'll be okay, Chef. You go."

He hesitated briefly, then tapped his apron pocket and followed Jackson out. But not before yelling: "Don't forget to get that eggplant *melanzane* into the oven!"

Then, when Jackson went to head right, he said, "No, this way" and led him along a narrow corridor and then out the service door and onto the open deck, where he promptly retrieved a packet of cigarettes and a lighter from his pocket.

As he lit up, he said, "So what do you want?"

Jackson smiled. It was a good thing this bloke wasn't front of house with that bedside manner. "I'm completing an incident report for the coroner and need to know where everyone was around the time Elsbeth Wynter went missing and subsequently drowned. For my records."

Sergio didn't query that as the others had, simply shrugged as he exhaled and said, "I was in the kitchen as always. Preparing for the lunch."

"Alone?"

"Freddy and Pasha came and went but yes, until that one arrived"—he shrugged his head inwards—"I'm always alone. You don't know why Captain thinks I need help suddenly, do you?"

Jackson did his own shrug. "And you never left the galley all afternoon?"

Jackson looked pointedly at the cigarette Sergio was sucking, and the chef released another plume of smoke and said:

"Sure, I take time for smoko, so?"

"What about a swim? Did you take time for a swim that day?"

He scoffed. "Who has time for swimming? Certainly not me."

"Yet you work on a yacht. Isn't that one of the fringe benefits?"

"Perhaps for Pasha and Freddy. I am not here for fun. I am here to pay my bills. They do not pay themselves. Although my pitiful salary barely helps."

Jackson glanced outwards at the rapidly darkening sea. "So did you happen to see anything of any interest out on the water during one of these smoking breaks? Anything around the time it happened, say between eleven forty-five and twelve forty-five that afternoon?"

Sergio stared at his cigarette and said, "Sure. I see."

Jackson turned back to look at him. He wasn't expecting that. "See? What did you see?"

"The pretty girl, the one in the gold bikini."

"Indya Wynter?" Sergio shrugged like he had no idea what her name was. "And what was she doing?" Jackson asked.

"She was on the pontoon."

"The one closest to the yacht?"

"No, no, the one further away. She was talking to somebody."

Jackson held a hand up. Tried to catch his breath. "Hang on, are you saying you saw Indya Wynter on pontoon two with somebody? What time was this?"

"I cannot recall. Like you said, around lunchtime."

"Think. Please. Try to be more specific."

He stared at his cigarette. "Okay, so… the last platters went up and I was having a break before they call me back, bitching for more lobster. They always want more lobster even though it is not as tasty as the swordfish and the mussels. These are so much better. But this lot. It is always about big and showy lobster, yes?"

Jackson didn't care about lobster. He might just have his first official suspect; could wrap this case up faster than he'd thought. "So let's get back to Indya. You saw her on the farthest pontoon just as lunch was about to start. Around noon?"

He shrugged. "Sure. Noon. Maybe bit after."

"Who was she talking with?"

"How can I know this? They were in a wetsuit."

He nodded. "What shape were they? Could it have been the deceased? An older lady? Short, thin?"

Sergio did his infuriating shrug again and said, "Perhaps, yes. But why you hassle me? Ask Gary. He saw them too."

Then he dragged on his cigarette casually like he hadn't just lobbed a grenade into the middle of the case.

~

Gary also seemed unruffled as he recounted a similar statement to Jackson ten minutes later. In fact, he was verging on annoyed that Jackson hadn't worked it out for himself.

"Indya didn't tell you about this?" he said.

Jackson shook his head. *Neither did you,* he wanted to say, but it wasn't time for recriminations. Not yet. He needed to get this story straight, had been holding his breath since his interview with Sergio and was now standing in the bridge with Liz, whose startled eyes mirrored his mood.

"Start at the beginning," she said to Gary. "Tell him exactly what you just told me—how you saw Indya talking to Elsbeth out on the second pontoon."

He nodded and relaxed into the command chair, like he was enjoying the attention. "Fine. So here's the thing. I couldn't sleep so I went for a walk. Clear my head a bit."

"So you weren't sleeping like you said in your earlier statement."

"Hey, you try sleeping in the middle of the day on a yacht full of holiday makers!"

That wasn't Jackson's point, but he let it drop and said, "So what time are we talking?"

Gary lifted a shoulder. "About twenty minutes or so before lunch. Anyway, there's binoculars at strategic points around the deck, for the guests, so I grabbed a set and had a look about. Just happened to see them all diving so I watched them for a bit."

"The guests? You're talking about all the guests at this stage?"

"Except the bald older bloke. He wasn't there. Or the bigwig who owns this yacht and his sexy mail-order bride."

Jackson knew he was referring to Claire but didn't have time to pull him up on his obscene racism either, just waved him on.

Gary said, "So yeah, the others were diving off pontoon one, Roland boring them senseless with his namby-pamby greenie crap, always banging on about the preservation of the bloody reef." He flashed Liz a look that spoke volumes. "Then Indya and James had a bit of a squabble and—"

"You saw them fighting, even from a distance?" Okay, this married with what Connor had said.

"Dumb Freddie could tell they were fighting, and yes, I am referring to our so-called butler." Another snide glance at the captain. "Indya was waving her hands about, and James was kind of treading water, you know? Just listening while she splashed him in the face and made a spectacle of herself."

"Then what happened?"

"Nothing. Dr Knobjockey swam over and must have shooed them back to the ship because they all started swimming back. But here's the thing." He leaned forward. "*She didn't.* Indya started to head back when she just dived under and vanished. Then I saw her resurface about five minutes later and climb onto the second pontoon. The old bird was already up there, and they started yacking for a bit."

Jackson and Liz shared a look, then Jackson said, "How can you be certain it was Elsbeth Wynter on the second pontoon?" Sergio hadn't been that confident.

"Who else would it be?" he replied.

Liz placed a hand at her mouth, unsure what to say. Jackson considered this for a moment, then asked, "And you're sure it was Indya you saw resurface? All bodies look similar in wetsuits from afar."

"Yeah, but she wasn't in a wetsuit, was she?" He smirked. "She was in a gold bikini, and that's pretty hard to miss even from afar."

"Then what happened?"

He shrugged. "I don't know. I went back to bed. Ask Sergio. He hung around to perve."

"So you didn't see anyone else in the water?"

He shook his head as Liz rubbed the back of her neck.

"Why are you only just telling us this now?" she demanded.

"Hey, don't start laying into me, boss!" he spat back. "*You* said it was an accident. *You* said there was nothing to see here. So I figured it wasn't important." He turned his sneer towards Jackson. "Then you began asking strange questions and I realised you'd been lying from the start, *Captain*." His eyes were back on Liz, and they were full of thunder. "If you'd been straight with me, I would've told you all this earlier. I'm your second in command. Does that count for nothing? I should have been told this man was a detective. I had a right to know."

"Really?" she shot back. "You're really going to talk about honesty and respect, Gary? Seriously?"

His jaw tightened but he didn't respond to that as he turned and stormed out of the room.

"Keep that information to yourself!" she called after him, then dropped her head into her hands.

"What was that about?" Jackson asked the moment Gary had cleared the bridge.

Liz looked up. "It's nothing. Just his own personal crap. So what do you think? Could Indya be the culprit?"

Her expression was half-hopeful, half-sceptical, and Jackson didn't feel vested one way or the other. "If you mean could she have pulled it off, sure. She's younger and stronger than the victim and certainly has a motive. Now we know she had means and opportunity. It's our best lead so far."

"If we believe Gary," she said.

His eyes narrowed. "You want to tell me what's going on?"

She shrugged. "I don't trust him, that's all. He'll probably come out with some fresh, far-fetched story tomorrow."

"What about Sergio? Do you trust your chef? Because he made a similar statement." She tried shrugging him off again but he wasn't having it. "Come on, Liz, you're the one who mentioned honesty and respect. I'm big on those things too. Speak to me."

Eventually, after a clear mental tussle with herself,

Liz said, "I do trust Sergio, but Gary?" She shook her head, causing her tight bun to loosen a little. "I just think he *wants* it to be murder, that's all. He wants a scandal; that would suit him very nicely."

"Why would he want that?"

"He wants to destroy me, that's why."

"You're sounding very paranoid, Captain."

"Well, it's hard not to be paranoid when you're me." She sighed. "We were both up for this job, Gary and I. Did Simon tell you that? Both of equal ranking before I clinched it. Gary thinks I only got it because I'm a woman and because of my name. Like it's my fault I happen to have the same surname as some poncy British navigator. Which is ludicrous and, frankly, insulting. Couldn't possibly have anything to do with his past record or the fact I'm a superior commander."

"Past record?"

She shook her head. "I don't have time to get into this. I have a new route to navigate and a lot of paperwork to get in order. All I'll say is Gary doesn't really care who goes down for Elsbeth's death as long as I'm the collateral damage."

CHAPTER 24
What Happened During Dinner

Alicia watched as Pasha filled her wineglass with a wink, then thanked her and glanced around the dining deck at all the individual tables. It was such a pity they didn't get to sit as a group, like on a regular cruise, or have the captain and Jackson join them for dinner. And as she smiled back at Perry, she couldn't help wishing it was her boyfriend sitting across from her under the sparkly, moonlit sky.

"I know what you're thinking," Perry said, plucking a marinated olive from the plate of antipasti in the centre of the table. "I could tussle my hair a bit and scratch myself if that helps."

She laughed. "Jackson's not that bad!" Laughed again. Then she leaned in towards him. "Sorry," she whispered. "It just reminds me of the last cruise we took. The *SS Orient*. My previous boyfriend was working that cruise too, and remember how that ended up?"

"Jackson's nowhere near as straight as Dr Anders was, Alicia. I'm sure Jackson will let you sneak into his cabin later. Just don't get caught, or everyone will think I can't satisfy my new bride."

Then he winked and popped the olive into his mouth.

James watched patiently as Indya scrolled through her phone looking for God knows what—her Instagram feed no doubt—while Pasha held out two bottles of wine.

"Could I interest you in a very smooth Margaret River shiraz or a cheeky little Semillon from the Hunter Valley?"

she asked, and he glanced up at her.

"I'd like a lager, thanks."

"Of course." Pasha turned to Indya, holding the bottles high.

The woman barely looked up as she said, "The white one please."

James glowered back at his wife. "You're wasting your time. There's no Wi-Fi out here. Babe...?"

Indy was staring at her screen and zeroing in on one shot. He sighed loudly and she finally looked up.

"Sorry, hon'. I was just checking my photos."

"Well, don't. Please."

She nodded and dropped the phone to the table as Pasha strode away to fetch the beer.

James watched as Indya scooped some ice from her waterglass and plopped it into her wine, and he tried not to glower again. Said, "Are we cool?"

She flicked the hair from her shoulders and barely met his eyes, so he leaned across and grabbed her hands in his.

"Come on, Indy, we can't let this ruin us."

She stared back at him, brown eyes wide. "I'm not the one who ruined—"

But Indya didn't get a chance to finish that sentence. There was a discreet cough beside her, and she swung around to find Freddy standing there now, an envelope in his hand.

"Sorry to disturb. A note for you, madame."

He handed it across, offering James a quick, curt nod, then left them alone again.

"What is it?" James asked as she opened it.

Shrugging nonchalantly, she pulled the note out and began to read, then stopped and looked up and around, her face ashen.

James sat forward. "What is it, Indy? What's going on?"

"Hmm?" She looked back, then shoved the note into its envelope and reached for a pink metallic pouch she'd dropped below her chair.

"Indy?" he said again.

"It's nothing." She shoved the note into the handbag. "Just one of the other guests. She... she just wants to know if I'm free for a catch-up."

"Okay, well, that's nice. See, they don't all think you're a monster." Then he smiled while Pasha returned with a bottle of Byron Bay Premium Lager.

Indya waited until Pasha had poured it into a tall glass for James and left, then said, "And yet you still do."

"Hmm?" said James now.

"*You* think I'm a monster, don't you?"

He went to deny that, then stopped and just lifted a shoulder, making her gasp.

"I knew it!" She grabbed her pouch and jumped to her feet. "I..." She glanced around. "I need to use the restroom."

From his lonely table on the other side of the deck, Boulder watched the interaction with a frown.

"More red wine, Mr Boulder?" said Pasha beside him, and he nodded irritably, sitting back so she could refill his glass.

As she did so, Boulder looked up and locked eyes with James, who rolled his eyes wearily before looking away.

"They're still fighting," Claire whispered to Simon as he drizzled olive oil on a slice of ciabatta. "James and his wife. I can just feel it. Sad really. I thought they were better this evening."

"Any idea why?" he whispered back, and she squished her lips to one side. "Come on, give me your best book club theory."

She smiled back. "Maybe Indya had something to do with Elsbeth's murder and he knows it. Can't forgive her."

He blinked. "You really think so? Because I've got my money on Boulder."

Now Claire was sneaking a peek at the elderly lawyer.

"How is that even possible? He doesn't swim or dive. He was nowhere near the body."

"Or so he says. How are we to know he's not a champion diver?"

She grinned back at him, impressed. "Good thinking, honey. We should look into that."

From their table, the Dudley-Pines were watching with interest, too, eyebrows drawing together as Indya fled the deck.

Cindy spat her olive pit into her serviette and pushed her chair back. "I think I'd better powder my nose," she said.

"You think that's wise?" whispered Connor, glancing around.

"She owes us, darling," Cindy hissed back. "It's time to pay up."

Then she too left the deck.

~

Lynette was whipping cream for dessert when she noticed the captain stroll in. It was the first time she'd seen her in the galley. In fact, it was the first time they'd officially "met" so they faked introductions, then Liz said:

"I'm sorry to disturb you both, but I'd like to fetch Jackson's dinner. Pasha and Freddy have got enough on their plates, keeping things smooth for the guests."

"Oh, I can put that together for him," said Lynette, glancing at Sergio, who was leaning into the oven, pulling out his barramundi, which looked and smelled lemony and delicious. "Can I get you something too?"

Liz firmly shook her head. "I'm not at all hungry. But thank you." Then she turned to Sergio. "Why didn't you tell me you'd seen Indya Wynter out on the pontoon, talking to Elsbeth that day, Serg?"

He looked up, shrugged, and then placed the sizzling

pan on a bench. "Is no big deal."

"I beg to differ," Liz replied. "I lost one of my precious passengers out on that water, and you had vital information that could have helped the coroner's assistant earlier."

"How so?" He pulled off his gloves and began inspecting the fish. "All I saw were two women talking. What has that to do with an old lady accidentally drowning?"

Lynette stared hard at Liz. It was a good question! Why was she pushing this? Was she trying to give the game away?

The captain wrapped her arms around herself. "We're supposed to be on the same side, Serg. If you saw something useful, you should have told me. I looked like a fool in front of Jackson, in front of *Gary*…"

Her voice wobbled suddenly, and Sergio turned to face her. Lynette expected him to explode. The mains hadn't yet been plated up, and he wouldn't want the fish to get cold. But he surprised her by stepping across and pulling Liz into a warm embrace.

"Is okay," he said, his voice oddly soothing. "You need to stop torturing yourself, Liz. Is just terrible accident. Two women have cat fight on pontoon, but that's all that happens. The old one, she swims off, the young one, she takes more stupid selfies, then she swims back. She no cause it. *You* no cause it. Is *accident*, okay?"

Liz sniffed, released herself, sniffed again. Then she glanced back towards Lynette, wiping away a tear and now looking embarrassed. "Sorry," she said. "I just feel so terrible… It's all been such a disaster."

"No, no," he said, grabbing her hands and shaking her. "Is all okay. Now you take dinner for Jackson, then come back later and I give you some of Lynette's crème brûlée, *sì*? She not bad cook for dish pig, hey?"

Both women laughed, and Lynette quickly plated up Jackson's meal, then handed over the tray.

After the captain had left, Lynette cocked her head at Sergio.

"What?" he said.

"You're a softie underneath that hard exterior, just like my crème brûlée."

He scoffed and told her to get back to work, but as she did so, Lynette wondered if Sergio wasn't just a softie but had a soft spot for his captain.

~

Jackson sat at the captain's desk for some time, digesting both the meal Liz had brought him and what he'd recently learned from Sergio and then Gary. Unless they were colluding, it blew the case wide open. And yet it didn't necessarily mean Indya was the killer. Or, at least, it didn't prove it, if indeed she was.

Sure, the two women could have had words out on that pontoon and she might have turned off the older woman's air tank before she continued her dive, but surely Elsbeth would have noticed? Isn't that what Roland said? That the knob was virtually foolproof?

Perhaps Indya waited until the woman slipped into the water and then followed, turning off the valve and then holding her under until she took her last breath. Then swam back to the yacht just in time for a late lunch.

That was the more likely scenario, but how could he prove it? He had to get Indya to confess, and what were the chances of that? She'd already dropped Boulder's name last time they spoke. He knew these rich folk. She would lawyer up the second she knew he was onto her.

Yet that's not what was worrying Jackson. At least not exclusively.

He wanted to know why so many people had lied to him about Indya's whereabouts that fateful afternoon, and he wasn't just talking about First Officer Gary. James, Cindy and Connor had all agreed that the four of them had swum back to the yacht together. Hadn't the divemaster, Roland, suggested that too?

And yet now he had two witnesses to say Indya swam *away* from the yacht when they all returned, and had interacted with the victim directly.

So why all the lies?

Had they colluded? Were they in it together? It made a certain kind of sense why James would provide his wife an alibi, but why would the Dudley-Pines lie for a stranger? Why would Dr Roland?

He threw his pen on the table and groaned. So much for wrapping this case up fast. Now he would have to re-interview the lot of them, starting with Ms Wynter. Glancing at the wall clock he could see it was almost eight thirty p.m. Wondered if he should interrupt her dinner when there was a sudden, insistent knocking at the office door.

He got up to open it and audibly gasped. Indya was standing just outside, tears streaming down her high cheek bones.

"It's all my fault!" she cried. "I killed my mother-in-law! I'm a terrible, terrible person!"

CHAPTER 25
True Confession or Crocodile Tears?

Lynette dragged on the cigarette and tried not to cough. It was times like this that she wished she actually smoked. Everything had gone quiet. The dinner shift was over, her brûlée had gone out (the ramekins returning satisfyingly licked clean), and all that was left was the clean-up, so Sergio suggested they take a "smoko" before they got stuck in.

"You smoke, right?" he said, like that was a given.

"Sure," she'd replied, not willing to lose an opportunity to grill him.

And so they'd headed out to his favourite deck and they'd dragged on cigarettes while she tried to find the right wording. In the end, after too much small talk amidst the coughing and spluttering, she decided on candour.

"Are you and the captain an item?"

He looked around at her and said, "Item? What is this?"

"You know what I mean. You two, you looked, well, kind of cosy back there earlier."

He snorted. "Don't be a fool. She was upset, I was helping."

Lynette nodded. "Sure, right." She wasn't convinced, but he'd nearly finished his cigarette and she had another more important question.

"Tell me about this old job of yours. The one in publishing." He looked across at her oddly, so she quickly added, "You made it sound so good I'm wondering if there's an opportunity for a sous chef turned dish pig."

He laughed. "Good luck with that one. No, they sacked all their kitchen staff. You can blame Uber Eats for that. Now they get the food brought in. In my day we had a big, sparkly kitchen and would cook up great feasts for the executives; it was the glory days."

"Sounds ideal. A publishing house you say? Like... books and stuff?"

She already suspected the answer but needed to feign ignorance, and he laughed again.

"Why you go on about books? No, no, is a magazine publisher. Gossip magazines, some fashion stuff too."

"Oh, right!" A feigned giggle, then a feigned look of surprise. "It's not the same company that the people on board own, is it?"

Lynette knew she was sailing close to the wind but also knew these smoke breaks were short and she might not get another opportunity.

His brow furrowed, but it was not her he was frowning at. "Yes, that is them. They happy to spend twenty grand each for a week on a yacht, but when it comes to cooking for their staff? *Then* they get stingy! The richest family in the country and they count their pennies."

That's why they're the richest, Lynette thought but just shook her head along with him.

"Typical," she said. "That must've really stung. When they sacked you."

He took a final drag of his smoke. "That is life, Lynette. Shit happens." Then as he turned to go, he added, "This is why I tell the captain is not her fault. Bad things can happen to rich people too, yes? Perhaps the Wynters have learned that lesson this week. Perhaps they still have more to learn."

Then he whistled merrily as he made his way back to the galley.

~

It took several slugs of Liz's whisky to calm Indya down, and even then, Jackson noticed her hands shaking as she placed the tumbler onto the table beside her metallic pink pouch. He didn't want to rush her, not if she was about to confess, but he did wish he had a witness present. Was half hoping Pasha would appear with her flirty smile again. The problem was, a witness might send Indya scurrying for her lawyer, so he waited until the colour had returned to her cheeks and she was settled back on the sofa. Ready to confess.

"I wasn't completely honest last night," she said, and he nodded. "I... I didn't come back to the yacht with the others after the dive. I... well, I'm not gonna lie, I was a bit pissed with my husband and with Elsbeth." She looked up, darkly pencilled eyebrows now arched. "She crashed my honeymoon. Can you believe she would do such a thing?"

Like Jackson hadn't heard that bit of gossip. He nodded vaguely and let her continue.

"So when I saw her swim off to that other pontoon, I thought I'd follow. Not to do her any harm. Honest! I just wanted a quiet word while no one else was around. It's *impossible* on this ship. We were promised privacy, but there's no privacy. We keep running into everyone. Especially that hideous spice woman."

"Cinnamon Dudley-Pine?"

"Yes! She's, like, everywhere, all the time. I... I just wanted to ask Elsbeth to give me a chance, to give *us* a chance—James and me. We just needed some time to ourselves. She's so... cringe." She waved manicured fingers in front of her face. "I can't even."

"And yet you told me earlier that you and your mother-in-law, what was the term?" He pretended to glance through his notes. "Got on like a house on fire."

She winced, shook her hair away. "Well, it's kind of not true. I mean, we did at first but then... Look, it doesn't even matter. The point is it's my *honeymoon*. She shouldn't have come. It was her fault, really. Really it was…"

She burst into tears suddenly, and he sat forward, holding out a box of tissues.

"So what did she say?"

Indya grabbed some and said, "Sorry?"

"Elsbeth? When you spoke to her at the pontoon?"

"Oh, she just laughed at me. Told me I was pathetic, that James would always love her more than me, that he would tire of me like all the others but that he would never tire of his *darling mother*. Then she dropped off the platform and dived away."

"And you followed her?" Jackson said as she blew her nose.

She frowned, tucked the tissue away. "Excuse me?"

"After she swam away, you followed, yes?"

"No. I stewed for a bit, then I gave up and shallow dived to the yacht." She looked embarrassed now. "I'm not a good diver. Not like the rest of them. They're all used to this life. I'm a country girl; only learnt to swim when I was, like, fifteen and that was for a *Vogue* shoot. I didn't grow up with pools and yachts and stuff like that."

He crooked his neck. Tried not to frown. "Hang on, so you're now saying the last you saw Elsbeth, she was diving deeper, heading away?" She nodded, gulped again. "And yet here's my quandary, Indya. You were the last person to see her alive."

"I know! That's why I feel so bad."

"How do I know you didn't follow her?"

"But I *didn't*. I swam back, went to my cabin and dressed for lunch. I swear it."

"Just like you swore that you'd returned with your husband earlier, hm? Just like you swore that you and your mother-in-law got along great." He let her lies sink in. "Are you absolutely sure you didn't follow her after she left the second pontoon?"

"Yes! I mean, no, I didn't follow her. I promise you, I'm telling the truth now. She was fine when I left her."

"So why did you say you killed her, Indya? Excuse me if I'm a little confused."

Indya looked confused herself and then blushed a beetroot red. "Oh, no, I didn't *kill her* kill her if that's what you mean. It's just... I left her, don't you see? *That's* why I feel so bad. Maybe if I had followed, I might have seen her get into trouble, might have been able to help. I might have saved her."

"A missed opportunity to get on her good side."

She flinched at that, but it was true. "I didn't like her very much, and she certainly didn't like me, but I promise I didn't hurt her. I couldn't. But I also didn't help her, right? And it's worse than that. I might have caused it."

He rubbed his neck now. She was all over the shop. "How do you mean?"

Indya reached for the pink purse and pulled out a compact mirror. "It's all I can think about since it happened..." She inspected her reflection, then wiped a finger below her puffy eyes. "Maybe by talking to Ellie, she lost valuable oxygen. Maybe it stressed her out, like, more than I realised. Roland said we go through air faster when we're in a flap. Maybe I did do it without meaning to. Maybe James is right, maybe I am a monster."

Then she dropped the compact into her lap and buckled over, sobbing again.

~

"Could be crocodile tears," said Alicia as she lay in Jackson's arms later that night. "A sneaky double bluff. Indya could be playing you like a violin, knowing you'd got wind of her whereabouts and is now pretending to blame herself while sneakily taking herself off the hook. Classic *femme fatale* behaviour."

Jackson thought about that. He didn't normally get

taken in by such nonsense, and yet there was some validity to what Alicia was saying. They'd been talking now for hours, going over the case detail by detail. Something was bugging Jackson, and nothing his girlfriend could say could assuage him. Nor the book club earlier that night.

They had all snuck into the captain's office after dinner, each with fresh theories, more elaborate than the next, including Lynette, whose suspicions about Liz and Sergio's "affair" didn't add up to murder in Jackson's books, and he'd quickly shooed them out.

All except Alicia that is.

First they'd compiled a list of things they wanted Ronnie and Missy to research back on *terra firma*, including more background on the guests and crew, then Jackson had emailed it from the office computer as Simon had suggested, before telling Alicia to wait five minutes, then follow him down to his cabin.

And here they were now, the night growing shorter as they pondered the case.

"You could be right," Jackson said, propping up on one elbow. "Maybe I need to stop complicating things. Indya is the most likely suspect. She's the one who stayed the longest out on the water that day, she's the one who was last seen talking to the victim—by two witnesses no less. Indya herself admits this. I only have her word for it that she swam straight back to the yacht. She must have been furious, the way Elsbeth laughed in her face. It would not have been premeditated. She simply would have seen an opportunity to free herself of the suffocating in-law. Indya could have slipped in after Elsbeth, turned her air valve off, then held her under until she drowned. She's much younger; it wouldn't have been difficult. Plus she's the only one on the yacht with an obvious motive."

"Oh *that* she has in spades," agreed Alicia. "If Indya plays her cards right, or the aforementioned violin, a sympathetic judge could be very lenient. I mean, her mother-in-law *crashed her honeymoon!*"

He smiled. "Yes, I had heard that." His frown returned. "I'm not sure Elsbeth Wynter deserved the death penalty though, Alicia. You ask me, James is the guilty party there. He should've put up boundaries. Should never have put his wife in that position." Jackson took her hand, stroked it. "I'd never let my mother get away with that nonsense."

"Good to hear," said Alicia, trying not to get excited by where his mind was heading. "So, what are you going to do now?"

"Now? I'm going to get some sleep." He lay back down and drew Alicia towards him. "Then first thing tomorrow, I'm going to arrest Indya Wynter for murder."

CHAPTER 26
The Body in the Jacuzzi

A cool morning breeze was blowing across the dining deck when Pasha stepped out to set the tables for breakfast. The yacht had sailed through the night and was now anchored to the east of Escape Reef, and boy was it magnificent! But the chief steward didn't have time to enjoy the view. She zipped her jacket up and glanced around. Hoped the gust settled down in time for breakfast or they'd have to relocate the diners to Nemo's Lounge. And that was always such a nuisance…

Speaking of nuisances, where the hell was Freddy?

"Sup?" said Freddy, strolling in casually, napkins and cutlery in hand.

"Hurry up!" she snapped back. "We've only got an hour before the hungry hordes will be here demanding their breakfast, and I'm determined to have an incident-free day today even if it kills us."

"Okay, *Karen*, chill out. And be careful what you say around here, yes?" said Freddy, snickering.

As they began laying the tables, she thought again how easy it was for other cruise liners with indoor dining. You could prepare everything the night before. This yacht's only dining space was the semi-exposed upper deck, so it all had to be done on the fly with their fingers crossed that a sudden swell or tropical storm didn't send them racing inside, the retractable roof no match for Mother Nature at her fiercest.

Pasha's eyes swept the area again to check everything

was in order. No stray towels, no half-empty wineglasses from last night, no casually dropped cigarette butts. And they were the *least* of her worries. Pasha recalled finding a dead seagull in the jacuzzi one morning. Thank the Lord she'd discovered the bedraggled creature before the haughty guests popped in for a pre-breaky soak. That would have put them right off their eggs benedict.

It was the reason Pasha had started covering the spa over properly at night. Well, that and the fact the water took a while to heat up and you never could tell who was going to want to—

Hang on a minute.

Pasha's eyes had drifted across to the large jacuzzi on the farthest edge of the deck, and she noticed the cover was already off. Oh for heaven's sake! Had it been left off all night?

"Did you open that?" she asked Freddy, pointing across to it.

"Oh yes, I had a little swim before breakfast. Of course not. Maybe you did not cover it yesterday."

"I think you'll find that's in your job description," she snapped back. "Or do you want to cry to the boss again about your overloaded work schedule?"

He gave her a death stare, but she didn't see it as she strode across, sighing.

Then the sighing stopped and suddenly she found herself screaming. Very loudly. Very hysterically. Rather unprofessionally if she were being honest, and yet she couldn't stop. Pasha's worst nightmare had just eventuated—there was another bedraggled creature floating facedown in the jacuzzi.

But this one wasn't a seagull.

~

The homicide detective was not happy. Hell, he was furious! Jackson's worst fears had also materialised, and his first reaction was to lash out at Simon for dragging Alicia and her crew onto this death ship in the first place.

"Jackson?" said Simon, eyes wide beside him. "You okay, mate?"

"Course *I'm* okay, Simon. It's the woman in the hot tub I'm worried about. We should have got everybody off at Cooktown. What were we thinking? Should have performed formal investigations. Proper procedure."

Simon blinked back at him and then down to the victim. Jackson followed his gaze and sighed.

Poor young Indya Wynter. As lifeless as her mother-in-law now and drowned, too, by the look of it, in the confines of the ship's jacuzzi. At least they had a proper crime scene this time.

"Where is James Wynter?" Jackson asked.

"Claire's with him now, and Freddy. I've asked them to detain him in his suite so he doesn't disturb the scene."

"Well, there's one thing we got right then. And the others?"

"The captain's asking everyone to assemble up in the lounge so she can break the grim news."

"Good. Then we'd better keep them there until I've checked all their alibis."

"She was definitely murdered then?" Simon had a trace of hope in his voice as his eyes returned to the victim. "She couldn't have, you know, taken a morning soak and drowned?"

Jackson tried not to snort at Simon's naivety. "Can't see why Ms Wynter would take a morning soak in her gym gear and sneakers, can you?"

Simon tried not to wince at the detective's sarcasm. He was only trying to help. He glanced down at Indya, who was actually dressed for yoga in brightly patterned fluoro leggings and a pink crop top. Lululemon by the look of the insignia. And not unlike the set he'd asked Queenie to order for Claire's last birthday until Queenie had suggested something less sporty and more vintage would be appropriate.

Poor Indya. There'd be no more birthdays for this young lass.

While Pasha had initially found the body floating facedown in the jacuzzi, it was Freddy who'd dragged her out of the water and attempted CPR, according to the captain. But like Roland before him, it was futile. He'd then propped her up on the spa step and raced down to the bridge to alert the captain, who sprang into action, first heading to the sun deck to see the spectacle for herself.

All that time, Pasha had remained frozen in spot, staring at Indya's icy-blue lips, hands now muzzling her own. Until Liz had barked at her to get her "shit together!" and then dispatched her to alert the rest of the staff, starting at the galley.

"While you're there, get yourself a strong coffee," she'd said. "Or a shot of bourbon if you need one. It's going to be a very long day, and I need all hands on deck."

Then she'd ordered Freddy to stay with the body while she fetched Simon, who in turn alerted Jackson. Considering he was the only genuine detective on board, Jackson was furious that he wasn't the first to view the scene. Anybody could have tampered with it, he'd told Simon, grumbling all the way to the top.

"Just be happy you weren't asked to break the news to James," said Simon. "Thank God the captain took Claire and Freddy with her for that grim task. James was irate when he learned about his mother. I can't imagine how he's taking this." He rubbed a hand through his thick, dark hair. "Now don't get smarmy with me, Jackson, but I have to ask, could it be a terrible accident? Perhaps she hit her head somehow and knocked herself out. Then fell in?"

Jackson didn't look up from his phone, which he was now using to snap photos of the victim. "I'm no coroner's assistant, despite what you might have heard"—a slim smile at Simon, which cheered him up—"but I'm not seeing any indication of that. No obvious head trauma in any case."

"What about suicide then? It's just that Claire told me about Indya's confession to you during dinner. How guilty she felt, being the last to see Elsbeth alive. Maybe she... I don't know... The guilt got to her?"

"Maybe," said Jackson, surprising Simon. He looked up again from his camera. "I'm not like the book club, mate. I'd like nothing more than to wrap this up quickly—claim that Indya killed Elsbeth, then took her own life out of remorse." He glanced back at the body. "Or at the very least, was so depressed about it all she swallowed a bottle of gin and accidentally drowned in the jacuzzi."

"But?" said Simon, sensing a *but*.

"But I can't make that assumption, not without an autopsy."

"So what do we do now?" Simon asked hopefully.

"We keep investigating, and it starts with the witnesses."

~

Pasha still looked a little shaky when she appeared at the top of the carriageway, and Jackson quickly diverted her away from the tub and into one of the deck chairs.

"How are you holding up?" he asked, because she did not look good.

"Oh, I'll be fine. Just fine," she replied. Unconvincingly.

Simon frowned. "I think you need to take the rest of the day off, Pasha. Head back to your cabin after this. I'll speak to the captain about it. Finding a body is very confronting—"

"No! Goodness, don't do that to me. I can't just wallow in my cabin, going over it in my head. I need to be busy. It's the only thing that will keep me sane."

Simon nodded uncertainly as Pasha turned to Jackson. "What do you need to know? Because I really have to get down to Nemo's and start setting that up for breakfast."

Her stoicism was honourable and appreciated, too, because Jackson did have some difficult questions. First he asked her to go over exactly what had happened that morning, leading up to the discovery of Indya's body. Was there anyone else about? Did she see anything unusual?

"No," she replied on both counts. "I wouldn't have even found her... poor Indya... if I hadn't noticed the jacuzzi cover was off."

"And that's unusual?"

"Yes. We always cover it at night, although I can't recall doing it, to be honest, and neither can Freddy."

"It had been a very distressing few days; that's understandable," said Simon.

She was shaking her head. Madly. "It's my fault isn't it? If I hadn't left the cover open, maybe she wouldn't have fallen in. Maybe..."

"Let's not go there," said Simon.

Jackson's eyes had narrowed. "You think she just slipped in?"

"Yes! Doing her yoga stretches. What else?"

That explained the gear, thought Jackson as he glanced around. "Did you see her doing yoga this morning?"

"Not this morning, no, but I'd seen her before. The first day at sea, I came out just on sunrise and she was in the middle of a pose, a rather tricky-looking balancing pose. I just wonder... well, did the boat lurch suddenly and send her flying into the open jacuzzi? It's a possibility, yes?"

Pasha's eyes mirrored Simon's earlier, and Jackson tried to give her an assured look, but he wasn't sure which answer was better: The fact that Pasha's tardiness might have caused the woman's death, or the fact that it could be entirely unrelated and there might very well be a killer amongst them. He chose to say nothing, just asked her to head back inside and send Freddy up.

But not before Simon attempted again to get the steward to take some time off.

"No, no," said Pasha. "Somebody's got to look after the guests, and I can't leave them in Freddy's hands. They'll be eating breakfast at dinner!"

Freddy arrived quickly—probably relieved to be out of James's cabin where he'd been assisting Claire—and from his demeanour, Jackson wondered why Pasha had such little faith in the bloke. Unlike her, he was surprisingly calm, certainly the one in control when Indya had been found.

"Pasha turned into a crazy person," Freddy told them. "I thought she was going to drop too. *Sheesh.*"

Like Pasha, however, he didn't recall seeing anyone else early that morning, nor did he recall whether he had applied the spa cover the evening before. Any case, he wasn't taking the blame for that one.

"No way she fall into the jacuzzi," he said of Indya. "There is a railing on one side, lounge chairs on the other. They would have stopped her."

"So what do you suggest happened?" asked Jackson.

He shrugged. "You are the detective. You tell me."

Simon flinched beside Jackson who said, "I'm the coroner's assistant, Freddy."

Freddy nodded. "Hundred percent. That is what I meant."

As they dismissed him, Jackson had to wonder if that was a genuine slip-up on Freddy's part or if Gary had spilt the beans to all of them. Perhaps it was time to come clean.

"Okay," said Jackson, "let's go see the irate hubby."

CHAPTER 27
The Husband and the Holdout

James Wynter did not look irate in the slightest. More like he'd had the wind knocked out of him. He was slumped in a velvet armchair in his cabin, arms limp by his side, mouth drooping open, eyes staring blankly out of the enormous porthole. Like he was stoned or dazed or both.

"Come in," whispered Claire when she opened the door to Jackson, Simon having detoured to the office to "make the grim calls".

"I've just sent Freddy back out to fetch a pot of sweet tea," Claire added.

"Might need a shot of something stronger," said Jackson as he walked in and caught sight of James.

"We tried that." Claire nodded towards a collection of miniature liquor bottles atop the mini-bar fridge. "Didn't work."

"Has he said anything?"

She shook her head. "Shall I leave you?"

"No, stay please."

He gave her hand a squeeze, then stepped across to James, who was still staring lifeless at the shifting horizon.

"Mr Wynter?" Jackson said softly. "I'm very sorry for your loss."

James blinked. Turned his eyes slowly to meet Jackson's. Blinked again and then slowly came to life. "Oh, Jackson, hey. Yeah. Wow, it's, um…" He rubbed a hand across his face. "It's a freakin' nightmare. I can't believe this is happening. First my mother, now my wife.

Why is this happening?"

"Not sure yet, James, but I will find out. I can promise you that."

James made a soft scoffing sound. "But you're just the coroner's assistant…"

Jackson cleared his throat. Now was as good a time as any.

"I'm actually a police homicide detective," he said, catching both James and Claire by surprise. "I was brought on board to investigate what happened to your mother."

"Sorry?" James still sounded dozy.

"The captain had some suspicions regarding your mother's death. I was brought on to look into it quietly, discreetly. Now, with your wife… well, I think that was the correct decision."

"Hang on, *what*?" Now James's voice was louder, more solid, his eyes no longer glazed over. "What are you saying? You think my mother was murdered?"

Jackson held a hand up. "That's what I'm investigating."

"And Indy? Are you saying she did it?"

"What? No, I'm not saying that at all." He blinked. "Do you have any information that supports that?"

"Huh? No. I just… I mean… Why is Indy dead? I don't understand… I don't understand any of this."

Jackson swapped a worried look with Claire, who said, "James, I think what Jackson is trying to say is that it's all still up in the air but he's looking into it. He'll find out what happened."

"I'll tell you what happened!" James said, suddenly roaring to life. "My wife's now dead and this guy—a *cop*—didn't think to stop it." He leapt to his feet and reared towards Jackson, who stood his ground. "What were you doing when my wife was in that jacuzzi, struggling to come to terms with her guilt? Hmmm? Were you *sleeping*? Because you certainly weren't doing your job, *Detective*!"

"For God's sake, let the man get his questions out!"

came a booming voice from the doorway, and both men swung around to find Boulder standing there, Claire now beside him. They hadn't heard him enter, but he'd clearly heard this exchange and he had no patience for it. His face was mottled red.

"We can worry about who didn't do what later, Jimmy. And don't even get me started on the deception played out by the ship's company." A glower at Claire then. "For now, we need to work out what happened to young Indya and your poor mother before that. So answer the man's questions, damn it!"

James looked like he was about to leap across the room and throttle the lawyer, when suddenly he dropped back into the chair, head in his hands, weeping.

Claire shot both men a fierce frown as she stepped across and gently patted James's back, then Boulder slumped down onto the unmade bed like the outburst had also left him deflated.

Jackson gave everyone a few minutes to collect themselves, then he pulled the desk chair out and sat across from James. "I will find out what happened, Mr Wynter, and if there was foul play, I will bring the perpetrator to justice. But right now I need to get some facts straight, starting with how your wife ended up in the jacuzzi in her yoga gear this morning."

James looked up, sniffed. "I… I don't know."

He nodded. "When did you last see Indya? She came to bed as normal last night?"

"Yes."

"And how was her demeanour?"

"Depressed of course! Shattered! We've *all* been shattered by what happened to Mother."

"Did she tell you that she came and spoke with me last night? After dinner?"

James shot a wary look at Boulder, who was now sitting straighter.

"What did she tell you?" the lawyer demanded.

"You can't use anything she said. You should not have interviewed her without me present."

Jackson ignored his rant and turned back to James. "So when *did* you last see your wife this morning?"

James glared at him for a moment, and then the air went out of him again. He slumped back and rubbed his face. "I don't know. She... she just wasn't there when I woke up. I assumed she was doing her sun salutations. It's what she does. Every morning. Crack of dawn. I... I went back to sleep." His eyes flitted across to Claire. "She woke me with the news. Her and the captain."

Jackson nodded. All this confirmed what Pasha had said about Indya's morning ritual. "Does anyone else know that your wife does yoga first thing?" James shrugged. "And she always does it alone? While on board?"

Now James looked bemused. "Who else would she do it with? It's not my thing."

"Is there any chance she was meeting with someone this morning? That you know of?"

"What? Why? I mean, you can't possibly think someone else did this to her... can you?"

James stared worriedly at Boulder, and Jackson was about to say something when the younger man jumped back up, eyes darting about.

"There was a note!" he cried out. "Last night. The waiter gave Indy a note at dinner."

"What kind of note?" asked Boulder, but James was now scrambling for the small vanity table, wading through his wife's things like a burglar.

He spotted her pink metallic pouch on the chair and scooped it up, opened it and pulled out a few items. "She seemed a bit shocked or something, then said one of the girls wanted to catch up. I didn't think anything of it..."

He turned the bag upside down, and a few things fell out—lip gloss, a tiny mirror, some digital ear buds—but there was no note.

"What girl?" asked Jackson. "Did she elaborate?"

"No. I... I would have asked but... Oh shit. Do you think someone lured her to the jacuzzi this morning? One of the other women?"

Then his eyes swept to Claire, who took a step backwards, palms out. "I'm not a yoga person, I can assure you."

"The other one? That newcomer?" said James. "Maria what's her name?"

"Has to be Cindy," said Boulder, eyes furtive. "My God, I should have listened to Elsbeth. When she first clapped eyes on that woman, she said she was shifty. Now I'm the one who should have been asking more questions."

"Yes," said James, nodding madly. "She's low-key weird! Sucking up to us all like nobody's business."

Jackson stood up. "Do you have any evidence against Mrs Dudley-Pine?" They shook their heads miserably. "Then let's all take a deep breath before we start throwing accusations around. I'll enquire about the note, but in the meantime—"

"I want to see Indy," said James. "I need to see my wife."

"Of course," said Jackson. "We're moving her now, so I'll get Claire to bring you down when..." He faltered, not knowing how to finish that sentence.

When we've had a chance find a spare body bag *and* a spare room? Because the cabins were all occupied and they could hardly place Indya down beside her nemesis.

He was saved by the arrival of Freddy, tea tray in hand, so he quickly said, "Have some tea first, and then we'll make it happen."

As James watched Freddy pour him a cup, it must have hit him. "You'll know! That note last night!"

The butler jumped like he'd been stung, spilling tea across the tray. "Oooh, sorry, sorry," he said, snatching up a serviette.

"The note you handed my wife during dinner," continued James, "who was it from?"

Freddy began mopping up the mess. "I do not know, sir. It was private."

Boulder snorted at that, but Jackson stepped forward, pulling Freddy to the side. "Tell me about the note."

The young man looked worried for the first time all morning. "It was just a note, sir. I mean, I think it was. It was in an official envelope, you know, from the set we put in every cabin. It did not have a name on the back, just hers on the front. It was obviously private. I did not open it. I swear!"

"Okay. So where did you find it?"

"Under her door." Freddy nodded towards the carpet. "I came to turn down the bed for the night like I always do, just after everyone had gone up to dinner, and I saw it lying there. I was not sure if it was, like, urgent so I gave it to the lady during dinner. I did not... I mean I would not..."

"So you have no idea who it was from or what the contents said?" asked Jackson.

"No sir."

"And the writing on the front? It was in handwriting?" He nodded. "Did you recognise it?"

He shook his head. "Can I go now please, sir. Pasha needs a hand with breakfast."

Jackson watched him for another moment, then nodded while James dropped his head into his hands as though the air had been sucked from him all over again.

CHAPTER 28
A Bleak Breakfast

All eyes in Nemo's Lounge were full of anxiety as the guests sipped cups of coffee and waited for the captain to return, but no one's more so than Cindy's. This cruise was not going according to plan. What a colossal disaster! And it was about to get a whole lot worse, she realised, when she spotted the coroner's assistant walk in and stare directly at her.

But then he casually looked away and towards Pasha, who was holding a tray of pastries, deep in conversation with Gary at the other end of the room. Jackson frowned and Cindy didn't blame him. She didn't like First Officer Gary. He had none of the captain's class, none of her decorum. None of the very calm manner she'd used when she'd knocked on their door that morning and calmly asked them to dress and assemble at Nemo's.

Liz wouldn't tell them any more than that, so Cindy assured Connor it was just a safety drill until the captain broke the shocking news once they'd all arrived. Well, half of them at least. She should have guessed what had happened when the young Wynter couple did not show.

Indya was dead. Found deceased in the spa that morning, the captain told them. "A terrible, terrible accident," Liz had called it, then politely asked them all to stay put and breakfast would be served here in the lounge.

Like anybody was going to want to eat after that news!

Various questions were thrown back at her, mostly by a stunned and surly Boulder, who refused to take her silence for an answer and stormed after her while the new couple kept shooting glances at the doorway like they, too, wanted to do a runner.

What fools the Tanners were, Cindy thought. They could have avoided all this if they'd accepted the refund she suspected they'd been offered. They must have been very hard up for a holiday!

"What are we going to—" began Connor.

She held a finger to her lips, watching as the captain reappeared with Simon, and both made a beeline for Jackson, who was now speaking furtively with Roland.

The four of them spoke for a few minutes more, whispering like they were sharing state secrets, and Cindy felt a fresh wave of anxiety.

This did not look good. There was more bad news to come, she knew it.

And then it happened.

The captain stepped forward and called them to attention again, what few of them remained. Because Boulder had not reappeared and no one had seen James or Claire all morning.

"Ladies and gentlemen," Liz called out. "I appreciate your patience, and once again I apologise for this second, dreadful incident. It has been very... very distressing."

"Incident? Is that what you're calling it?" said Connor, his tone loaded, his whole body twitching.

Cindy shot her husband a worried look, then turned back in time to see Liz offer the coroner's assistant a very similar glance before she cleared her throat and said:

"At this stage we're not exactly sure what's happened. That's still being determined. But in the interests of finding out properly and moving forward, I'd like to introduce you to Detective Inspector Liam Jackson."

Cindy blinked. Stared at the coroner's assistant and blinked again.

"Detective?" someone said.

It was Connor, eyes darting between his wife and

Jackson. "You mean, he's *not* working for the coroner?"

Jackson stepped forward to stand beside the captain. "Indirectly actually, yes, I am. But I'm not a coroner's assistant no. I work for the NSW Serious Crimes Division. Have been flown in on the authority of the police commissioner."

"Hang on, what is this?" said Freddy now. "What is going on?"

Now it was Simon's turn to step forward. "The fact is, we had some suspicions regarding Mrs Wynter's... Mrs *Elsbeth* Wynter's death, but we didn't know for sure. Still don't." Now his eyes darted across to Jackson. "We didn't want to upset anybody's honeymoon, so the captain and I decided to bring DI Jackson on board to investigate quietly."

"You've got to be joking!" This was Connor again, and he had risen to his feet, chest puffing out.

Cindy tried to grab his hand, pull him back, but he was having none of it.

"You've been investigating a suspicious death and you told us it was an accident? A drowning. You lied to us?"

"I understand your concerns, Connor," Simon began, "but it wasn't like—"

"It's a betrayal of our rights! A bloody outrage! You were trying to protect yourself, that's what you were doing. Why else wouldn't you tell us? We had a right to know."

"We believed it was for the best—"

"Tell that to Indya Wynter!" Connor shot back, and Simon seemed to shrink to half his size while the captain grew taller.

"Mr Dudley-Pine," she said firmly, "please sit down. This is distressing enough for everybody, and you are *not* helping."

That did the trick.

Connor dropped back into his seat, shooting Cindy a look that she would have repaid with a scowl if it wasn't for the fact that everybody was now staring at them.

"Please," the captain said again, more gently. "I appreciate that there will be a lot of strong emotions today, a lot of distress and worry and concern, and that's why I think it's a *positive* thing that we have one of the country's top detectives here to help us. We hope and strongly suspect that both incidents *were* just tragic drownings—"

There was a loud scoff. Cindy did not know where from, but the captain forged on:

"Until we confirm that, I ask all of you to stay calm and stay strong. We will get to the bottom of this, I assure you. And to my crew…" She waved a hand towards Pasha and Freddy by the buffet and Roland, who had his hands thrust into his jeans at the back, looking almost sheepish beside Gary. "We have to pull together, work as a team, try to assist DI Jackson in any way we can and find out what really happened to both Elsbeth and to Indya. We owe them that."

"You owe us all," muttered Connor, his voice now a low growl. "We should sue you for this drama, that's what we should do."

"You can worry about making money out of all this later," Jackson said, his tone droll. "For now, my only concern is the two deceased women. They're my priority. Which means the honeymoon's over, folks. And I mean that literally. I've instructed Captain Flinders to begin sailing immediately back to Cairns, and I will ask the rest of you to remain in this room until I have had a chance to speak to you individually. Starting with you, Mr and Mrs Dudley-Pine."

Connor scoffed again at that, and Cindy tried not to glare at her idiotic husband.

Well done, Mr Pecs, she thought. You couldn't have made us more of a target if you'd painted red circles on our foreheads yourself.

~

"Psst!" came a hiss from the swinging doorway, and Alicia looked around to see that Lynette had followed her into the restroom just off the lounge. She had an empty coffeepot in one hand, an excitable look on her face.

"I just heard Jackson out himself," she said, and Alicia held a finger to her lips and then inspected the two empty cubicles before waving her in.

"How long have you been lurking outside, listening in?" Alicia asked.

"Who cares? What do you think? Should we all come clean?"

"Lord no. Who's that going to help?"

"Me. Then I can get off kitchen duty and start properly investigating."

"You *are* investigating. We need you to stay undercover." Lynette groaned, and Alicia gave her arm a rub. "Look, I haven't had a chance to speak to Jackson this morning, but I don't think he wants to blow our cover. If he did, he would have said something back there when he blew his own. Captain didn't say a word either, so we stay on the down-low."

There was another groan from Lynette. "And what did Liz mean it's a tragic drowning. Surely Indya was murdered?"

"I guess they're trying to keep the horses calm again. Like I said, I haven't got the full story yet. What has Sergio said?"

"Nothing. But he's grumpy. Extra grumpy. Which is annoying because he shuts down when he's grumpy. That's why I might as well come clean—"

"No. Not unless we have to. You and I know how useful it is to fly below the radar; we've done it plenty of times before. Jackson's now official, so they'll clam right up on him. We could be the only chance of finding the killer. If indeed there is one."

"Oh, there is one," said Lynette. Then, "Fine. But it's not going to stay quiet forever. I think Sergio suspects something anyway; he's no fool. Neither is Freddy for that matter. They know the captain's already lied to them about Jackson, so they're bound to work it out."

"Until then, we zip it," said Alicia. "Now go, get back to the kitchen, or Sergio will be out here with a meat cleaver. Oh, and while you're back there, can you top up that pot? I'm gagging for another coffee."

Lynette glowered at her sister as she snuck back out of the restroom.

CHAPTER 29
Liars and Traitors

DI Jackson opened the door to the captain's office and then kicked himself for not dragging Simon in with him. The ship's owner had detoured to the bridge again, and Jackson wondered momentarily if he should fetch him back. He didn't need Boulder's lecture to know it wasn't proper procedure to interview suspects alone, but then nothing about this case had been done properly, so why start now?

Turning back to the Dudley-Pines, he said, "I'll speak to you first, Mrs—"

"Cindy please," she said, not for the first time.

He nodded, eyes back on her husband. "If you could wait out here, Mr—"

"I will not be waiting anywhere!" Connor began.

Cindy swivelled to face him. "Connor please. Just do as the man says." Then she turned and followed Jackson into the office. As she took her seat in front of the desk, she apologised for her husband. "He's just in shock, as are we all. And not just about Indya. The fact that *we* would be under any kind of suspicion. Well, it is rather unsettling. As I'm sure you understand."

Jackson stared at her. "I never suggested that either of you are under any kind of suspicion. In fact, the captain made it quite clear it could be another accidental drowning."

She smiled. "And yet here we are, being questioned." She slowly crossed her muscular legs again. "What is it you need to know, *Detective?*"

Jackson leaned back in his seat. She was a smart one, he decided, and he would have to tread carefully. Pulling out his notepad, he found a fresh page and jotted something down, then looked up and said, "First thing I need to know is if you had any interactions with the deceased—Indya Wynter—any time after we all retired to bed last night or first thing this morning."

She answered immediately. "No, I did not."

"So you never met with her on the top deck this morning? For a pre-arranged yoga session perhaps?"

Cindy looked genuinely surprised. "Why would you think that?"

He stared at the bulging bicep she was now scratching, and she dropped her hand to her lap. Smiled.

"I like to stay fit, Detective, thanks for noticing, but I'm a weights junkie, not a hippie. Just ask Roland. He's had to bring some dumbbells to my cabin. I'm surprised the boat's not listing to one side. But no, Indya and I were not exactly besties. She barely gave me the time of day if I'm honest. Certainly no invitations to yoga. I think I would have been the last person she'd ask."

"Perhaps you asked her?"

She blinked; stayed mute.

He said, "I'd like to know what was in the note you left under her door last night."

Cindy's voice was steady as she said, "I'm sorry. You've lost me. What note?"

He sat back, watched her for a moment. "During dinner last night, Ms Wynter received a note. She told her husband it was from a woman on this ship. I believe that note is pivotal to this case, and I believe the woman who sent it was you."

Now Cindy was sitting back, biting her lip. She waited a few moments, then said very casually, "I don't see why. There are other women on this yacht; we haven't all been murdered. At least not yet." A fleeting smile.

"Everyone will be questioned," he replied.

"That's a relief. For a moment there I thought you were playing favourites, Detective."

"Favourites?"

She shrugged. "From what I can see, several of the other women have been flirting rather outrageously with you, including our newcomer, Marie Tanner—which doesn't bode well for her marriage I must say."

Jackson tried not to react. He'd have to tell Alicia her acting skills were not up to scratch.

Cindy continued: "And the only other female passenger is sleeping with the owner, so you're hardly going to accuse her now are you?"

"I wasn't aware I was accusing anyone of anything, but let me assure you, both Ms Hargreaves and, er, Mrs Tanner, will be asked the same questions as you. Starting with: Do you know anything about the note that was handed to Indya Wynter during dinner last night?"

"No, I do not. It wasn't my note. So…" More biting of the lip.

"Why did you lie to me yesterday about Indya's return to the yacht?"

The question caught the otherwise unflappable Cindy off guard, and he noticed she took another moment to collect her thoughts but masked it with feigned stupidity.

"I'm sorry. What are you saying? I'm confused."

He doubted she'd ever had a confused moment in her life. "I'm referring to our interview that first night I arrived on board. I asked you when you returned to the yacht post-dive and with whom. You told me you came back with your husband and with both James and Indya Wynter. But I have since learned that Indya was not with you."

Cindy smudged her lips downwards. "Sorry, is this in relation to her death or to Elsbeth's? I can't keep up."

"It's in relation to the fact that your answers can't necessarily be trusted. But I'll ask again anyway. Why did you tell me Indya was with you at the time Elsbeth was missing when she wasn't?"

"Oh, I was just *confused*. I mean, we were all so upset and shocked, I couldn't really recall who swam back when and with whom."

He felt like rolling his eyes, not buying it for a moment, and she went to say something but then thought better of it and sighed.

"Okay, if you must know, I was just trying to help a fellow sister." She smiled, waved a hand like it was irrelevant. "At that stage we didn't believe—*were not told*—that there were any suspicions regarding Elsbeth's death, so I didn't think it really mattered where everyone was and when."

"The truth always matters, Cindy. In any death, no matter the circumstances."

"Well, yes, of course, I get that." She sounded impatient. "But Indya was so distressed about it all, and I had an inkling she was the last one to see the old dragon, so—"

"Why would you think that?"

"Because she didn't swim back with us, of course, so I just assumed."

"Did you see something?"

"No, of course not. But I knew what you'd all assume, and I didn't think it would be very nice to dump her in it. Poor child was stressed enough as it was."

He smiled. "And yet she barely gave you the time of day?" His smile dropped. "Did somebody ask you to lie for Indya? James or Boulder perhaps?"

"Why would they do that?"

"And you had no prior relationship with the Wynters before you boarded this vessel?"

"I told you that already, didn't I?" She sounded impatient again, and he slapped her with a frown. She sat forward. "In retrospect, yes, I should not have lied about Indya. Here!" She produced her wrists. "Lock me up and throw away the key!" She dropped her wrists again.

"I thought I was helping, but I can see now how foolish I have been. And with Indya now dead… Well, I am deeply, deeply sorry I didn't speak up sooner."

Then she swept her hair back and sat forward. "Now, if that's all, I really am famished. I know it seems in bad taste to be hungry after such drama, but I'm going to need to refuel if I'm going to stay looking this fit." She waved a hand across her muscular arms, then got to her feet, adding, "No need to get up. I'll let my husband in."

He ignored that and followed her to the door anyway. Jackson knew exactly what Cindy was doing and didn't want to give her the opportunity to collude with her husband out in the corridor. Cindy might be fit, but she was also very slippery…

~

Back in Nemo's Lounge, Pasha was deep in thought as she poured Alicia a second cup of coffee.

"Are you okay?" Alicia asked.

The stewardess almost missed the cup as she snapped herself out of it. "Sorry, yes. In fact, I should be asking you that, Marie. I'm so sorry this cruise has been such a… a…"

"Tragedy?" offered Alicia.

She nodded. "I was going to say disaster, but you're very kind. Very calm in fact." Pasha's eyes narrowed at Alicia and then turned towards Perry, who was speaking with Roland at the bar. "You're both being very civil about all this, unlike… well, *others*. Are you regretting your decision to come on board?"

Alicia baulked a little. Had they been *too* calm? *Too* civil? Would that give the game away? She waved Pasha closer and said, "To be honest, Pasha, I don't feel calm at all. I'm just trying not to make it any worse, especially for you. I believe you're the one who found her?"

Pasha nodded. "Poor darling was doing her yoga, just trying to stay healthy, and look what happened! At first I thought she'd slipped, but now..." She leaned in closer. "I have to wonder if there's something more sinister going on."

Alicia feigned surprise. "Do you suspect one of the other passengers?"

Pasha blinked at her, startled. "Goodness, that's not what I'm saying! Or at least, I sincerely hope not, otherwise you have every right to be furious with the captain."

"The captain?"

"Yes! She should never have let you board in Cooktown. It was very negligent of Liz. She must have had suspicions if she dragged a detective on board, and yet she let you waltz on like nobody's business. At the very least you should have been informed there'd been a suspicious death."

"We don't know that for sure though, do we?" said Alicia, trying to placate her as Jackson had placated Connor earlier.

But Pasha was tsking now and shaking her head. "It's all very well for the captain to tell us to pull our heads in, but she lied, didn't she? To all of us! And who's to know what else will happen?"

Alicia sat back. "You really think there's going to be another... *suspicious death?*"

Pasha gave her a pointed look, then scooped the pot up and headed back to the buffet table.

As she watched the stewardess move platters around, Alicia wondered about that. If Pasha really was concerned for the guests, whispering about "suspicious deaths" was hardly going to make things better. And what a traitor she'd turned out to be! So much for pulling together as the captain had pleaded. Pasha was all but telling Alicia there was a killer on the loose and she should lay the blame firmly at her boss's feet.

Now why would she do that, she wondered?

~

The dive instructor was standing at the drinks station, filling two jugs with orange juice, when Perry first approached.

"Are you going to drop a few shots of vodka in that?" Perry said, and Roland looked up with a start. "Sorry," added Perry. "You were miles away."

Roland offered a grim smile. "Perhaps you wish you were, right about now."

Perry went to deny that, then realised, as Alicia had, that they were not acting shocked enough. "I am very disturbed," he said. "What do you think happened to the young woman?"

Roland stared down at the jugs again. "Accident, I guess. Must've hit her head. I can't say."

"You didn't see her? This morning?"

He looked up startled. "Why would you think I saw her?"

"I just assumed you might have been assisting Pasha up on the dining deck, you know, when she found her?"

"Oh no, I'm helping out now, but really my job in the mornings is down the other end of the yacht—getting the swim gear ready for the dive. Not that we'll get a chance now…"

"But you were up at that hour?"

He nodded. "Double-checking the apparatus." He gave Perry a strained look. "I was determined not to lose another passenger, but look how that's turned out."

Then he shook his head sadly, picked up both jugs and walked them across to the buffet.

~

Connor had none of the slippery calm of his wife. The fury he showed in Nemo's Lounge now spilled over as Jackson interrogated him in the captain's office.

Or at least attempted to.

"I don't have to sit here like an obedient little schoolboy and answer your questions!" Connor announced the moment he had sat down. "You have no authority over me."

Jackson leaned back in his seat. "I think you'll find I do."

"I should be allowed to have a lawyer at the very least."

"And you're welcome to one. In fact, if you give me a moment, I can ask Mr Boulder to join us. That would make it all official. Very official."

Connor blinked rapidly, rubbed a hand across his closely shaved jaw. "No... well... that is to say, I couldn't afford Boulder. He was Elsbeth's lawyer. Can you imagine the hourly rate he charges?"

"Then how about I ask my questions anyway and see how we go?"

Connor held his chin high, gave it some thought and then dropped his chin again. "Fine. What do you want to know?"

"For starters, why you lied to me about Indya Wynter's whereabouts immediately after the dive two days ago."

"Sorry? I thought this was about Indya's death, not Elsbeth's."

"You and your wife told me that Indya had swum back to the yacht with you just before lunch on the day Elsbeth died. Care to explain why you lied?"

His chin was back up. "I just assumed."

"Or did James ask you to?"

"What? Is that what Cindy said?"

Jackson remained quiet.

He shrugged. "I don't wish to comment."

Jackson nodded. "Can you tell me the last time you saw Indya alive?"

A flicker of fresh concern. "You mean last night?"

"Whenever."

Another chin jut. "I don't wish to comment."

"When did your wife last see Indya alive?"

A flicker of concern then another "No comment".

Jackson pretended to jot a note in his pad and then looked up with a breezy smile. "Okay, thanks for your time, Connor. Your lack of cooperation has been duly noted. You can see yourself out."

Connor blinked furiously and stared down at the pad, then shifted uneasily in his seat, so Jackson added, "Unless there's anything else you'd like to tell me, you'll want to get back and get your money's worth before all the croissants run out."

CHAPTER 30
Lies and Videotape

Cindy scowled at her husband as he sat in a corner shovelling down his breakfast (cold scrambled eggs as it happens). Then she quickly replaced it with a smile and glanced around the room. Everyone was busy eating— or attempting to. She turned back to Connor, scowl back in place and hissed, "You really are as thick as you look."

He glanced up, startled. "What?"

"What do you mean you said 'no comment' to every question? Are you trying to get us locked away?"

"No. I just don't think it's any of his damn business."

"He's a *detective*, you idiot. It's his only business. You answer his questions, and then he's off our case."

She growled below her breath and glanced around the room, noticing the first officer reappear with a worried expression before heading back out again. Cindy wedged her smile wider, then leaned in even closer to her husband and said, "And what were you thinking before? Carrying on in front of everybody like a headless chook."

"You don't agree with me that it was an outrage that we were lied to? That we shouldn't sue the pants off this boat?"

"Of course I agree," she hissed through her teeth. "But we don't need to make a spectacle of ourselves while we do it. How is that helping?"

"I don't care about the captain—"

"I'm talking about *us*." She sighed. Shook her head. "Just finish your breakfast and let's hope to God the copper locks on to someone else before he puts two and two together and gets…"

"Zero?" said Conner, a sneer now on his face.

~

Claire wanted nothing more than to leave James Wynter's cabin and get back into the comforting arms of her husband—or, better yet, the book club—but Jackson had asked her to remain until Indya's body was ready for viewing. And she understood why.

Boulder clearly wanted James alone, and no sooner had Jackson left, he suggested Claire do so too. "Get yourself some breakfast," he said.

She shook her head. She wasn't giving them a chance to collude, if indeed that was his plan. "I'll stay with James until his wife is ready for him," she said firmly, and he frowned but let it go.

For his part James was back to dazed and confused, and it occurred to Claire that he was taking his wife's death worse than his mother's. That was a surprise. From what she had seen, Elsbeth had been his favourite, would always come first. Yet here he was, clearly heartbroken or… She studied him closely.

Was there some guilt in there?

Was it an act?

A sudden knock on the door caught them all by surprise, and Claire opened it to find Gary standing there, a grim look on his face.

"She's ready. If you'd like to follow me?"

Claire turned to James, who rubbed a hand over his face, then stood up and followed, Boulder close behind.

Claire trailed them down to the staff quarters where she saw Jackson standing at the door to what looked like a storage room. He mouthed a quick thank-you and waved her off, and she felt a rush of relief as she finally made her way to the lounge.

Inside the storage room, Indya looked peaceful, the most peaceful she'd looked all cruise. Sheets had been draped over various boxes, and a makeshift bed had been set up in the centre where Indya lay, also draped in a sheet to her neck. For a moment they all just stood at the door, staring inwards.

James put a hand to his lips and choked back a sob, then said, "I'm sorry… I can't…"

And he fled back down the corridor.

"Oh, for pity's sake," said Boulder below his breath as he marched in.

"I have to get back to the bridge," Gary told Jackson. "We need to get this yacht moving."

Jackson excused him, then followed the older man into the room and over to the lifeless body.

They both stared at Indya for a few moments, then Boulder said, "It's all my fault, you know."

Jackson rubbed his stubble. This was another confession of guilt but not of murder, he could tell, but still it surprised him. Boulder was the type to insist he was innocent even when the gun in his hand was still smoking. It took a few minutes, but eventually Boulder found his words.

"She came to me, Indya, just before the wedding." He reached a hand down to touch her before Jackson caught his wrist.

"Best you don't," he said, and Boulder nodded and pulled his hand back.

"Indya asked me… no, she *begged* me to keep Elsbeth away," he continued. "Just give them the honeymoon, she said, just give her that week. But I didn't. I ignored her. She wasn't my boss. Elsbeth was. So when Ellie showed up with her ludicrous scheme to crash her son's honeymoon, I didn't tell her she was being an old fool. I didn't tell her she wasn't wanted, not even by her son, who was the biggest fool of all. Mistook his mother's smothering for love… No, I let Elsbeth have her way, as I always did. She's been getting her way for decades, and I never had the courage to stop her."

Boulder offered another weary sigh, quickly glancing at Jackson and back. "I thought it would be a bit of fun, to be honest. I thought it would be harmless. I never suspected it would end like this…"

"Like what?" said Jackson quietly. "Is there anything you know that you're not telling me?"

Boulder looked up at him sharply. "I know that two women are dead and a young man has been left bereft, and you *Detective Inspector* have done bugger all about it."

"Then help me fix this," said Jackson. "I need your honest opinion. Could James have something to do with this?"

Boulder wasn't as enflamed by that question as Jackson was expecting.

"I have wondered about James," he said eventually. "I wonder if he suspected that his wife had killed his mother. I could see it in him, the pain, the disappointment… Had he pushed his new wife too far? Had we all? Could Indya see no escape from Elsbeth? Is that why she snapped?"

"You believe Indya killed Elsbeth, and then what? James avenged his mother?"

Now Boulder was enflamed. "Of course I don't believe that! That's not what I was saying! I think Indya killed Elsbeth and then she killed herself."

There it was again, the murder-suicide theory.

"I suspect after we return to shore," continued Boulder, "and a proper autopsy is carried out, you will find barbiturates or something similar in Indya's system. I think she couldn't live with the guilt and so she took something strong and just… let herself go."

Jackson must have looked sceptical because Boulder turned to face him, head-on. "You saw how distraught Indya was. How riddled with guilt. Of course she killed herself. What else could have happened? Nothing else makes sense."

"Who stood to gain by both deaths?" Jackson asked calmly.

"Not James if that's what you're implying."

"James *doesn't* inherit all his mother's fortune now? Doesn't have to share it with the young wife you both suspected of killing Elsbeth?"

Boulder's face turned an ugly shade of red. "That is not what I was saying, and you know it."

"Did you write up Elsbeth's Last Will and Testament? You're the family lawyer, you must know what it contains."

"Of course I'm the executor and of course Jimmy inherits everything. That's no secret. But it's a massive fortune. Having to share it with Indya is hardly grounds for murder. Besides, I could've had the marriage annulled in five seconds, especially after what happened. It would not have been a problem. There's no way Jimmy killed his wife for money; it's absurd."

"Maybe it was more about revenge then?"

"Poppycock! I've known that lad his whole life. He doesn't have it in him. Jimmy's a good boy, but he's weak, doesn't have the gumption. Hence the reason he couldn't stand up to Elsbeth."

"What about you? What do you inherit from Elsbeth's Will?"

Boulder's blush drained away. "Not a brass razoo." He smiled suddenly, incongruously. "So now you think I did it, hmm? I walked on water across to Elsbeth did I? I wasn't diving that day remember, Detective?"

"And this morning?"

"This morning I was tucked up in bed, fast asleep." He went to go, then turned back and said, "As were *you*. Jimmy's quite right about that. You call yourself a detective and yet you were snoring happily while a young woman was taking her final breaths. Fat lot of good you've been."

Then he slouched out of the room while Jackson turned his gaze back to young Indya and he thought, *Okay, now it's my turn to feel guilty.*

~

"If you're cooking more eggs, don't do it, bro'," said Freddy as he stepped into the steamy kitchen. "Nobody is eating; they just want more coffee."

"*Again?*" said Lynette, taking the two empty pots from him to get it brewing. "How's it going out there? Apart from the caffeine fetish that is."

"You getting all the drama on film like last time?" added Sergio, smirking at the butler.

Freddy gaped back at him. "Low blow, grandpa, low blow."

He sounded disappointed with Sergio as he left the galley, but Lynette was delighted. Had she just stumbled upon another suspect?

Trying to sound casual, she asked, "What did you mean by that, Sergio? About the filming? Is Freddy a bit of a perve? A voyeur maybe? Should I be worried?"

"You? *Pft!* No, no, you are not famous enough for Freddy."

"How do you mean?"

"I am just teasing you. Come on, back to work."

Lynette let it go for now, but she was feeling buoyed. It sounded to her like Freddy was shifty. Very shifty. And the case was now shifting in a very different direction.

CHAPTER 31
The Missing Piece

A thorough search of James and Indya's suite was long overdue, but it had been one of those mornings, and it was getting away from Jackson fast. He hadn't even had a chance to officially report the death to the police commissioner, let alone homicide headquarters. Couldn't even be sure it was another homicide, if you believed half the suspects.

No, thanks to the book club's pretence, Jackson also had to pretend, which meant wasting valuable time interviewing *them*, just as he'd interviewed the others. So, after securing Indya's body, he'd returned to the lounge and made a show of dragging them up to his office, one by one.

First he spoke to "Marie", then "Bob", then Claire.

Alicia wanted to give him a hug and fetch him breakfast and then asked how she could help, and he'd told her to return to the lounge and watch the others like a hawk. Perry was more interested in the dirt—"How was Indya found? What did she look like? Was she *naked?*"— while Claire provided one very useful titbit, something she'd wanted to mention earlier up in James's cabin.

"I saw the butler hand Indya that note last night during dinner," she told him. "And whatever it said, it wasn't a happy catch-up with a fellow passenger I can tell you that. Indya looked very rattled. I thought it was because of something James said, but now I wonder whether it was the note that distressed her because she ran from the deck soon after she got it and didn't return for ages. But here's the thing: someone else fled the deck around the same time. Cindy!"

That piqued Jackson's interest but only just. He'd already quizzed Cindy about the note, and she'd already denied sending it. Wasn't sure his time would be well spent going another round with the slippery eel. Besides, what could Cindy possibly say in the note that would lead to murder? As far as he could tell, she had no clear motive to hurt either woman.

So he tucked that away and headed back to James Wynter's cabin to properly search through his wife's possessions, an important step in any investigation. Perhaps he'd get lucky and find a suicide note while he was at it.

This time, however, he did corral Simon, who was still holed up in the bridge. He was tapping furiously at a laptop and told Jackson, "I'm emailing the board of directors. It's all turning to shit fast."

Jackson wasn't sure his company board were the priority, but he didn't comment, just asked him to accompany him to James's cabin so he could record the search on his phone—another important part of the process.

After ten minutes sifting through Indya's possessions, it became clear to Jackson that something else was missing, not just that note.

"Where did your wife keep her mobile phone?" he asked James, who was watching with vague interest from his bed, a plate of untouched pastries beside him.

James blinked. Sat up. "Why do you need her mobile phone?"

Because she's a digital native, Jackson wanted to say, part of the generation whose mobile devices contained their entire lives. Each photo, text message and past Google search a potential trail of clues. Jackson could learn more from a young woman's Instagram account than any interview.

"It may contain something useful," he said simply.

James still looked confused. "You didn't find it on her? That's sus. Indy never went anywhere without her phone. It *must* have been on her. Did you look around the deck where… you know…?"

Jackson frowned. No, not properly. That was also on his to-do list. He glanced at Simon, who read his mind, then said, "I'll do it now" before exiting the cabin.

"If she did leave it here, where might it be?" Jackson asked James again, and they both turned to look at the bedside table.

Jackson saw a small lamp, a copy of Italian *Vogue*, a few pieces of chunky jewellery and some vials of hand cream, but no phone. Then he went through her belongings, slowly, methodically, through each handbag, every pocket, in her drawers, under her pillow, behind the bed. He searched her bathroom, found her gold string bikini hanging on the showerhead, like the entrails of a life now extinguished, and a set of tacky, matching flippers that had been dropped into the bathtub. No use for any of it now. But still no sign of her iPhone.

Ten minutes later, Simon was back from searching the sun deck, equally empty-handed. There would be no digital breadcrumbs for Jackson today.

"Hang on," said James. "Now you're telling me my wife's phone has been stolen? Who would do such a thing?"

The killer, Jackson would have told him, if he didn't look so shell-shocked already.

~

Pasha had a killer smile when she walked into the bar, seafood platters in hand, and Alicia wondered why she bothered—with both the fake bravado and the buffet.

None of the guests were very hungry, and if their shifty sideways glances were any indication, they weren't buying the "she'll be right" attitude either. One drowning was an accident. Two a genuine concern.

"You okay?" asked Perry. "You look a little peaky."

"I'm fine," said Alicia.

"You're worried."

"Who wouldn't be?" Then she leaned closer and said, "But I'm also more intrigued than ever now. Can you believe poor Indya might have been murdered? Right under our noses. I'm so grateful that we're here to help."

"That's what I love about you," said Perry. "Your mind is on overload and you're still relishing it."

"Relish is a bad word," she retorted, glancing around in case anyone overheard.

But Cindy and Connor were having their own furtive conversation at a small table on one side and Claire had been cornered at the buffet table by Boulder since she'd come in. He was the only guest who looked vaguely hungry, munching on a chicken wing.

"Can't wait to talk to Claire privately," said Alicia. "See how James is handling it."

"That will probably depend on whether the man's a killer or just an innocent bystander who's just lost the two loves of his life. Jackson tell you about the note Indya got during dinner last night?"

Alicia nodded. "I didn't notice that myself, but I have to wonder whether it was the reason she left the deck for so long. She didn't come back until we were well into mains." She leaned forward. "I really should have followed her out. Done my job. Maybe I would have seen her meeting with her killer."

Perry dropped his head to one side. "Or maybe you would have seen her throw her dinner up in the toilet. And I'm not saying that because I think she's bulimic. I mean, I'm bad but I'm not that bitchy!"

He offered her a wink. "No, after seeing her sobbing yesterday out on that deck, I wonder if Indya was worried sick about something. Or *someone*."

He gave her a knowing look. "Maybe the note's a red herring. Indya was with her husband right before she dashed out, yes? Maybe James said something to her? Or worse, maybe she was scared of him and she knew what was coming."

Now Alicia did look peaky as she digested that comment.

~

The captain was seated at her desk, finally getting some coffee into her system, when the first officer burst in.

"What is it now, Gary?" she said, not in the mood for more of his tantrums.

"Oh, I'm sorry, am I interrupting your tea break?" He stared down at her cup. "Need I remind you, I'm the one who hasn't had any sleep yet?"

She dropped the coffee to the table and rubbed the back of her neck. "Sorry. It's been a nightmare."

"And it's about to get a whole lot worse. The engine's stuffed. I'm sorry to say, Captain, but for now, we're stranded."

CHAPTER 32
Floating Aimlessly

Liz sat forward, nearly toppling her cup over. "I'm sorry, did you just say the engines aren't working?"

"Just one," said Gary. "I think it's a cooling-system failure. I'm troubleshooting it now, but I thought you should know. See? I like to share information. Not withhold it from my crew."

She ignored that slur and said, "But that's ridiculous. I mean, they're top-notch Caterpillar Diesel engines. Almost new!"

"Another thing you can bring up with your best mate Simon then."

"Gary…"

He held up a hand. "We're supposed to be on the same team, *Liz,* and you have lied to me—to all of us—from the start. We didn't even know Simon was the boat's owner. I should have been informed at the very least. Then when that cop came on board…" He glowered at her, thrust his hands into his pockets. "You talk about pulling together, and yet you've done nothing but work behind our backs from the minute this cruise set sail."

"Come on, Gary, there's no need—"

"I don't have time for this. I have an engine to repair. And I don't need you down there, by the way. We both know I'm the expert on engines. I can do it myself."

Then he left her staring into her cup, her expression as dark as its contents. He was right. She had played this all wrong right from the beginning. She should have come clean about everything. Who the hell was she protecting? Really?

She pushed the beverage away and dropped her head onto the table.

"Bad time?" came a voice from the doorway, and Liz looked up to see Jackson standing there.

"Has there been a good time since you boarded?" she said, then held out a hand. "Sorry." She sounded like sulky Gary. She stood up. "You want this office back, yes?"

"No hurry, but I do need to call my boss, let them know what's happened."

"Good luck with that." She nodded towards the handsheld receiver. "Satellite's down again. Might click in later if we get lucky. But I did notice email got through at some stage today. There's one addressed to you on the desktop."

"Well, that's something," he said, glancing at the computer in front of her, then across to the phone. "What's wrong with the Wi-Fi? Is it something suspicious?"

"Let's not jump to conclusions. I've got enough headaches. No, it always plays up." She pushed herself up and from the desk. "I have to get down to the engine room."

He glanced out the porthole. "Yes, good, it's vital we get cracking on to Cairns."

The captain paled even further. "I'm afraid I have some more bad news."

She proceeded to explain what Gary had just told her about the faulty engine. "It may be nothing. We're all a bit shaky; maybe he's overlooking something. I'll investigate."

"And if it's *not* nothing?" asked Jackson. "How do you repair a faulty engine out here in the middle of nowhere?"

"Depends what the fault is. Any luck yet? With the investigation?" She quickly added an *s* to that word, and he shook his head.

"From my perspective, things seem to be going from bad to worse too. I've now discovered that Indya's phone has gone missing, and I suspect the killer has stolen it."

"What? Why would they do that?"

"Perhaps it had some incriminating evidence on it, or they feared it did. I can't say."

"Oh dear. Should we search everyone's cabins?"

He shook his head. "It's probably already been thrown overboard. I want to get to the bottom of a note that was handed to Indya at dinner last night. I'm guessing you didn't send it?"

Liz looked confused, so he quickly added, "It may be nothing." Then he proceeded to describe what James had told him. "He says it was from a woman, but we don't even know that for sure. It might have been a lie, a way to lure her to a secluded area early this morning."

Liz dropped back into the seat like that was more than she could bear. "So the note could have been from *anybody*?"

"Yep. It's a pity Freddy hadn't been a little sneakier, we might have our answer."

"Freddy?"

"He was the one who found the note and handed it to Indya."

Liz looked startled by that. "Oh, okay. Right."

He frowned. "He didn't tell you?"

"No, he did not. Turns out my crew aren't telling me anything anymore." She scraped a strand of hair from her face as her eyes drifted across to the captain's hat she'd dumped on the desk. "We all used to be close until I got this promotion." Then, worriedly, "Do you have any idea what's happened? To Indya? I mean, we played a good game of Don't Ask Don't Tell down there, but... could it be an accident? Suicide perhaps?"

Her expression was as hopeful as the others, but he just shrugged. "Without an autopsy, it's impossible to say, but as you know, I assume murder and work back from there.

Forced drowning is my best guess. There're no obvious marks, so I think she was tripped or thrown into the jacuzzi and then held under."

The captain's eyes filled with tears. She held a hand to her lips, like she wanted to vomit. But still he had to ask:

"What time were you up and about this morning? Out of interest."

Liz smiled slimly. "I'll try not to be offended by that. Um... I woke at five, as I always do, got to the bridge at exactly five thirty. That's when I relieve Gary. And no, I didn't see anyone about, if that's what you're suggesting. I was too busy steering around the reef, putting down safe anchor. God... if only I had seen something."

"Don't beat yourself up," said Jackson. "It doesn't make you feel any better. Trust me, I've tried."

Smiling wearily now, she got back to her feet and scooped up her cap. "I'd better go and see about this engine."

After the captain had departed, Jackson reached for the satellite phone and found that it was, indeed, dead. He felt an odd mixture of anger and relief.

Anger because he should be phoning headquarters, reporting the second suspected homicide, discussing his findings, seeking their help. Relief because he had no idea what he would tell them, just as he couldn't really answer the captain's question earlier.

What *did* happen to Indya Wynter up in that tub? Maybe it was suicide. Or a very tragic accident. Or maybe it was cold-blooded murder. He felt as muddled as Liz had looked.

And that wasn't all. No matter what happened at the jacuzzi this morning, one thing was certain. He had let the young woman down. Indya was clearly struggling with something yesterday, and he had not taken the time to find out what. He didn't need James and Boulder's recriminations to know he'd failed her.

Jackson's mind strayed to Detective Inspector Indira Singh then, his partner back in Sydney. His *senior* partner, in fact. Why hadn't he called Singho last night or sent her that email he'd sent to Missy and Ronnie? She'd be spitting chips if she knew he was relying on a group of amateur sleuths to do his research. Was that why it was all crumbling around him? Had he relied on them too much?

Groaning, he tried the phone again, then he turned to the computer and clicked open the email that was marked: ATTN: LIAM JACKSON, CORONER'S ASSISTANT.

He exhaled. It was from Ronnie, who didn't yet know that his ruse was up. She had provided a Miss Marple-style commentary on all the suspects, and despite himself, he began to smile as he read through it. They might be amateurs, the book club, but they didn't miss a beat. He digested her comments, then read through them again:

"• Dr Roland Brown—seems tickety-boo. Long career on the reef, keen interest in saving it, judging by his Facebook feed. A girlfriend back in Cairns, no kids, no dirt we can find. Bit of a bleeding-heart leftie (good on him, I say!).

• Pasha Patel—less concerned about the planet than promoting herself as @GoddessOfCruising (her "handle", Missy tells me). Lots of vacuous Instagram posts including gleaming "selfies" from various decks—nothing sinister apart from that smile. Does she really think people are buying it?

• Freddy Cruz—he's a ghost. Can't find anything on any Freddy Cruz who works in the cruising industry (or anything similar). Will keep digging…

• Sergio Aloisio—it's as you thought. Was executive chef at Wynter Publishing for fifteen years before the work was 'outsourced'—their euphemism in a press release. Can't find any nasty tweets or FB messages threatening to turn postal on them. Will keep hunting.

• Gary Andrews—employed with a major cruise liner for a decade before leaving three years ago and then joining Simon's company a year later. No effusive press release to thank him for his service or explain his departure. Could be something in it or maybe he just got bored with drunken yobbos?

• The Dudley-Pines—Cindy does own an investment company called Cinnamon & Spice. Very glossy website, big promises of suspiciously high returns, but I've never heard of them."

Then a final note: "Still looking into Connor and his gymnasium. I do know Arne Boulder but only by association, will also enquire. And Captain Flinders' record, from what I can see, is impeccable. Could get Queeny to explore further? (She's been holed up at work since this happened. Simon's quite the taskmaster!)"

Jackson made a few notes but couldn't see any startling revelations in the material, nothing that would dramatically progress the case.

He tapped his pen on the desk, grumpy again. Another reason he should have phoned DI Singh earlier. Ronnie's notes were colourful, but there was only so much information amateur detectives could uncover. He needed *real* intel, background information like warrants and arrests. He threw the pen on the table, then glanced at the computer again.

An email had got through to the office at some point. Maybe an email could also get back out?

Hastily he tapped a fresh set of questions, this time to the real detective, then crossed his fingers and pressed Send just as he heard a loud knocking coming from the door. He jumped up to find Freddy standing there, a sheepish look in his eyes.

"Cap'n said you wanted to see me."

Jackson stepped back. "I'm not sure I asked her to—"

"I read the note!" Freddy blurted. "The note Indya got. Not gonna lie. I know exactly what it said."

CHAPTER 33
Worth Noting

Jackson's mood improved quickly. Finally a decent break in the case!

Trying not to get ahead of himself, he waited until Freddy had settled into a seat in front of the desk, then he perched on the edge, hovering over him, and said, "So tell me, what did the note say?"

Freddy looked suitably contrite. "I do not normally read other people's mail, yes? But... well, it was open. The envelope. And I wanted to see how urgent it was—if I must get to Mrs Wynter fast, you know? Or just leave it on her pillow like. I had so much work to do and I was not sure I had the time, so—"

"What did it say, Freddy?" he repeated.

Freddy nodded quickly. "It said, 'I have kept your secret, now I would like you to pay up.' Or something like this."

Jackson almost laughed. It was like something from one of Alicia's crime novels. And oddly polite for what sounded suspiciously like extortion. Jackson repeated the words: "I have kept your secret, now I would like you to pay up?" Freddy nodded. "And who was the note addressed from?"

"I do not know."

"You don't know?" He shook his head. "There was no name?"

"Oh, there was a name, sure. But it was scribbled like. I could not read the writing. I did not really try... I was running late, so I just put it back in the envelope and I pass it on."

Freddy held Jackson's gaze, his big brown eyes blinking innocently, but the detective didn't quite believe him. There was something slightly off about this kid. Jackson leaned forward and said, "You're certain about that?" Freddy nodded and Jackson leaned back.

"What's your full name please, Freddy?"

The butler blinked rapidly now. "Freddy Cruz."

"Freddy doesn't sound very Filipino."

"I told you, I am Aussie."

"Still." Jackson waited.

A belligerent sigh. "It is *Vilfredo de la Cruz*, but Freddy is better, yes? Easier for the guests."

Was that a slight snarl in his tone? "No middle name?" Jackson asked.

He shook his head, so Jackson made a note of it, then sent him on his way but not before giving him a lecture about reading private messages.

"Yes, yes, Cap'n has already chewed me out. But the way I see it, it is a *good thing* I read the note, because I am helping the case, yes?"

Jackson just waved him away, wasn't going to give the liar absolution on that count.

Still, the detective did feel more hopeful now. As far as he was concerned, the contents of the note changed everything. Or at the very least, it clicked a few pieces back into place.

Perhaps his first instinct was correct. Perhaps Indya really did drown her mother-in-law that afternoon on the water, and someone saw it happen, then tried to buy her silence.

What other secret would Indya pay to keep quiet?

It had to be an extortion attempt. And if that was the case, then it narrowed down his suspect list considerably. The guests were all super wealthy—why would any of them need to extort money? Oh no, it was a crew member, he just knew it. And not just any crew member. It was most likely someone who had seen Indya out on the second pontoon that day.

And as far as Jackson knew, there were only two crew who had admitted to just that.

And both of them had also whined to him recently about their "pitiful" salaries.

~

Sergio scowled deeply when Jackson appeared at the galley. So did Lynette.

"No way! No can do!" he yelled and scurried into the pantry.

Lynette dragged Jackson back out into the corridor. "You've really got to learn to pick your times, Jackson. We've got to get the afternoon tea going."

"Bloody hell, how much food do rich people consume?" Jackson groaned. "Fine. I'll come back in twenty."

"Before you go…" Lynette glanced into the galley, then dragged him further down the corridor. "There's something you should know about Freddy…"

~

Captain Flinders was emerging from the engine room when Pasha appeared, a prawn salad sandwich in hand.

"I thought you and Gary might need some nourishment," she said, holding the plate out.

It looked like a meal for one, and Liz knew exactly what she was doing. "You can fuss over Gary later, Pasha. He needs to focus."

She ignored that snipe and said, "Everything okay?" Glanced curiously into the room behind her.

"It'll be fine," Liz said, or at least she hoped it would.

Gary was right. He was the one with the engineering

background. *Perhaps he should have been the one to score the captaincy,* she thought, stroking the epaulet on her shoulder.

"Captain?" This was Pasha, perhaps for the second time.

"Sorry, what were you saying?"

"The animals are getting restless. No one's very hungry and there's only so much coffee we can produce."

Liz stared at her. Felt nauseated. "Okay, um, if Detective Jackson's finished with them, I can't see why they can't return to their cabins."

"Cabins? No, no, that's not going to work. They're demanding some fresh air. Or at least Cindy is. Boulder says it's time to get the yacht moving." Another sideways glance towards the engine.

"Boulder isn't the captain of this boat!" Liz barked back. "We'll get moving when I say we get moving and not a minute sooner." She slapped a hand to her lips and took a calming breath. "Sorry. Look, get that sandwich back to the galley and let everyone know we'll be moving soon enough, but until then they're welcome to use the lower deck and dive platform. But make sure they stay well away from the sun deck and that jacuzzi, got it? And no one is to go into the water. Not a soul. Is that clear?"

Pasha blinked. "You think there's going to be another drowning?"

"Of course I don't," she replied, but she didn't sound very certain.

~

Claire found her new husband head down at the large chart table in the centre of the bridge, studying some notes. He barely looked up when she entered.

"How's it all going?" she asked.

"What? Oh, not good. I've had a very heated conversation with Tommo. He seems to blame me for all of this."

"That's ridiculous." He shrugged and looked down again. "Can I help in any way?" she asked. "Simon?"

"Hmm?"

"Can I—"

"Look, honey, I really need to put out a few fires. All good down there?"

She frowned. "You mean apart from the two body bags and stressed-out passengers? Sure, it's *ridgy-didge*."

Finally he looked at her properly. Stepped out from the desk and towards her. "Sorry, Claire, I know I've been a bit absent. It's just... well, I've got so much to handle at my end. I'm trying to contain the damage. I've got to cancel the next few cruises, and once the shareholders find out about this, my company—*our* company—it could all go south."

Claire frowned harder and stepped back. "It's fine. Focus on your company." *It's what you really love*, she would have added if she had more of Boulder's gumption. "I'll get back to where I'm wanted. Needed. Back to my book club friends."

Then she strode out, feeling like sulky Indya now and not liking the feeling one bit.

~

Gary was leaning against a wall in the engine room, chewing on a prawn sandwich, when DI Jackson strode in.

"If you're after Liz, you just missed her," he said. "You'll find her snoring blissfully in bed."

He ignored the obvious jibe and said, "Actually it's you I'm after. Got a minute?"

"Am I even allowed to say no?"

Jackson smiled. "Thanks for your enthusiastic cooperation, Gary. I won't keep you long. I hear the engine's playing up."

"Nothing I can't handle."

"Good, because I'm anxious to get moving."

Gary finished the sandwich and put the plate aside. "So what do you want?"

"I want to know if you were on the sun deck early this morning."

"No mate, I was too busy navigating from the bridge."

"What time was your shift?"

"I started driving the boat after dinner at eleven, and Captain relieved me at five thirty. That's when Liz decides to finally get up and do her job. She took over command, I returned to my cabin."

"Which way do you return to your cabin?"

"Not past the jacuzzi if that's what you're inferring."

"Did you happen to see Indya Wynter doing her morning yoga while you were at the bridge?"

"Ah, *no*. Now let me do *your* job for you, Detective, and remind you that you can't see the sun deck from the bridge below. So I wouldn't have, would I?"

Jackson smudged his lips sideways. "She had to get up there though, didn't she? How do I know you didn't see Indya stride past while you were working all alone? Hm? How do I know you didn't slip out and attack her?"

"*Attack* her?" Gary's smarminess had given way to fury, and his hands were now fists at his sides. "Where did that come from? Why would I do that? What the hell!"

"I'm just saying—"

"I've never hurt a woman in my life. It's a lie. I'm not violent."

"Okay, take it easy." Jackson glanced pointedly down at his fists. "I'm not saying you meant to do it, Gary, but I do have to wonder if things got out of hand. Did you tell her you'd seen her out there on the pontoon with Elsbeth and did she panic, perhaps?"

"Hang on, what are you saying?"

"I'm saying you were one of the few people who knew Indya was with Elsbeth before she died. Did you try to use that knowledge to your advantage by extorting money from the young woman? And did she fight back? Did you hurt her in the process?"

Gary surprised him then by relaxing the fists and bursting into laughter, like he hadn't just been accused of blackmail and murder. When he finally gathered himself, he said, "You're not real bright are ya, mate?" Another chuckle, a shake of the head. "Besides, if that really happened, do you think I'm going to stand here and tell you all about it? I'm not a fool, although you clearly are."

Jackson glowered now. "You were a witness to what happened out there on the water that day, Mr Andrews, so you can cut the attitude. I think you saw Indya sabotage Elsbeth's tank, and I think you tried to use that to your advantage."

"Er no, I never saw Indya go anywhere near the old woman's tank. I told you that. And I'm not the only one who saw her, remember? Sergio was up there too, and it was Sergio who hung around perving long after I left. You should be questioning him. And while you're at it, ask him what *he* was doing up on the bridge deck so early this morning. Because the last time I looked, that wasn't the direct route from his bed to the galley."

CHAPTER 34
Camera Trouble

The water slapped playfully at the stern, glistening at the guests as though winking at them, welcoming them in, but no one took up the offer. They didn't dare. There were six of them on the dive deck that afternoon—Alicia, Perry, Claire, Boulder, Connor and Cindy—and they all looked wary.

Although Cindy tried her damnedest not to.

"Don't worry," she joked to Roland who was also there, watching as she lathered on some sunscreen, "this brand is super organic, won't hurt the little fishies."

He smiled vaguely while Boulder gave an exaggerated groan.

"Although it does leave my hands very oily," Cindy added, "not so good for taking photos."

Then she picked up her phone with two fingers and held it out to her husband. "Be a darl' and get a picture of us all, as a group, while we have a chance."

"What do you mean by that?" demanded Boulder from a banana lounge. "You think someone else is going to die?"

"Of course not! I'm just trying to be friendly."

"I'll do it," said Roland, taking the camera from her and waving the group together around Boulder, who clearly wasn't about to get up.

Claire wasn't exactly thrilled with this idea either. Group happy snaps didn't feel appropriate given the circumstances, and if one of these people turned out to be the killer, she wasn't sure Simon would want her being photographed alongside them. His precious shareholders would have a fit!

She was just considering how to extricate herself when something marvellous happened. Roland dropped Cindy's phone into the water.

"Oh my God!" he said. "Oh no!" Then he flicked off his shoes and dived in after it while Cindy gasped and Connor began yelling abuse.

"There go all our holiday photos, you dimwit!" he cried out as Roland splashed about trying to see where it had landed. "This is a disaster!"

The others rushed to the side, trying to spot the device in the glassy water below the platform—perhaps it had come to rest on a reef? But Claire's mind was now back on another reef, another day, another disaster.

And another iPhone. Indya's iPhone. The one she was snapping selfies with out on the water the day Elsbeth was murdered.

Except she can't have been using her missing iPhone, Claire suddenly realised. Because they shared the same model and it was not waterproof. Indya wouldn't have taken that phone into the water; she must have been using a different camera. A waterproof camera! And the more Claire thought about it, the more it started to take shape in her mind.

Yes, it was a blue one, thicker, chunkier…

~

Lynette had her hands in sudsy water when Jackson returned, and she shook her head.

"You missed him. He's out on the deck, having a ciggie."

"I thought he was busy."

"Never too busy for lung cancer," she told him as she continued scrubbing an oily pot. "Seems weird to me that the staff all have to keep working while there's a maniac on the loose."

"Do you feel unsafe down here?" Jackson asked.

"Not at all. I'm just whining. You wouldn't recognise me if I didn't. Besides, Sergio's never gone for long."

"It's him I'm worried about."

"Really? Why?" Her eyes narrowed. "What have you learned?"

"What time did he get to the galley this morning? Do you know?"

She shrugged a shoulder, then used it to wipe some sweat from her brow. "He was already here when I got in around six thirty. Why? When did Indya die?"

"Can't say for sure, but I might have narrowed it down to between five thirty and seven this morning, if Gary and Pasha can be believed, that is."

"You don't trust them?"

"Not Gary. And I don't trust Sergio either. How did he appear when you arrived this morning?"

"Stressed, dripping with sweat…" Then, as Jackson's eyebrows lifted, she added, "Like every chef on the planet. It's no fun in these hot kitchens. I wouldn't read anything into it. You don't really think he did it, do you? What about Freddy? Did you ask the captain about his sneaky filming?"

"Haven't had a chance, but I think it's a distraction. He was serving lunch at the time Elsbeth was killed, remember?" She nodded, grumpily. "Look, like I told you, keep your wits about you and—"

"Why?" This was Sergio, now standing at the galley door. "Why does she have to keep her wits about her?"

Jackson turned to face the chef.

~

It took a little scheming to get James Wynter out of his cabin. But it had to be done before Claire could begin her search for Indya's blue waterproof camera. She wasn't sure if James was involved in the murders, but if he was, he'd hardly just hand over potential evidence.

She had to be discreet.

So, as the kerfuffle broke out on the deck, Claire gave Alicia and Perry a sly look, then nodded downwards. She slipped away first, then Alicia congratulated Roland, who was now holding Cindy's dripping iPhone up jubilantly while Connor was shouting abuse.

"Come on, Bob," Alicia said loudly to Perry, "let's get some rice from the kitchen to dry the phone out."

Then they too scuttled away.

By the time they'd caught up with Claire, she was standing just outside James's stateroom and quickly filled them in: "Jackson's been looking for the wrong phone, or camera, really. Because I think there's a second camera, a waterproof camera, and it might hold some clues to what happened to Elsbeth."

"You think Indya photographed the killer that day?" said Perry.

"Maybe inadvertently. She took selfies as regularly as you and I breathe. So the chances are pretty good. Perhaps she snapped someone in the background, lurking, ready to kill Elsbeth."

"Or perhaps the killer just *thinks* she did," said Alicia, catching on, "and they stole her iPhone assuming that's what she used."

"But she didn't!" finished Perry. "Wow, brilliant, Claire. Now what?"

"Now we need to find that waterproof camera, and that means we need to get James out of his cabin in case he's hiding it. Or tries to sabotage it like Roland did just now."

"You think the divemaster dropped Cindy's phone into the water deliberately?" said Perry. "Why would he do such a thing?"

"Ooo!" said Alicia, clicking her fingers. "It's just like

The Woman in Cabin 10! You know? When the only evidence of the missing woman, the camera, gets 'accidentally' knocked into the hot tub!"

Perry scoffed but Claire was fervently nodding. "How do we know he didn't do that on purpose? Hmm? I don't trust anybody on this yacht anymore."

"Welcome to my mind, Claire," Alicia said, laughing.

"So what do you suggest?" asked Perry just as Freddy turned the corner, singing a hip-hop tune.

He stopped when he saw them together. Squinted. "Sup?"

Claire winked subtly at Perry and turned to the butler.

"Actually, we're very worried about James," she said. "He needs some fresh air and could really do with his room made up. Do you think you could knock and ask him to vacate the cabin please?"

"Shouldn't we just leave him? Mr Boulder told me to—"

"Forget about Boulder," she said, her tone uncharacteristically stern. "He doesn't own this yacht, my husband does, and James could really do with a change of scenery and some fresh sheets. Now, let's make it snappy!"

Alicia and Perry shared an impressed look—Mrs Barrier was feisty!—as the butler quickly tapped on James's door.

It took a few more taps before James appeared, his hair tufted up, his blue eyes red and puffy.

"What do you want now?" he mumbled, staring at Claire, and for a moment she felt deeply sorry for him.

Then she snapped herself out of it. "I'm sorry to disturb you, James. But Freddy has orders to clean your room, so I thought I'd ask, er, Marie here to escort you outside to get some lovely sunshine. It might perk you up a bit."

"I don't care about—"

"Please, Mr Wynter," said Freddy now. "I will get sacked if I do not do it."

Now all three book club friends were swapping a look,

impressed at Freddy's ability to lie so easily.

James shoved a hand through his hair and said, "Fine, let me get my door key."

~

The chef looked thunderous as he stared down Jackson. "What are you saying to Lynette? Hmm? Why should she keep her wits about her?"

"Two women are dead, Sergio. Does she need any more reason than that?"

Sergio glared at him for a moment longer, then marched in. "Why are you in my kitchen? What do you want?"

"I'm questioning everybody regarding their whereabouts this morning," Jackson replied. "And I'd like to know where you were between five and seven this morning."

Sergio tucked a cigarette packet into his apron pocket and went to the sink, dunking his hands in the water Lynette was using. He rinsed them and then reached for a tea towel.

"Where I always am," he said. "I fire up the ovens, get the bread baking at five."

"See anyone at that hour?"

"You mean did I see a woman drowning in a hot tub?"

"If that's what happened, yes."

Sergio scoffed. "No, that was your job, and you failed. Me? I just went straight from my cabin to here like I always do. The bread does not bake itself."

"Is that so?" said Jackson, leaning now against a bench. "Because I have a witness who places you up near that sun deck around five thirty this morning."

The thunderous look was back and he let out a steam of obscenities in Italian. "Did Gary tell you I killed her too? Did he tell you that? Because I never saw that poor young lady and I went nowhere near that jacuzzi. I was at the bridge, that is all."

Jackson watched him for a moment. "What were you doing at the bridge this morning?"

"I was sailing the boat, what else?" He scoffed. "I took the captain some breakfast. We had a chat, then I came back here."

Jackson tried not to glance at Lynette then, remembering what she'd told him last night about Sergio and Liz's embrace. Were they in a relationship? Was it even relevant? And, more importantly, why hadn't Liz mentioned this to him when he asked about her whereabouts this morning? He really needed to speak to Liz again.

"What did you *chat* about?" Jackson prodded.

"Does it matter?" Then, hands in the air, "I am not happy about all of this. I told her that. I knew you were a fraud, and you're not the only one. She needed to know that. There are too many liars on this yacht."

Jackson did lock eyes with Lynette then. Hers had widened. He said, "What do you mean, Sergio? Who else is lying? And what are they lying about?"

The chef waved his hands again and turned towards the stove. "I have no time for you! The guests will go hungry if I don't get moving. Now go, scoot."

"Mr Aloisio," Jackson said sternly, "if there's any information you have that could assist with my enquiries, you need to tell me now. Who do you believe is lying to me?"

"To you? I do not know! To me?" He swivelled back to the sink. "This one! She is too nosey. I know she is working for you!"

Lynette blushed crimson red and gaped back at him. "Chef…," she began, but he was shaking a set of tongs at Jackson now.

"Get out, Mr Detective, and take your spy with you!"

CHAPTER 35
Not So Happy Snaps

James's stateroom looked just as it had that morning, the only real mess the crumpled bed that he had clearly returned to. Claire felt bad for pulling him from his blessed slumber, but this was important. They needed to find that camera. And they needed to do it while Alicia was distracting James and before Freddy returned with fresh sheets and towels to make up the room. Time was of the essence.

"Come on," said Claire to Perry. "Where would you hide a waterproof camera if you had one?"

Perry glanced around, then smoothed down his goatee. "I wouldn't. Hide it I mean. Especially if I didn't know it contained evidence of a murder."

"*If* it contains evidence of a murder," said Claire, not wanting to get her hopes up.

"When did she last use it?" he asked, opening a drawer and rifling through. "Because I don't recall any waterproof camera when we were all snorkelling yesterday."

"No," said Claire, "that's probably why I didn't remember it. I have a feeling the only time she used it was that first fateful dive." She glanced around. "Let's think about it logically. Indya was running late for lunch that day, I know that, but she was also fully clothed in a sundress if I recall. Which means she must have come back here first, was probably still dripping wet…"

She stopped, turned, then headed straight for the bathroom, Perry fast on her heels. In there she looked around, then spotted the golden flippers still sitting idle at the bottom of the bath, and she leapt upon them. Within seconds, she was pulling out a small plastic contraption that had been wedged up inside one flipper.

It was the small, blue waterproof camera, a single-use disposable one.

Perry was impressed. "Nice work, honey!"

Claire beamed. Oh how she had missed all of this! Investigating with her friends, and doing it so well. So naturally...

"Do you think Indya hid it in the fin deliberately?" Perry was asking.

"Maybe, or maybe she just popped it in there for safe keeping when she was making her way back to her cabin."

They both inspected the camera excitedly until Claire turned it over and their excitement evaporated. The camera was loaded with Kodak film.

"What a nuisance," said Claire. "If this gadget does contain evidence, we won't know about it until we get to shore." Then she peered out the porthole and added, "Because there ain't no photo processing labs out here in the Pacific."

~

Alicia was regretting letting James divert them to Nemo's Lounge. He seemed intoxicated to her, stumbling over several times as they made their way in, even though the boat was immobile and barely listing. She watched him snatch a beer from the unmanned bar, then slug it back in just a few mouthfuls before grabbing another and knew she should be stopping him. But what could she do? He was a grown man, and he had just lost two family members in less than three days.

She wasn't sure if James was guilty of killing them, but he sure was beating himself up about something.

Well, kind of.

"Should never have let Mother come on this yacht," he told her as he stumbled with the beer to a leather armchair. "Boulder's such a yes man. He should have stopped her. Hell, I shouldn't have mentioned the cruise in the first place!" He glanced at Alicia sheepishly as he dropped into it and took a long swig of his beer. "She begged me not to, you know? Indy. I should've known it would all end in tears."

Another good swig of his ale.

"But you couldn't have known it would end in murder, surely?" she replied, taking the seat beside him.

"No, perhapshhh not," he slurred now. "But I was playing with fire, wasn't I? And with my mother's life." He leaned in closer, reeking of whisky, oddly. "You wanna know the truth?" He held a finger to his lips. "Shhh! Don't tell anybody."

Alicia pretended to lock her lips.

"I was teshhting Indy." James winked slowly. "There. I said it!"

Then his mouth drooped downwards, his eyes glazed over, and he looked like he was about to doze off, so Alicia coughed and said:

"What do you mean you were testing her, James? What did you do?"

"Hmm?" He looked up. Scowled like she was stupid. "I brought her here, didn't I? On the shh...stupid yacht."

Alicia nodded, hoping he'd continue. And he did, eventually, his eyes now drifting around the room.

"She was always so cool, Indy," he said. "Cool ash... ash a cucumber with my mum. I wanted to see if she was bluffing. Wanted to see what she'd be like... how she'd handle it... But she didn't, did she? It all went..." He made crashing sound, followed by explosions. Half chuckled, tears in his eyes. "She failed me, like they all do, just one big disappointment." Then he held up a wobbly finger and said, "I told her that. I said, 'You can't jushhh kill my mum, babe, and get away with it.' Thash not ash… ass… assheptible…"

Alicia felt her stomach drop and leaned in closer. "What are you saying, James?"

He looked back, his expression dark and bleak. "Hmm?"

"What really happened to your mother? And your wife? Do you know?"

James nodded, very certainly now. "My failure of a wife killed my beautiful mother of courshh. Then I—"

"James!" came a roar from the other side of the room.

They both swung around to see Boulder standing at the bottom of the stairs, arms akimbo, his thick cheeks a splotchy red. "What are you doing out of your cabin?"

"That's my fault," said Alicia, leaping to her feet. "Freddy had to make up the room, so I was keeping James company. Just trying to help."

Boulder brushed past and pulled James to his feet. "Come on, Jimmy, let's get you back to bed."

Then he glowered at Alicia like he knew exactly what she was doing and it had nothing to do with housekeeping.

~

"I'm mortified!" Lynette said as she followed Jackson back up and along the bridge deck towards the office. "I didn't realise Sergio knew. Do you think he suspects Alicia and Perry too? Is that what he means by 'too many liars on this yacht'?"

"Maybe," said Jackson. "Or maybe someone else is pulling the wool over my eyes. But who?"

"Has to be Freddy," she said. "He's clearly dodgy, filming the guests on the sly."

"He's also twenty, Lynette. That generation films themselves in their sleep. I really wouldn't read into it. Besides, he has an ironclad alibi, at least for Elsbeth's murder. There's no… Hang on, is that Simon waving?"

They were just passing the bridge and could see him

through the large window, waving the satellite phone towards them. "Phone call!" he mouthed through the glass.

"Finally, it's working," said Jackson, dashing in. "Must be Singho."

He was referring to his partner, DI Indira Singh, but it turned out to be Ronnie, and he would have been disappointed if she didn't sound so thrilled to hear his voice.

"You had us so worried!" she said. "We've been trying you all morning."

"Reception's dodgy," he told her, then sighed heavily and added, "And that's not all. The engine's playing up and there's been another murder."

"Yes, we know! About the murder. The press is going berserk back here."

"What? How?" Jackson slumped into the seat Simon had vacated, thinking how grumpy the police commissioner would be, while Lynette located the Speaker button so they could listen in.

"We'll worry about all that later," Ronnie said. "Missy is with me, but I'm afraid the line will drop out again, so we haven't much time. Have you got a suspect yet?"

"I've got too many suspects," said Jackson, "and not nearly enough evidence." He glanced around the control centre to make sure it was just the three of them, then said, "I'm particularly concerned about Gary Andrews and Sergio Aloisio, the chef. But at this point, I don't have anything concrete. And I haven't even begun to properly investigate the dive instructor or James and Boulder."

"Arne Boulder?" said Ronnie. "You really think he could have done it?"

"I'm not sure," said Jackson. "He's got his own agenda, that I do know. He's trying to blame Indya Wynter for all of this, but I can't help wondering if he's deflecting. Says he's the executor of Elsbeth's Will and gets nothing from her death, but he could be lying. I've emailed and asked headquarters to look into it, but it could take time, especially if they have to get search warrants and the like."

"Leave it with me," said Ronnie. "I play bridge with one of his law partner's wives. I'll have a quiet word. But do you really think Boulder's responsible?"

"He's not a front-runner, no, certainly not for Elsbeth. He's not a diver, and he's a big bloke, so for him to slip in and swim across without anyone seeing is unlikely. Besides, the timing doesn't work."

"Can you look into Freddy Cruz too?" said Lynette, breaking her silence. "He's very shifty."

"Hey Lynny!" came Missy's voice now. Then less excitedly, "You're right, he *is* shifty. I can't find anything on him, which is super weird because he's Gen Z. He should be all over TikTok, right?"

Jackson grappled for his notes. "His full name's Vilfredo de la Cruz, but I'm not sure I'd waste time with him, Missy. Like I keep telling Lynette"—a pointed look at her then—"his alibi for Elsbeth's murder is strong."

"Okay then, possum, worth a try," she replied while Ronnie cut back in.

"Listen folks, that's not the reason we've called, so let's get to the point before we get cut off. There's something else we've discovered about one of the passengers. I've just been on the blower with my friend Reginald Firskin. He sits on the board of the Securities and Exchange Commission, and what he's just told me in confidence might crack the case wide open."

CHAPTER 36
Another Spicy Interview

Cindy Dudley-Pine looked the picture of innocence as she sat twiddling her Tag Heuer and smiling towards Jackson. She smelled of sea salt and sunscreen and clearly had no idea what was coming.

Jackson tried not to look too smug as he sat across from her at the desk, back in the captain's office. Lynette had dashed off to "do a little more sleuthing" before Sergio blew her cover, and Simon looked so stressed he didn't have the heart to drag him from the bridge to bear witness. Besides, Cindy was so slippery this was better done solo.

"How's your business going?" he asked, and she looked surprised, her smile slipping ever so slightly.

"Why? Do you have a spare million you'd like to invest?"

Her eyes twinkled as brightly as her watch, but Jackson shook his head.

"If I had a spare million, I'd want to hold on to it, Cindy. Not hand it to a criminal."

Her smile vanished, but she didn't say a word, so he sat forward and gave her a victorious smile of his own.

"I've just discovered that your investment company is currently being investigated for illegal practices, insider trading to be precise. Care to elaborate on that?"

Now her eyes were sparkling with fury. She held up one finger. "Er, no, I believe you have that wrong, Detective. My business partner, *Warren Spice*, is being investigated for insider trading, and so far they've found nothing. It's all just a terrible misunderstanding and has nothing to do with me."

"Except business has nosedived, Cindy. According to my sources, you're close to bankruptcy."

The finger was now waving. "No, no, we're not done yet. I will turn it all around. You'll see."

"Is that why you're here? To snag yourself a rich investor? Someone like Indya Wynter perhaps?"

She shifted uneasily and said nothing, so he leaned forward, soothed his tone.

"I'm not actually interested in what trouble you're in on the mainland," he said, "except where it encroaches on this vessel, and I have a feeling it did just that."

"I don't know what you mean."

"I'm talking about the note you sent Indya Wynter last night. I'm talking about your extortion attempt!"

Jackson was yelling suddenly, but he was over this woman and her lies.

"I told you this morning," she shot back calmly. "I never sent Indya a note."

"Forgive me, Cindy, if I no longer believe a word that comes out of your fraudulent mouth. You also told me you saw Indya swim back with you to the yacht that first morning, then you confessed to lying."

"Ah, no, I just confessed to helping the distressed woman out. I was simply motivated by kindness."

He scoffed. "Your so-called motivation doesn't make it less of a lie."

She sat forward, looking desperate suddenly. Not her usual self. "I didn't send her a note. I didn't." Then, brow knotted, she asked, "What did it say?"

"You threatened her and asked her to bail you out."

"No, I did not."

"You sent her that note, then the minute she received it, she left the dining deck and you followed her out. I have several witnesses who will attest to that."

"No," she said again, less convincingly.

"You met with her and demanded she pay up in return for your silence."

"No! I mean, it wasn't like that, I can assure you."

"What was it like then? Tell me."

Cindy sat back then, chewing her lower lip, and he knew she was choosing her words, wondered how many of them would be lies.

"Look, I don't know about any note," she said eventually. "But... okay." She exhaled. "I did head to the toilets around the same time as Indya. I happened to find her in there, and we had a little chat."

Happened to indeed! "What did you *chat* about?"

"I just mentioned how I'd helped her out with you, had provided her an alibi. I wanted her to know that I'd done her a favour and perhaps she could do me one in return."

"I thought you were concerned about Indya's distress levels."

"Yeah, well, I'm more concerned about *my* distress levels. Because, yes, I am experiencing a bit of trouble if you must know. But like I said, it's all just a terrible misunderstanding. Things are flat at the moment, that's all. I just need a few more clients, a few big fish to lure back the tadpoles."

"Enter Indya Wynter. A very big fish."

"Hardly! She's just a very pretty goldfish married to a big fish. It's really James Wynter I wanted. Look, I can see how it might have been misconstrued... I just thought I'd explain to Indya how much I had helped her. How, if she thought about it—about how I'd perjured myself for her sake—she might want to convince her hubby to sign up. My God, he's got more money than he knows what to do with! That's all it was. Just a business proposal."

"So you invited her to the jacuzzi early this morning."

"What? No! I spoke with her last night in the bathroom, like I said." She sat forward. "But here's the thing. I barely got a word out. The moment I told her I'd seen her out there with Elsbeth on the pontoon, she turned ghostly pale and said 'Oh God, not you too!' or something like that. Then dashed out without even using the loo."

Jackson stared hard at her. "*You* saw that, too? What time was all this?"

She shrugged. "Between entrée and mains?"

He thought about that. That would have been around the time Indya showed up at his door to make her confession. There could be some truth in what Cindy was saying. Perhaps—just perhaps—Cindy didn't send the threatening note, someone else did (had to be Gary or Sergio, had to be!). Perhaps Cindy's conversation was the final straw. Indya could see the wagons circling; the truth was coming out. She must have decided then and there that it was time to come clean about being the last to see Elsbeth alive.

But Indya hadn't confessed to murder, not to Jackson last night and not to Cindy either…

"Is that all?" the woman asked, heartened by the way he'd drifted off.

He shook his head. "Here's my problem with all this. How do I know you aren't lying again? Perhaps you wouldn't take no for an answer. Perhaps you followed her to the sun deck this morning, had another little chat, but this time it ended badly. Things could've got out of hand, you didn't mean to do it…"

Cindy was snorting now, shaking her head. "What a load of rubbish," she said, "and are you really going to lecture me about lying? You! It's clear you think something dodgy is going on and you haven't got the decency to tell us. What's worse"—she was on her feet now—"you seem to want to plant it all on me. Well, I won't have it. All I'm guilty of is some bad investment luck and trying to grab an opportunity to turn that luck around. I poured all my life's savings into this blasted cruise. Do you have any idea how much a ticket costs? It's daylight robbery! But I paid up so

I could rub shoulders with Mr Wynter, and all I've had is the cold shoulder. I just thought Indya might act as a go-between. Where's the harm in that? And I can tell you this for nothing: killing that poor child is not going to make that happen now is it? My business is still in the toilet, and you're no closer to solving two murders!"

~

Lynette found Freddy in Nemo's Lounge, pulling glasses out of a dishwasher, and he looked up, surprised, when she strode in.

"I've been redirected to help you," she said by way of explanation.

It was a lie, of course, but he didn't question it.

"Cool! I have too much work to do before the old people come for cocktails." He reached for a tequila bottle and said, "But first…"

Lynette's eyes lit up as he poured her a shot.

~

Cindy's words echoed in the detective's ears as he sat at the captain's desk and tried to make sense of the case. Another day was nearly over, sundowners fast approaching, and Jackson needed to get his thoughts together. Fast.

He scooped up the office phone to call DI Singh but found it was dead. Again! Groaning, he returned it to its cradle, then checked the computer, but there was no reply email from her either. Another loud groan, then he got to his feet.

He could sit here all alone in the captain's office, waiting for the Wi-Fi to click in, or he could do what had worked so well in the past and throw it around with somebody.

When he got back to the bridge, Simon was at a side

table, wading through files. He looked up expectantly as Jackson approached.

"Please tell me Mrs Dudley-Pine just confessed to everything and this nightmare is over," Simon said, following it up with a weary smile.

"I wish," said Jackson, glancing around. "Where's the captain, by the way? I haven't seen her for ages."

"She's getting some shut-eye, will be on navigation duty this evening."

"I thought Gary was joking about that. Isn't he on night shift?"

"Usually, yes, but he hasn't had a chance to rest. Liz is doing that now so he can focus on the engine."

"I guess that makes sense," said Jackson. Then, "I know you're busy, but can you do me a favour and gather the book club together? In your cabin? I'll see if I can find Lynette and meet you there in ten. Just don't be obvious about it. I don't want the others knowing."

"You want to consult the club again?"

"Why not?" he said. "It's always worked well in the past."

~

Lynette pretended to sip her tequila as they continued setting up glasses in Nemo's Lounge and noticed that Freddy downed two shots while she was still on her first.

Good. Perhaps that would loosen his tongue.

"Ever get any cool celebs on the yacht?" she asked as casually as she could muster.

"This is only my second cruise, yes?" he replied.

"Yeah, but…"

"But sure, yachts like this are full of the rich and famous. We had that lady with the blue hair. You know? The one who sings that trash song about butterflies. She was on the last cruise."

"Really? How exciting!" said Lynette. "Did you get her

autograph or a selfie with her or something?"

"No, no, she was too stuck-up. Plus the captain gets aggro if we try to make friends with the guests. Says we have to keep our distance, like, that is what they pay for." Then he sniggered and added, "It is not all they will pay for, yes? Especially when they are pressed."

"Oh yeah?" said Lynette, eyes lighting up just as a dark shadow appeared in the doorway...

CHAPTER 37
Three Official Theories

Connor peeked through the open gap in his door and frowned. "There's something going down," he whispered across to his wife. "I've just seen the Tanners slip into the Barriers' room like they are up to something."

"They're probably just enquiring about getting the chopper back and fleeing, and we really should have too. Back in Cooktown. What was I thinking?"

"Oops, here comes the detective, and he's got someone with him. I can't see—"

Cindy rushed across and yanked Connor from the door, then closed it as quietly as she could. "For God's sake!" she hissed. "Don't let him see you. The last thing I need is another Spanish Inquisition. If he knocks, do not answer it!"

Connor slumped down on the bed. "The copper really thinks you did this?"

"They all do. What do you think they're talking about down in that cabin?" She jiggled her ample shoulders, then sat at the vanity table and began peeling off her gold jewellery. "Come on, let's start getting ready for sundowners."

"You're going to go to drinks? After what's just happened?"

"I'm going to drinks *because of* what's happened. You should know this, Mr Pecs. When they've got you cornered, you come out fighting." Then she stood up and reached for a fresh towel. "Now fetch my pearls from the safe, darling, while I have a shower. It's time to put our masks back on."

~

Lynette wanted to smack Jackson across the head.

"I nearly had him!" she said as they made their way along the corridor to Claire and Simon's stateroom. "Freddy was about to spill his guts until you walked in the bar. I reckon he films the guests in salacious positions, then blackmails them for the footage. He's our extortionist, for sure."

"I told you, Lynette, that makes no sense," said Jackson, tapping softly on the cabin door. "*He* came to me with the note's contents, remember? He could've pretended he never read it or said it was trivial, some words of sympathy. Doesn't add up, so just drop it, okay? Ah, hey Claire."

"*Hello*," she whispered excitedly, letting them in.

The others were all there, spread across the chairs and bed, so Jackson leaned against the dresser while Lynette dropped onto the plush carpet.

"Okay, gang, let's try not to take too long," said Jackson. "Your fancy cocktails are in an hour, and we need to get out of here before then. Connor's just spotted us together, and Sergio's already outed Lynette."

"Oh no," said Alicia. "I was wondering how you got away at the witching hour."

"Told you he was smart," Lynette said. "Perhaps it's time we all came clean."

"Not yet," said Jackson. "It's too much of a distraction. I want things to settle down again. That's when we get slip-ups. I've emailed HQ and asked for background checks on everyone. Should have asked a lot earlier. But, knowing what we currently know, I want to go through it methodically with you all and see if we can't narrow down this suspect list before we get to Cairns."

"Would help if we got moving," said Perry, staring out through the balcony's sliding door. "Why are we still sitting here?"

"Engine trouble," said Simon, his tone grim.

"Was it sabotaged?" asked Alicia, and Jackson wanted to tell her it was her overactive imagination, but he'd thought the same thing.

"At least it gives us more time to investigate," said Perry.

Simon gasped. "We're marooned in the middle of nowhere with a potential serial killer, and you think that's a positive, Perry?"

"They all do," said Jackson, shaking his head. "You still don't quite get this club, Simon." *Or your wife*, he could have added, but the bloke looked startled enough. "Okay, let's get back to it. We have two women drowned within two days of each other, so we have to assume there's a link. I've had a good think about it, and as far as I'm concerned, there are three likely theories we should consider."

He held up a finger. "The first theory, the one Boulder is rooting for, is that Indya killed her mother-in-law during a moment of madness while out diving and then, stricken with guilt, drowned herself, either deliberately or because she was under the influence of something."

"Helps explain why she was crying when we ran into her jogging yesterday," said Perry.

"I like this theory," said Simon.

Jackson knew why. "Yes, it is ideal because it wraps everything up very neatly and means we no longer have a killer roaming the yacht. It also reduces the urgency of this case, because there's not much more we can do until we get to shore and an autopsy is performed. For those reasons, I say we put that theory aside."

Simon looked disappointed, but Jackson was only warming up. "Which brings me to my second theory, and it runs along similar lines—Indya killed Elsbeth in a rage and then somebody else killed Indya to avenge Elsbeth."

"Has to be James or Boulder then," said Claire. "Who else would care enough? Elsbeth didn't exactly make friends on this ship."

Alicia sat forward. "I've got my money on James," she said, then described his slurred revelations in the lounge bar earlier. "He was stonking drunk and really maudlin, inches from confessing to me, I'm sure of it. But then Boulder walked in and sent him back to bed. He's protecting him, I know it."

"But James didn't actually confess?" asked Jackson.

Alicia swished her lips to one side. "I'm telling you, he was close. You should grill him, Jackson. You'd get it out of him in five seconds."

The detective shook his head. "If James is as intoxicated as you say, then any confession is as good as useless. It'll have to wait until morning when he sobers up. It also reduces the urgency because the risk to the passengers is minimal—and not just because it sounds like he's now passed out in bed. He has no motive to kill anyone else."

"We hope!" said Simon. "Okay so what's the third theory?"

"Ah." Jackson leaned back on the dresser. "The third theory is a lot more complex, a lot more urgent, and, quite frankly, is doing my head in."

~

Sergio stared at the young chef, one hand waving above his head. "I told you I do not want you here!" he said as Lynette stepped into the galley. "Why are you back in my kitchen?"

Alicia had asked her the same thing just moments ago when she fled Claire's cabin midway through Jackson's third theory. "Sergio knows you're investigating, and he could be the killer. Stay with us. Stay safe!"

But Lynette was determined to help with the dinner prep. "I'm more use in the galley," she'd proclaimed, "and I'm not just talking the case. Sergio is relying on me tonight. I'd promised to make another special dessert. We think it'll help settle the horses."

"You've changed your tune since this morning," Alicia had shot back. "And what if the horse happens to be a murderous chef?"

"Well, it's not like I haven't dealt with that kind of beast before."

And so here she was, holding her ground in the galley entryway as Sergio continued to rail.

"Go away, little girl," he said. "I have no need for liars and traitors here."

She stepped in regardless. "I'm sorry I lied to you, Chef. I was just trying to help find Elsbeth's killer."

"You're *really* a detective?" He looked at her with disbelief. "But you can cook!"

She smiled. "I'm glad you noticed." Her smile dropped. "I am a chef, Sergio. I was brought on with Jackson to do a little sleuthing while giving you a hand at the same time."

He scoffed. "Why would they let a chef do this?"

"You'll be surprised what they let you do when they're as desperate for discretion as they are answers."

"I do not care. You should not have lied to me, Lynette. I have no use for liars."

She dropped her head to one side. "So you *don't* want my help, is that what you're saying? Have you even started prepping my mango-and-coconut pudding?" Lynette sniffed the air and added, "And that better not be my crab tartlets I can smell burning in the oven."

He glowered, then turned away. Said nothing for a second, then growled, "Hurry up then. They won't crawl out on their own you know!"

She grinned as she reached for an oven mitt.

~

Back in Claire's cabin, the team were mulling over Jackson's third theory, and now all their heads were boggling and not just because it cracked the case wide open.

"I strongly suspect both women were killed by a third party," Jackson told them, "and that third party is still amongst us, alive and kicking. Which means the risk is still grave and we have to keep digging. Let's start from the top, the obvious suspect, and work our way through."

"Hang on," said Alicia. "So you're assuming the *same* person killed *both* women?"

Jackson scratched his stubble. "I hate making assumptions, but yes, in the interest of time, let's do that too. Whoever killed Elsbeth also killed Indya, but why?"

"I know why," said Claire, producing the waterproof camera from the safe box in her cabin. She'd wrapped it in a bin bag and handed it to Jackson now as she explained what it was and where she and Perry had found it.

"Great work," Jackson said, inspecting it through the plastic and making her bristle with pride. "Pity we can't process it yet, but you're quite right, Claire. There could be evidence on that camera, or the perpetrator just thinks there is. Which brings us back to the likeliest scenario— the simplest scenario—that Elsbeth was the only target and Indya was killed simply because she was in the wrong place at the wrong time. She saw the killer out on the reef that day, might even have photographed them, ergo she had to be silenced."

"That's a lot of assumptions," said Alicia, wincing. She knew from experience that assumptions were dangerous.

"I'm telling you, my head is muddled and the clock is ticking. Right, so who does that fit in with? Who wanted Elsbeth Wynter dead? And why? Or, more specifically, who had the most to gain by Elsbeth's death?"

"That brings us back to James Wynter, heir to all that

luscious fortune, surely?" said Perry.

"No way," said Claire. "Elsbeth was elderly and doted on James. Why kill her now? It was all coming to him soon anyway."

"Maybe it wasn't about the money," said Perry. "Maybe it was more personal than that. Elsbeth's arrival on the yacht was the final straw. He was finally standing up to his mum, protecting his marriage."

"So why go on and kill Indya if he wanted to protect his marriage?" asked Alicia, one eyebrow cocked.

Perry shrugged and Claire said, "Nope, I can't see James as the culprit. I mean, I can see him drowning Indya in a jacuzzi easily enough."

"You can?" said Simon, gulping.

She ignored him completely. "But I can't see him hurting his mother. He adored her too much. Worse than that, he was in awe of her, almost feared her I'd say. He wouldn't have been able to do it."

"Boulder would agree with you," said Jackson. "Says Jimmy doesn't have the gumption."

"What about Boulder then?" said Alicia. "He has plenty of gumption. He could have killed Elsbeth to free his beloved Jimmy and then killed Indya because he feared she'd seen him out there."

"But Boulder wasn't in the water, doesn't swim, doesn't dive," said Simon.

"*We think*," said Claire. "And what about Captain Flinders? Have we looked at her closely enough?"

All eyes swept to Jackson, and he brushed a strand of sandy hair from his face. "No, we have not. She doesn't have a solid alibi for either murder—all alone in the bridge apparently—but what would be her motive?"

"Has none," said Simon. "And if she did, why would she bring this lot on board?"

"I believe you're the one to blame for that," shot back Jackson.

"Touché," Simon retorted. "Still, Captain Flinders has

no motive. If anything, it's made her life worse. I've been on the phone to the office all day—"

"You have?" said Jackson. "I thought the Wi-Fi has been down most of the day."

He shrugged. "The phone in the bridge is working okay. Anyway, as I was saying, my business partner and I agree, we're going to struggle to keep Captain Flinders on. The board of directors have lost all confidence in her."

"But it's hardly Liz's fault," said Claire, aghast. "If we confirm she's innocent, then surely it's just bad luck."

"It's a marketing disaster, Claire," he replied. "Perception is everything in this industry. I know that's a harsh thing to say, but would you take another cruise with a commander who oversaw two murders and a faulty engine? I know I wouldn't."

Claire tsked and sat back, glowering at him, and Jackson swapped looks with the others. But there was no time for marital friction.

"Let's move on to the Dudley-Pines," he said, taking a moment to reveal what Ronnie told him about Cindy's business partner and the allegations of insider trading out against him.

That got them excited again as he knew it would. He added, "I wonder if I've been reading Cindy all wrong. This isn't about money or at least not directly. It's about protecting her dirty secret. I know she came on this boat to try to sign James Wynter up as a client, so it must have been a great shock when Elsbeth said she recognised Cindy's name from somewhere."

"That first night at dinner," said Claire.

Jackson nodded. "Perhaps Elsbeth had sources at the Securities and Exchange Commission, like Ronnie, or one of her financial mags was about to break the story. Cindy might have feared Elsbeth would work it out and spill the beans to James, and it would all be for nothing. She'd never get him to invest in her business after that, so she killed Elsbeth to shut her up."

"Cindy did come to lunch very late that day after diving," said Claire.

"So where does that leave Connor?" asked Alicia. "Were they working together, do you think?"

"Most likely," said Jackson. "And I still think Cindy was blackmailing Indya even though she stridently denies it."

"But by that logic, Cindy would have *no reason* to blackmail Indya if she was the one who had really killed Elsbeth," said Perry.

Jackson had to think about that for a moment before conceding he was right.

Perry added, "You know, folks, we're being very Agatha Christie about this."

"What's that now?" said Simon.

"Agatha is often accused of classism, especially in books like *Evil Under the Sun*," explained Claire, her tone a little impatient. "She had a tendency to ignore the domestic servants in a murder case, as though they weren't quite sentient beings."

"Oh, she did it for convenience," said Alicia. "Too many suspects can be unwieldy."

"Tell me about it," said Jackson, checking his watch. "Let's look at the crew then. What do we think about the first officer, Gary Andrews? His alibis are also weak at the time of both murders, and he has a very special beef with the captain."

"He does?" said Simon.

Jackson sounded impatient now. "I thought you'd know this. Yes, Liz says they were both up for the captaincy and Gary hasn't forgiven her for clinching it. In fact, do you have any idea what happened at his last posting? With the large cruise company? He left abruptly; could be a red flag."

Simon shrugged dismissively. "I have a human resources department that deals with recruitment, that sort of thing."

"Right," said Jackson, "well, I have to wonder if there's something there. Liz tells me Gary covets her job, thinks she's not worthy. Maybe Gary didn't have a motive to hurt the Wynters, and it was Captain Flinders he was trying to destroy."

"By destroying the boat?" gulped Simon.

"Goodness," said Claire. "That's one hell of a chip. Would you really kill two innocent people because you hate your boss?"

"If so, you better pop Pasha on the suspect list," said Alicia, telling them all now about their exchange during breakfast that morning. "She was gunning for the captain, all but told me to blame her and sue the ship."

Simon dropped his head into his hands, and Claire softened then, reaching across and giving his back a quick rub. "Don't worry, nobody's suing anybody, but again, Pasha can't have killed Elsbeth, she was working when it happened, remember?"

"Sure, but she's thick as thieves with Gary," said Perry. "I've seen them sniggering together in the corner. And *his* alibi's as weak as his abs. They could be in *cahoots*."

"If that's what you're thinking, I should also tell you that Lynette has suspicions about the butler, Freddy," said Jackson. "Thinks he sneaks photos of celebrity guests and blackmails them or something." He held up a hand. "Before you get excited, I've all but discounted him from my enquiry. He has an alibi for the first murder and would hardly tell me the contents of Indya's note if he then went on to kill her. He's a scumbag, but I'm not sure he's smart enough to be the killer."

"What about the chef then?" said Perry. "He's clearly smart if he's outed Lynette. And his motive's decent. Elsbeth took away his beloved publishing job."

Jackson nodded. "His alibis are also shaky. I know he was watching Elsbeth and Indya together on the pontoon the day she died. He could have slipped in unnoticed after Indya returned and killed Elsbeth out of anger or spite while everyone was distracted at lunch."

"Bit of a risk though," said Claire. "Freddy or Pasha could have noticed him missing when they went to the galley to replenish the platters."

"Maybe it was a risk worth taking," said Jackson. "He was angry with Elsbeth for sacking him. I know for a fact that Sergio was also in the vicinity of Indya's murder, on the bridge deck this morning." Again, he held up a hand to quell their visible excitement. "Could be a red herring. Lynette thinks Sergio might be in a relationship with the captain."

"Liz and Sergio?" said Simon. "That's not the impression I get."

Jackson wasn't surprised. The guy had about as much intuition as a rodent. "One more reason to interrogate Liz again."

"Can we move on to Dr Roland?" asked Alicia now. "He's also been getting a free pass. And from what I can tell, he, too, has no alibi."

"You can't possibly suspect our esteemed marine biologist!" gasped Simon. "He's in as much hot water as the captain. He'd hardly engineer a murder during one of his dives. He'll be lucky to ever work again. And he's the one who found her dead, remember?"

"But did he? Really? How do we know he didn't kill her while he was 'pretending' to rescue her? Hmm."

"Why would he do that?"

She shrugged like it was inconsequential, but Perry was now warming to this theory.

"I do know he was up and about very early this morning," he said. "He admitted as much to me. Said he was prepping the dive deck. So he has no alibi for Indya's murder either."

"And Roland did fling Cindy's phone into the water this afternoon!" added Claire, her voice animated again. "Maybe he was worried she also had incriminating photos and was covering all his bases?"

"Okay, and his motive?" asked Jackson. "Because Simon's right. He's done himself no favours. He'll be dragged through the coroner's court over Elsbeth's drowning. It won't be pretty."

Alicia chewed her lip and sat back. "It's just a theory."

"And a typical book club one at that," said Jackson, grinning at her as he got to his feet. "Okay, time's up. We need to get out of here before anyone gets suspicious." He stretched, then turned for the door. Turned back. "Listen, I'm not sure we can rely on that waterproof camera. It may contain nothing. We need to find more evidence, and we need to find it fast. As far I'm concerned, there's still a murderer on this yacht and they may strike again."

Then, lessening the blow, he quickly added, "Just keep your eyes open and stick together. And get word to Lynette, please Alicia. I don't want her sleeping down on that crew deck alone tonight. She can bunk in with Perry while you're in with me."

"Surely someone's going to notice all this bed-hopping," said Simon. "Didn't you say Connor was already onto us? And Sergio knows about Lynette. Won't they all start gossiping?"

"They can gossip all they like," said Jackson. "As long as there's no more killing."

CHAPTER 38
Revving Up

Liz Flinders never thought she'd want to give Gary Andrews a giant hug, but when she finally heard the heavy drone of the engines kick in and then felt the boat lurch, she almost raced to the engine room to do just that.

But first she needed to face the music.

So, after a revitalising shower, Liz dressed in a fresh uniform, slicked her hair back as she always did with argan oil, and pulled her cap on, then made her way straight to Nemo's Lounge where she knew the guests were gathering for the final night of cocktails.

All except for James.

"He's sleeping and is not to be disturbed," Boulder told her gruffly when she spotted the lawyer alone at the bar.

"Of course," she replied. "I'll get word to the crew."

"It's not the crew I'm worried about," he muttered.

Liz swapped a look with the butler, then turned to face the others. Once again everyone was in attendance, including all the crew except Gary, who was now turning the yacht towards Cairns. She locked eyes with Jackson, and he gave her the nod, so she stepped into the centre of the room and took a good, deep breath.

"Hello everybody!" she called out, bringing them to silence. "Thanks again for your understanding and patience. I know it's been…" A fluttering smile. "Well, thank you." She waved towards a window. "As you may have heard, we had a spot of engine trouble, but that is now clearly in the past."

There was a "tsk" from somewhere, but she pretended not to hear it. She just needed to get through this.

"First Officer Gary is currently clearing the reef, and I will take over from him shortly. However, we have lost valuable time, so we will continue sailing through dinner tonight and expect to be docking in Cairns mid-morning tomorrow. That means dinner will be a little rockier than I like, but it's vital we keep going. I do hope you understand."

No one made a sound of complaint now. They all looked exhausted, tentative. Worried. And she wondered how this cruise could have nosedived so quickly.

"I do believe the top deck is still out of bounds..." A quick glance at Jackson, who nodded, so she turned to Pasha. "I think it's best we serve dinner buffet-style down here in Nemo's Lounge."

"What happens when we get to Cairns?" asked Cindy now.

Another glance at Jackson, who stepped forward to join Liz in the centre.

"A forensics team will be meeting us at the port, and there will be further interviews, I'm afraid."

Now they found their voices and there were grumbles all around.

Jackson watched as Boulder began to moan about his "precious time". He was now seated beside Cindy and Connor, who was nodding along. The detective felt like giving them a good shake. Two people had been murdered—*by someone on this ship*. What were they expecting when they got back to Cairns? Dancing girls? A marching band?

He studied them some more and wondered that they were still so calm. *He* wasn't even feeling calm, would be worried sick until he got them all safely off this boat, starting with Alicia and her book club friends.

That is, if he *did* get them all off in Cairns. Perhaps it

was time for a little straight-talking.

"Listen up, people," he called out, bringing them to silence. "In the light of what's happened, I suggest you stay together as a group tonight, and after dinner, you return directly to your cabins with your partners, and you stay there until morning. If you're on your own, apply the chain lock, and don't let anyone inside except for me."

"Crikey!" cried out Connor. "Are you trying to alarm us?"

"I'm trying to pre-arm you," he shot back. "Like the captain, I appreciate how calm you're being, but let's not be foolhardy. Until I've firmly established what's happened on this yacht, it's important to take precautions. Please stay in your rooms and meet back here as a group at, say, eight in the morning."

"You do not mean the crew, surely?" called out Sergio. "We have to get breakfast ready."

"Forget about breakfast," Jackson said, making him scowl. "We can rustle something up together later. For now, the priority is everyone's safety. I don't want anyone up early, moving about the boat on their own. Except of course myself and the captain, who I believe will be on duty then?"

Liz nodded.

"It sounds like you're alleging one of us is a killer," said Boulder.

Again Jackson wanted to give him a shake. He could stick to his murder-suicide theory all he liked, but Jackson was no longer convinced Indya was the culprit.

"Please, Mr Boulder," Liz was saying now, flashing Jackson a frown. "No one's accusing anyone of anything, but he's quite right. We do have to play it safe. I'm sure this will all make sense when we get to land and get some autopsies done, but until then, please do as DI Jackson asks. Let's just keep our cool and keep our buddies close."

"Ooooh, it sounds like we're diving all over again," said Cindy, almost breezily.

"Let's hope it doesn't go the way of the first dive," Boulder mumbled below his breath.

~

"Did you really need to frighten them, Jackson?" Captain Flinders asked as they made their way back to the bridge deck.

"I'm trying to protect them," he said. "*And you*. You'll be alone in the bridge all night, and that worries me."

She blinked rapidly then. Reached a hand to her throat. "Oh God, I hadn't thought of that. I'll… I'll deadlock the bridge door from the inside. That should keep me safe."

"Good idea." He nodded. "That was kind of you to give Gary the night off."

Her hand dropped back to her side. "I'm not doing it for Gary. I'm doing it so we don't run into the reef. The guy's exhausted. Now if you'll excuse me…"

They had reached the control room, but Jackson held his ground. "Actually, I do have some more questions while I'm here."

She did not look surprised. "I thought I'd got off lightly. Okay, can you give me five? I'll take over from Gary and will be all yours after that."

He agreed and left her to it, then continued upwards to the now abandoned dining deck and that infamous jacuzzi. Glancing around, he could see it was exactly as they'd left it that morning, the tub cover off, but otherwise looking oddly tranquil. Like a woman had not been found dead there just twelve hours earlier. He felt a pang of sadness for Indya and a fresh stab of regret. Knew he hadn't kept her safe and feared it might not be over yet.

Turning, he dashed back down to the bridge deck and into the captain's office. He stared at the phone that still sat lifeless on the desk. Then, through the large window, he spotted Gary leaving the bridge next door, and he jumped up and called him in.

"Any idea how to get this phone working? It's been playing up."

Gary frowned. "Don't see why. The weather's been fine; there should be no interference. Is it even connected?" He grabbed it from the cradle and listened to the receiver, then began to play around with the digital controls. "It's switched off."

"What?"

"Via the settings," Gary added and began tapping away. He waited a few moments and then handed the phone across. "All good now."

Jackson frowned. "Why would it be switched off?"

"Don't get paranoid, mate. These phones are pretty sketchy and can switch themselves off, especially in storms. It's not a big deal. You just go into settings and switch it back on again. Did nobody explain that to you?"

No, he thought, *including you*. "But the weather's been fine."

He shrugged again. "It's not an exact science."

Then he left Jackson to his thoughts, which were, indeed, bordering on paranoid. He went to call DI Singh, then realised he'd better not keep the captain waiting, so he turned and made his way back to the bridge.

Liz was standing at the helm, staring as though mesmerised out at the moon-dappled ocean as the yacht ploughed southward. She looked peaceful, almost serene, and Jackson didn't have the heart to interrupt her moment of reprieve, but time was of the essence.

"Captain?" he said gently, and she swung around.

"Ah, come in, Jackson." She smiled and looked outwards again. "Sometimes you can forget all your woes when you're up here. Feels like it's just you and the sea. The best view in the house."

"You love your job, don't you?"

She nodded. A sad sigh. Then dropped into the command seat. "I have a hunch it's now ruined."

Jackson didn't have the heart to tell her her hunch was correct, judging by Simon's comments earlier. "Can I ask, did you switch the satellite phone off? The one in your office?"

She glanced up with a start. "God no, why would I do that? It's our lifeline out here."

"Who has access to that phone, apart from you and me?"

She shrugged. "All the crew. Everyone is given an access key to both the office and the bridge, just in case there's an emergency and they need to call for help. What's going on, Jackson? What are you saying?"

He shook his head. There was no time to explain. "You're not going to like the next question, but are you and Sergio in a relationship?"

That also caught her by surprise, then her expression relaxed and she said, "Ah, Lynette's gossiping out of school I see." Then, more crisply, "This is important I assume?"

"I'm verifying his alibi. Sergio was seen in the vicinity early this morning, claims he was on his way to see you."

"He's not lying." She swivelled on the chair. "But there's nothing sinister about it or salacious. I drop into the galley most mornings to grab some breaky on my way to the bridge, but I didn't today. I was stressed and I was distracted, so Serg brought some up to me. That's all it was. Well, that and a chance to whinge about you. He clocked you were a cop quite early, but I managed to assuage his fears." Her brow crinkled. "I'm happy to lie to Gary and Pasha, but I really don't enjoy lying to Serg. He's too much of a friend. But that's all he is."

Jackson nodded. "Good to know."

"Sergio's a good man, Jackson. He's the only one on this yacht who has my back. Gary and Pasha have been so unsupportive it's bordering on mutiny, and I will be demanding they're removed from their positions the minute this matter gets sorted."

She wouldn't get the chance, Jackson thought, but again he let it drop. "What about Freddy?"

"What about him?"

"Is he supportive?"

She shrugged. "He's new, not so important. In fact, Gary and Pasha have been bullying him, too, from what I can see."

"Where did he come from? Young Freddy?"

She shrugged again. "You'd have to ask Simon. His company takes care of hiring and firing. Look, I know Freddy's green. Got a lot to learn. But he'll get there if they give him a chance. As for Serg? He's been my shoulder to cry on, but that's all he is. And I can assure you, he had nothing to do with—"

She didn't get to finish that sentence because the satellite phone was now ringing.

"Excuse me," she said and picked it up. She listened for a moment, then held it out to Jackson. "It's for you. Says she's your partner in crime."

As Liz turned back to her monitors, Jackson leapt upon the phone and said, "Singho?"

"Who? No, no, this is Ronnie again."

He tried not to sound disappointed as he stepped away. "Hey Ronnie, what's new?"

"Well!" she began with a flourish. "Missy's been looking into the butler, Freddy, and started googling the name you gave us, and we've come up with something very interesting. You said his full name was Vilfredo, yes? Well we've found details of an 'Afraido' who may or may not be the same man."

"Okay, but I told you—"

"If you'll allow me to finish! Afraido has a blog and a steady stream of what they call followers, and while he dubs himself a photojournalist, he is, in fact, judging by the images all over the media, nothing more than a common paparazzi, and there are a few pictures that look like they might have been taken from a yacht. Some tarted-up popstar with dreadful blue hair. Missy seemed to know who it is. Anyhoo, what I find more interesting is that this Afraido character got into some trouble not so long ago, sneaking into a celebrity wedding and spilling it all over the web. Beat the gossip magazines to the punch and at least one of them had paid big bickies for the exclusive."

"Okay, that is interesting, I'll grant you that," said Jackson, and worrying considering Freddy's current position on this yacht. It was no doubt Freddy who alerted the public of Indya's death. "But I'm still not sure it's important, Ronnie, and if you'll let *me* finish, I'll explain why. I'm not sure about Indya, but Freddy is one of the few suspects who absolutely could not have killed Elsbeth Wynter. He was serving lunch the whole time. Sadly, Claire and Simon are his alibi."

"Oh, that is annoying," she replied. A heavy sigh. "We were both rather excited by that. The Wynters own gossip mags. We figured Elsbeth must have recognised him and threatened to out him and had to be murdered."

He smiled to himself, imagining the book club friends nursing cups of tea, theorising as the others had done just before sundowners. "Brilliant theory," he said, "but not possible, unless he was working with someone." And the way he was being bullied by the others suggested otherwise. "What about James Wynter?" he asked. "And Arne Boulder? Anything more on them?"

"James, no. Just lots more gossip about being such a mummy's boy," said Ronnie. "I spoke with a dear friend's granddaughter, whom he was courting for all of five minutes, and she shivers at the mere mention of Elsbeth. Said the only time James would be free of his mother was when she was six feet under, although I'm not sure she meant to be quite so insensitive.

"As for Boulder? Annoyingly, he isn't lying to you about Elsbeth's Will. He is executor, and according to my sources, he absolutely does *not* feature in it, at least not as a recipient. Every last dime goes straight to James, so

Boulder's motive just got shot to pieces."

"At least there's another name I can cross off the suspect list."

"Not so fast," said Ronnie. "You also mentioned he didn't dive, and I wonder where you got that idea from?"

Jackson blinked at the phone. "He told me that, I think. Or maybe Claire and Simon did. Any case I believe Boulder wasn't diving the day Elsbeth died."

He looked up and Liz was nodding, giving him the thumbs-up on that one.

"Don't be so sure about that," said Ronnie, sounding confident again. "According to my friend at his law firm, he's a terrific diver."

"Okay… so why would he lie about that?" Jackson stared at Liz now, and she was holding her palms out, questioning.

"Why indeed," said Ronnie. "I only found out as I was saying goodbye. My friend made a quip about how at least Boulder got a free dive out of the old biddy. When I enquired further, he said, 'Of course he dives! We went diving together in the Maldives pre-COVID.' He might look like a large, clumsy fellow but apparently, underwater, he's as swift as a sea lion."

CHAPTER 39
Butting Horns

The sea lion was currently having words with Simon and Claire, and they did not sound pretty.

"You had better prepare your company," he told Simon while sipping a fresh martini. "I do believe there will be some pretty hefty lawsuits at the end of this cruise."

Claire gasped and shot a look at her husband, but he seemed unfazed.

"And you will be leading the charge, I suppose?" said Simon.

Boulder chuckled. "I think you'll find Connor Dudley-Pine will take that honour. He's already had a word with me." Another casual sip. "This isn't personal, Simon, but he does have a point. This cruise hasn't been at all as advertised."

"Advertised?" said Claire.

"Yes, we were promised a relaxing cruise on the Great Barrier Reef."

"Ah, no you weren't," she replied. "You were promised a romantic honeymoon cruise of which you were not entitled. You're not even married, nor was Elsbeth."

"Either way," he continued, shooting Simon an almost convivial eye roll. "We were not expecting bloodshed; we had a right to expect safety and calm."

"Safety and calm?" shot back Claire. "After what you did!"

"*Claire*," cautioned Simon.

She shook her glossy black hair. "I'm sorry, Simon,

but it has to be said. Boulder brought a fake bride on board with the deliberate intent of disrupting a marriage. You wonder why there was bloodshed? You didn't just set a cat amongst the pigeons, as Dame Agatha would say, it was the emotional equivalent of screaming 'shark!' in the water and expecting 'safety and calm'!"

Boulder didn't look so amused now. "You're going to blame the victims for all of this?"

"I'm going to blame a mother who was allowed to overstep in the grossest possible way and her paid lackey who enabled it! And you honestly thought there would be no consequences? I believe you are at least partially responsible for what's happened on this yacht. If you hadn't accompanied Elsbeth on board, she would still be alive and so would Indya! Now if you'll excuse me"— a quick glance at her startled husband—"I'm going to find some more palatable company."

Then she stood up and stormed away.

Boulder was back to mottled red, looking flustered, and Simon blew some air from his lips. Then he smiled. Widely. Turns out, marrying Claire Hargreaves was the best investment he'd ever made.

~

"What was that about?" asked Alicia after she'd followed Claire out and found her in the restroom, leaning against the sink, breathing heavily.

"Sorry," she said. "I had to get out of there before I said something I'd really regret. I hate confrontation, you know that, Alicia, but the hide of that man! Who does he think he is?"

"He's a lawyer, Claire. He doesn't think. Not about other people's feelings."

Claire splashed some water on her face, took some deep calming breaths.

"Your hubby looked proud of you in there," added

Alicia, but it didn't make Claire smile as she'd hoped.

"All he cares about is this yacht," she said so quietly Alicia almost missed it.

"What? That's not true. He adores you." *Doesn't he?*

Claire reached for a hand towel and dabbed at her face. Then stopped and turned back to Alicia. "Do you think I rushed into it too fast? This marriage? Do you think…?"

The words fell away as her eyes filled with tears.

Alicia grabbed her hands and squeezed them. "I think you're still getting to know each other, and that's not such a bad thing. Jackson and I are still trying to work each other out too."

"Yes, but you're not married and changing your whole life for each other, are you?"

Alicia frowned. "What's really going on, Claire?"

Claire shook her off. Pulled a lipstick from a hidden pocket in her wide, tulle skirt. "So what do you think?" she said as she began to apply a thick layer. "About Boulder?"

Alicia frowned. "I think Simon should be worried. He's a lawyer, he's naturally litigious."

"No, I don't care about that, not really." Claire smacked her lips together. "I mean, is he bluffing? It could all just be a distraction from the fact Boulder's the culprit."

Alicia thought about that as Claire returned the lipstick to her pocket. "I'm not sure the timing works though, does it?" Alicia told her. "At least not for Elsbeth's murder. Haven't we narrowed that down to around twelve thirty, which is when Indya returned to the yacht? He was at lunch by then, wasn't he?"

She frowned. "Yes, annoyingly. I would've loved to plant it at his fat, ugly feet." She blinked at her reflection. "I'm turning nasty, aren't I?"

Alicia put an arm around her shoulders. "No, Claire. Compared to Boulder, you're just a sweet little pebble."

~

Back in the bridge, Jackson mulled over Ronnie's words as Freddy appeared with two trays, both containing dinner plates covered with a silver cloche, both smelling delicious.

Jackson took his tray and turned to Liz. "I'm going to leave you to it and get back to the office."

"Rightio," she said, then raised an eyebrow at Freddy. "I'm not sure why you're up here, feeding us first. The passengers are the priority. You know that."

"But Sergio said—"

"Just head back to the lounge please. And thank you."

He nodded, looking grumpy, and Jackson followed him out.

Back in the office, Jackson took a moment to enjoy the meal, marvelling yet again at Sergio's culinary prowess. Then he pushed the plate aside, picked up the phone, and finally put in a call to his partner back in Sydney.

"Well, hello, stranger!" said DI Indira Singh, her voice just slightly scratchy. "Where the hell have you been?"

"Phone's been on the blink," he said, not wanting to elaborate.

"No, it hasn't," she shot back. "I left a message earlier with some fellow."

Jackson nearly fell off his chair. "What fellow? Wasn't Gary, was it?"

"Not sure…" There was a scrambling sound. "His name's here somewhere…" More scrambling as Jackson smiled. He was just relieved to hear her voice.

"Forget about him for now, Singho," he said, "and tell me you have something for me. Tell me there's someone on this yacht with a criminal record I can plant this all on."

"*Someone?*" She scoffed. "Jacko, I don't know what kind of company your friends are keeping, but there are *three* people on that yacht who've had warrants out against them. One for illegal trespass, one for assault and one for break and enter."

Then she laughed at his gobsmacked silence and said, "So which one do you want to hear about first?"

CHAPTER 40
Hero or Villain?

"You have got to be kidding me," said Gary when he opened the door to Jackson ten minutes later. "I need sleep, okay? I've been up for three days straight."

"You can get your beauty sleep later," said Jackson, pushing past him and into his cabin.

The room was dramatically smaller than the guests', a lot less plush, and looked like a bomb had hit it, revealing at least a secret or two amongst the debris. Jackson used a stray coat hanger to pick up a lacy white bra and said, "Pasha Patel's, I presume?"

Gary smirked as he made his way back to the rumpled bed. "So what? We're both adults. It's not illegal."

"That is true, but it is illegal to assault someone."

That got the man's attention. He swung around. "What are you talking about?"

"I'm talking about the assault you were charged with on a commercial cruise to Fiji three years ago. It's the reason you left your post so quickly and took a demotion with this job."

"So she told you, did she? Traitor."

"Who?"

"The captain of course."

"No, Gary. I did my job, like you told me to do, found out all by my lonesome. So you put a passenger into a coma?"

He snorted.

"You cops are all the same. I stopped a drunken

passenger from attacking a vulnerable young woman, that's all I was doing."

"Really? Because that's not what the 'drunken passenger' said when he finally came out of the coma. Or the vulnerable woman for that matter."

Gary eye-rolled him now. "She was also drunk, that's why she was vulnerable. That's why she didn't remember it clearly. But I was there and I was sober. The dirtbag grabbed her after she got out of the lift, and I went to her defence. The CCTV proved it. That's why the charges were dropped. And that's the truth."

Jackson nodded. "The truth, hey?"

Why did that feel like such an elusive thing on this yacht? And what a pity the *Living Large* didn't have closed circuit television too.

"You see, I've been thinking Indya was killed because somebody wanted money or because she witnessed something," said Jackson, "but maybe it was more impulsive than that. More lecherous. Maybe she was attacked purely because she was young and vulnerable. Maybe you saw a pretty young thing strolling past in tight gym gear and you took advantage."

Jackson steeled himself, expecting Gary to explode, but he seemed oddly amused suddenly.

"That's what you're going with now? Seriously? Once again, mate, you've got your wires crossed. Oh, there were advantages taken of pretty young things on this boat, but it wasn't by me, I can assure you of that."

"What does that even mean?" Jackson demanded.

"It means you are so far off the mark you can't see the wood for the trees. You think my history with cruising is dodgy? Well, at least I have a history."

"You're talking in riddles again, Gary."

"Then riddle me this: Who else on this yacht is hiding their relationship? Who else has worked Pacific Island cruises? And who has always had a thing for the pretty young crew?"

~

Perry sat in Nemo's Lounge and watched as Connor helped himself to the buffet dinner that had now been presented, then tried not to smile as he saw the man drop his plate beside his wife and excuse himself before striding up the stairs and out.

Waiting a beat, Perry pushed his own plate aside, gave Alicia a quick wink, then followed.

For a brief moment though, he lost him. He was just about to check the men's toilets when he spotted a muscular figure through the service door, leaning on the railing.

Perry smiled again as he stepped outside to join him.

"Busted," said Connor, holding up a packet of cigarettes. "Don't tell Cindy. She'll have a coronary. I promised I'd give it up for the marriage."

"Is that all you're giving up?" asked Perry, his eyebrows high.

Connor's eyes narrowed. Then narrowed again. He offered the packet to Perry, who refused, then pulled one out and lit up—no mean feat considering the howling wind.

Eventually he got it going, then inhaled deeply before releasing a long plume of smoke.

"I wondered when we were going to come clean," Connor said, offering Perry a wink. "I picked you from the start."

"You recognised me from the media?" Perry asked, and Connor looked confused.

"What? Oh no, it was that woeful kiss you planted on your poor 'wife'." He made the quote marks with his fingers, then dragged on the cigarette again. "That was the first giveaway you were gay. That and your rather funky citrus jacket. And don't get me started on that goatee. And you?"

"I'm a member of your gym."

"Of course you are." He smiled. "Busted again."

"So you married Cindy to help her business along?"

Connor snorted. "It's not the olden days, Bob! No, no, we're not really married, just very old friends." He leaned in. "I'm as bad as Boulder. I provided her 'plus one' so she could get on this honeymoon cruise. You?"

Perry blinked, then fabricated an excuse. "Oh, Marie wants children. Her folks are very conservative."

"Really?" Connor looked amused.

"So why did Cindy need to come on this cruise so badly?" Perry prodded.

Connor released more smoke. "To meet James Wynter of course. I'd heard through the grapevine that he was honeymooning on this yacht. Well, through the *gayvine* really. My hairdresser happens to know his hairdresser... the usual story. It was all very last minute, and we were stunned when we managed to secure a cabin too. Cindy has grand plans of signing him up but... well..." He sighed at his cigarette. "That's now gone up in smoke."

Then his smile turned lascivious, and he nudged his eyebrows up and down.

Perry chuckled. "Not going to happen."

"Oh well, a man can try. I thought I might have had a chance with Freddy. A very pretty young lad if ever there was one. But I already busted him cuddling up the back of the boat. Sadly, our butler is well and truly taken."

"Really?"

Connor chuckled now. "I know! Turns out I'm not the only one with a penchant for pretty young things."

Then he sighed wistfully again as he stubbed out his cigarette.

~

Jackson glanced around Nemo's Lounge, looking for Simon. Found him perched at the bar with Claire and her book club friends, feasting on a meal that was identical to the one he'd just consumed. He strode across and tapped him on the shoulder. "Got a minute?"

Simon looked around and frowned, then apologised to the others who were staring at Jackson wide-eyed. He gave a very subtle shake of his head.

Yes, he'd love to fill them in, but no, there simply wasn't time.

Out in the corridor, Simon said, "Okay, what is it now?" Like he had better things to do.

Jackson swung around. "I'm trying to solve two murders, mate, and prevent a third one. You want to help me or not?"

"Of course. I'm sorry. I was just trying to make up some precious time with Claire... How can I help?"

Jackson's anger dissolved. "I'm glad you're finally getting your priorities straight, but this is important. I need some proper background on the crew."

"Didn't Liz give you the staff files?"

"They tell me nothing. I want to see the full employment records, the résumés, references, the lot. I know it's late, but I also know you have Queenie on speed dial and she can access your HR department. I need you to get her on the phone now. Because I think at least one crew member has lied on their résumé and that's not all they're lying about. Someone on this yacht is here under false pretences, and it might explain everything that's happened since."

~

It was now nine p.m. The meals had all been despatched, and the cooks were enjoying a moment of reprieve before the dishes boomeranged back. Sergio was lighting his cigarette at the entrance to the galley, like the rules had been thrown overboard.

And who could blame him? Lynette thought, munching on some leftover salad as she watched him, her head to one side. "You haven't told anyone," she said eventually, "about me."

About her ruse.

Lynette had searched for signs in both Pasha and Freddy, but they acted normally as they took the platters out—Freddy still flirting hard with his big brown eyes, Pasha staring straight through her like she was utterly irrelevant.

Sergio lifted a shoulder as he released a quick puff of smoke. "Who would I tell? I don't trust anyone on this boat anymore."

"Not even the captain?" She raised her eyebrows mischievously.

"Get your mind out of the gutter, girl. I told you before, she is a friend, that is all."

Lynette wondered whether to buy it. Dropped her eyebrows. "Who do you think's behind all this?"

"You mean who is the killer? You want me to do that job for you?"

"If it gets us off this yacht alive, sure."

He dragged on his cigarette for a bit as she continued eating.

"How do you know it is not me?" he said eventually. "Why are you not scared, little girl, in here all alone with me? I could just hit you over the head, tip you over the side... no one would hear you scream."

Lynette skewered a tomato and shrugged. "If you're trying to scare me, Chef, it's not working."

He stared at her for a moment, then chuckled. "You have balls, you know."

"And you're not as tough as you make out. Now come on, who would you put money on if you had to pick the killer?"

He offered a shoulder shrug and dragged some more on his cigarette. "I have no idea. But it is not me, because I know you thought that I did it. It's the reason you are here."

"Oh, only for a few minutes. Stop taking it personally. Everyone's been a suspect at some stage. You were a pretty good one for five seconds there, Serg. I mean, you were very angry with Wynter magazines."

"Wynter magazines?" he scoffed. "I do not care about the magazines. It was Elsbeth Wynter I did not like. She is the one who fired me. But I am not so pathetic that I must kill her for it."

"Fair enough," said Lynette, now popping some arugula into her mouth.

They continued in silence for a while, Lynette chewing, Sergio dragging on his smoke.

Then he said, quite casually, "You know, if you think it's the magazines that caused all this mayhem and murder, then there is someone else you should be nagging. Somebody who also likes salad and goes on and on about the Wynter family magazines and the danger they are doing to all of this."

Lynette looked up, eyes wide. "To all of what?"

He waved his cigarette outward, through the porthole to the pitch-black sea beyond, and said, "The ocean. The reef. The planet, of course."

~

Jackson had only recently hung up from Simon's PA, Queenie, his worst fears confirmed, when he heard a knock on the door and opened it to find Dr Roland Brown standing there, a sheepish look on his sunburned face. It was proving a familiar expression.

"Don't tell me," said Jackson, waving him in. "You have a confession to make? You're the one who wrote that note to Indya Wynter."

The dive instructor looked surprised then ashamed and said, "Yep, that was me, but it's not why I'm here. It's time to come clean about Elsbeth Wynter and what really happened out there on the water."

Jackson nodded knowingly as he closed the door behind him.

CHAPTER 41
The Grand Reveal

As the sun poked out from behind the horizon, struggling to get ahead of the clouds, Jackson watched it from the door of his cabin, then glanced down to the body in the sheets.

Alicia was still fast asleep. He wasn't sure how she'd managed it. Knew what a nightmare her imagination could be. Suspected it was because she'd snuck in again last night, as planned, and held on to him like a flotation device until she'd drifted off. But not before adding one final piece of evidence to the messy montage this case had created, telling him what Perry had learned from Connor, about Freddy and his so-called lover.

But Jackson already knew about that, and it wasn't what they all thought. Hell, nothing and no one was what they expected on this yacht. It's the reason he'd left Alicia sleeping soundly and patrolled the boat all night. He was keeping an eye on the most dangerous fraud of all.

But enough was enough. It was now time to rip off the masks and reveal some home truths. So he closed the door behind him and gently woke Alicia.

Opening her eyes, she could see that he had solved the case and she couldn't help smiling. "Don't tell me, the bumbling detective outwits the amateur sleuths this time?" Then her smile plateaued. "Time for the grand denouement?"

"It's long overdue," he replied. "But first I need your book club."

Sometime later, Jackson was squinting hard against the morning sun that now flooded the top deck, the clouds long gone. The temperature was still mild, the breeze gentle, an ideal morning to enjoy a romantic breakfast outdoors, and yet the "honeymooners" were gathering as a group inside again, down in Nemo's Lounge, along with all the crew.

At least he hoped they were. Would have to hand in his badge if he lost another one.

Spotting the jacuzzi from the corner of his eye, he strode across and looked down. He'd already checked it this morning but still felt a foolish rush of relief when he saw it was empty.

"All clear?" came a voice behind him, and he swung around to see the captain.

"I've just stalled the engines," she told him, "so we can gather as you requested."

He nodded. "You sailed all night. You must be exhausted."

"Relieved actually." She glanced towards the horizon. "Cairns is not far off."

"Then let's get down there and get this out of the way."

She smiled warmly, but there was a touch of anxiety in her eyes and a smidge of sadness too.

Down in Nemo's Lounge, looking out at the group now, those were the dominant emotions Jackson could see—anxiety, sadness and warmth. The latter was radiating from the book club members who had met with him and Simon earlier and knew exactly what was coming. They were seated together at one table, all except Lynette, who was standing at the back next to Sergio, still in her chef uniform.

Despite Jackson's strict instructions, the chefs had defied him and met early to prepare a quick breakfast of fresh fruit and pastries, yogurts and cereals, and jugs of coffee, tea and juice. And the guests looked relieved to see it all, filling plates like their hunger was finally back, or perhaps they were refuelling for what they, too, suspected was on the horizon.

Jackson waited until things had settled, then he gave Captain Flinders the nod.

She removed her cap, placing it gently on the bar top, smoothed down her sleek chignon, then stepped to the centre of the room again and called them all to attention.

"It is such a relief to see you all here this morning," she said, and there was a nervous murmur through the group. "It has been a very, very distressing few days, but it's nearly over folks and, yet again, I thank you for your strength and resilience. I'm now going to hand over to Detective Inspector Jackson, who has asked to speak with you."

"This better not be more of your ugly questions," rumbled Boulder, seated beside James.

The latter looked like he'd been through the ringer, no longer the cocky newlywed who'd stepped from a gleaming helicopter.

Jackson turned his gaze to Boulder. "Oh no, I have answers now, and I'm sorry to say, none of them are pretty."

"You know what happened to the two women?" gasped Pasha. She was seated at a back table beside Gary, Freddy and Roland at another, the latter nervously tapping his leg. "Was it an accident? Drowning?"

Still donning her mask, Jackson thought. "I'm afraid not, Pasha. There is a murderer on this boat, and they have been on this boat from the beginning."

And with those words, the group finally looked genuinely scared, staring at each other suspiciously and shifting closer to their companions.

He held out a hand. "Before I go into details, I'd like to make a comment. Something that needs to be said." Jackson pulled his shoulders back and cleared his throat.

"From the moment I set foot on this yacht, there have been multiple attempts to pervert the course of justice, and it is verging on criminal. This entire ordeal could have been brought to a close a lot earlier if it had not been for a constant flow of lies and misinformation from almost everybody in this room."

In fact, he thought quietly, as his eyes darted from couple to couple and crew member to crew member, the lying started long before Jackson got on this ship. Before any of them did.

It started when a young man promised to love and cherish his wife above all others, then continued to put his mother first. And when that mother lied to wangle her way onto a honeymoon cruise, and her lawyer lied to enable it. There were lies about who was diving and when, even who could dive—he slapped Boulder with a frown then. There were lies about relationships, loyalties, the satellite phone, even the state of the engine. But he said none of that now because the truth was, Jackson was also guilty, and he could hear Boulder mumbling something to that effect from his table.

The detective held both hands up now. "Yep, I've done my share of lying too, it has to be said. But no more. The lying stops now. And the truth starts by introducing my team."

"Team?" said Connor, who'd also been grumbling.

"That one!" yelled out Pasha, a finger pointing firmly at Lynette. "She's not a cook, she's a police officer. I can tell."

"Hey, I *am* a cook," said Lynette. "And I'm certainly not a copper. But it's true. I am part of Jackson's team."

"So am I," said Alicia, waving a hand.

"And me!" called out Perry, offering Connor an apologetic shrug.

There were gasps of surprise all around, then Cindy said, "If you're not cops, then who are you people?"

"They're my people," said Claire loudly, proudly.

"They're the Murder Mystery Book Club."

There was a moment of silence as everyone caught up, then Connor turned his eyes to the captain. "Did you seriously bring a bunch of book nerds on this yacht to try to solve a murder?"

"They're not nerds," said Simon, springing to their defence. "And they didn't just try, Connor. Thanks to their diligence and hard work, not to mention courage in the face of danger, they have succeeded." He gave his wife a loving look before glaring back at Connor. "So I suggest you shut up, sit back and for once in your life just listen."

Connor smudged his lips together and slunk back behind Cindy while Claire offered Simon a grateful smile.

Jackson stepped forward again. "While we're on the subject of lies, let's start with you Mr and Mrs Dudley-Pine."

Now Cindy was sliding back into her seat.

Jackson originally suspected Cindy because she had lied to him from the start, and he told her that now. "You should have done as your fake husband did and made no comment, because your lies only left you looking guilty."

Connor slapped Cindy with a smarmy look as Jackson continued: "First you lied about seeing Indya swim back to the yacht with you after that first dive. Then you lied about why you lied. You didn't do it to help out a 'fellow sister', you did it to help yourself to the Wynter fortune, or at least you hoped some of it would rain down on you after providing Indya with an alibi. But she didn't want your alibi, did she, Cindy? She just wanted the truth to come out, and so, soon after receiving that threatening note, she came to me to confess but not before you'd accosted her in the women's toilets and tried to extort money from her."

"I never! I didn't!" said Cindy, eyes on James and Boulder. "I told you, I had nothing to do with that note."

"That is true," said Jackson. "About the only true thing you've said all trip. You threatened Indya, but you didn't do it on paper. You're smarter than that. That foolish honour goes to Dr Roland Brown."

She blinked, her eyes searching the room for the divemaster who was hiding behind a coffee mug, looking contrite. Across from him James was twitching.

"*You* wrote that note?" he said, and Roland paled considerably. "You threatened my wife?"

"No! I mean, I wrote the note, but it wasn't a threat, it wasn't like that." He cleared his throat nervously. "I was just asking Indya for her help, that's all. Look, I knew she hadn't come back from the dive at midday with the rest of you. I could see her scuba gear was missing. But I never thought she had anything to do with Mrs Wynter's drowning, honest! And even if she did, well, I just thought, good riddance, you know?"

There were gasps of outrage around the room, and James was staring at Roland like he was trying to interpret exactly what he'd said.

Roland held his own palms out defensively. "I'm sorry," he said quickly, "that came out wrong. What I'm trying to say is the planet is a better place for it, that's all. It's just... well, your mother's magazines have smothered climate debate for decades, James. Worse that that..." He looked at Jackson now. "You talk about lies? Wynter publishing is as bad as Murdoch, pedalling the fossil fuel industry's misinformation all so they can sell magazines and keep enjoying their luxury reef holidays. All at the expense of our grandchildren's future!"

"Oh, here he goes," said Boulder, eyes rolling dramatically. "I knew you were one of those green Nazis. Do you also throw eggs at famous paintings and disrupt the traffic all for some stupid idea that the world is warming? Hmm?"

"It *is* warming, you ignoramus," Roland spat back, "but no, I never disrupt anyone. Well, apart from that fracking operation in Northern NSW, but I was there on the invitation of the landholder, and I shouldn't have got done for illegal trespass. All I'm trying to do is educate."

"And you're doing a splendid job," said Pasha, as though trying to keep the peace. "You've made me reconsider the sunscreen we use on this yacht, the plastics…"

"Oh, for Pete's sake!" said James. "What has any of that got to do with my wife?"

"That's what I'm trying to tell you," Roland responded. "I was simply asking for her support. I spoke to Indya after dinner. I told her I'd covered for her that day on the water and asked if she'd repay the favour and be an advocate for climate action. We need young people to get on board, young people with real clout. Influencers. But I never killed her."

"That is true," said Jackson. "The note was a dead end, a waste of precious time." A quick frown at Roland then, but it was himself he was angry with because he had not got around to interviewing Roland properly earlier. "We'll get back to Roland in a minute. For now, while we have your attention, let's focus on you, Mr Wynter."

Now all eyes were shifting to James, but he did not shrink under their scrutiny. "I had nothing to do with any of this."

There was a loud snort from another table, and he saw Alicia shaking her head, so too Claire and Perry.

"What?" he demanded.

"I'm sorry too, James," said Alicia. "I know you've been through the wringer, but I don't think that's a fair statement. What Claire said to Boulder last night is quite correct. By telling your mother about the honeymoon cruise, by allowing her to stay on board and interfere in your life, you inadvertently caused her death."

"That's an outrageous slur!" he yelled, jumping to his feet.

"I did use the word *inadvertent*," she said calmly,

"because we agree. You were guilty of plenty of things, including being dangerously careless with your wife's feelings. You brought the two women together to test Indya out, like she was a two-bit candidate on Love Island, and she failed you. But we don't believe you played a part in either murder."

"So James *didn't* do it?" said Connor, trying to keep up.

"Of course I didn't do it," James said, glowering at him, then back at Jackson. "So what is all this? Are you suggesting that because I brought the women together, it forced Indy's hand? That's why she killed Mother and then herself?"

Now Jackson tried not to snort. "No, James, that's not what we're suggesting at all, although I know you and Boulder wanted me to think that. Talk about pedalling agendas. I did start to wonder if you were trying to divert suspicion from yourselves, but now I think it's even sadder. Alicia's right. You're just a lousy husband, James. You had no faith in your wife. Indya was an innocent player in all this, and yet she was condemned, not just by herself but by the man who should have been her greatest supporter. Your wife didn't kill anyone, including herself in that jacuzzi. Somebody else did that, and while it might not have been you, James, you played your part."

"Leave the lad alone," croaked Boulder, reaching out to pat James's back.

The younger man had returned to his seat, speechless, not even attempting to defend himself, let alone his wife.

But Boulder could try. "Poor Jimmy has suffered enough. And who can blame him for thinking it was Indya, hmm? Let's face it, we all did. She was the last person to return from the dive."

"Yes, let's focus on that dive for a moment," said Jackson. "Would you like to explain why you lied about your diving experience?" He turned his eyes to the group. "Turns out Mr Boulder is an excellent diver."

"*You can dive?*" said Roland.

"Of course I can dive!" Boulder shot back. "But if I'd said that, I'd never have got away from Ellie." An apologetic glance at James now. "I loved your mother dearly, you know that, boy. But even I deserved some time out."

James didn't appear to be listening now, but Cindy was sitting forward, eyes narrowed.

"So how do we know you didn't sneak into the water that day and kill Mrs Wynter?"

"Because I loved her, I told you. And because I didn't have the gear anyway."

"You could have pinched one of our sets when we returned," she persisted. "Mine had a bit of air left in it, I noticed that. You could have swum over there while we were dressing for lunch."

"Do the timing, you silly woman!" Boulder rumbled. "Sure, I can dive, but I'm not Aquaman. I couldn't have pulled it off even if I wanted to. Besides, why would I want to hurt my dear friend?"

"To protect your dear friend's son?" suggested Connor now, warming to how this denouement worked. "You clearly love him, too. Perhaps you knew Elsbeth would never leave him be, so you did it to save him. So 'Jimmy' could finally be free."

Boulder snorted at that. "Free? Look at the man! He's a mess!"

As they all stared worriedly at James, his hair tufted messily, his eyes red and dazed, Boulder's own eyes turned to the captain, who was now leaning against the bar, watching the proceedings with a look of utter dismay, like she simply couldn't work out how and when it had all gone so terribly off course.

"Are you going to just stand there, Captain," Boulder bellowed again, "and allow this two-bit detective to insult us all like this?"

She crossed her arms. "I'm sorry, Mr Boulder. But it's not up to me. I have no authority here."

"That'd be right," came a mutter from the back, and Jackson locked eyes with Gary, who was the only one in the bar looking both smug and delighted. He met Jackson's gaze. "I'm just saying—"

"Don't bother." Jackson cut him off. "You've said nothing of any substance from the start. Like the others, you spoke in riddles and released information as you saw fit. You have played a game and a very dangerous one. If you had spoken up earlier, been candid with me, Indya might still be alive. You're as culpable as James and Boulder, and I'm not just referring to your assault charges."

"What assault charges?" demanded Boulder. "Why am I only learning about this now?"

"You can catch up on that later," said Jackson. "That's not what's worrying me now. What I want to know is, why you faked the engine failure yesterday, Gary."

There was a momentary silence, and then the captain was gasping. "The engine wasn't faulty?" Liz said. "You lied to me about that?"

"Oh, because you've been the poster girl for honesty," the first officer replied. "Besides, if you were half the captain you think you are, you would have been able to work it out for yourself."

"I trusted you!"

"But I don't trust *you*! None of us do!" A nod towards Pasha, who was staring idly up at the ceiling, trying hard not to look complicit. "I did it to buy the dumb detective more time. Jackson should be thanking me."

"Oh, you did this for *me*?" Jackson faked a chuckle. "Really, Gary? Or did you do it to make your captain look even worse than she already did?"

The other man shrugged. "If there's a fringe benefit, who am I to complain?"

"So why switch off the Wi-Fi phone?" Jackson asked now. "Why not pass on the message from my partner?"

"Huh?" said Gary. "I told you, that office phone is

temperamental. It switches itself off."

"And, er..." This was Simon, hand in the air. "I might have forgotten to pass that message on, Jackson. I'm so sorry. I... I was preoccupied... you know, with LLE."

"Oh, for heaven's sake," said Jackson as Cindy now raised a hand.

"I'm sorry, but I am very confused. If Gary didn't do it, who did? Who's left?"

Her eyes danced around the group and landed first on Freddy, then on Sergio.

The chef puffed his chest out. "I've already told this lot, I might not have liked Elsbeth Wynter, but I did not kill anybody."

"And I could not have done it," said Freddy, also looking a little too smug considering the tension. "I was working at lunch, yes?"

"That is true," said Jackson. "But it doesn't mean it wasn't done *for* you."

"Wha'?" Freddy's smirk dissolved. He looked muddled for a moment, then his eyes darted across the room to the one person Jackson knew he would look to. The one person Jackson should have looked to from the very beginning.

"You killed the two women, didn't you, Captain Flinders?" the detective said. "Of everyone on this yacht, it turns out you are the biggest liar of us all."

CHAPTER 42
The Grand Reveal Gets Real

Liz Flinders had been largely quiet throughout the proceedings. Mostly hanging back, feigning bemusement. That was often a clue that someone was guilty, but it wasn't evidence, and Jackson knew he had to tread carefully. He couldn't be sure Indya's waterproof camera had vision of the captain in the water that day, so he needed her confession.

He waited a few moments while the group digested what he had said, most staring incredulously towards Liz. Including young Freddy, who was now on his feet.

"That is bullshit," he said. Then, less certainly, "Right, Cap'n?"

Liz rolled her eyes. "Of course, Freddy. It's utterly absurd. Now sit down and stop being dramatic. He's just going through the suspects like it's some corny detective novel. And now it's my turn."

Pushing herself up from the bar, Liz straightened down her jacket, then idly glanced around the group. "Unlike the rest of you, I had absolutely no reason to hurt anybody. No motive whatsoever. And that's not even the silliest part of all this." Her eyes were on Jackson again. "Half my crew might have no faith in me, but I wouldn't be so stupid. I'd hardly kill a woman and then knowingly invite the police on to investigate would I? Let alone his silly little book club friends."

That seemed to appease Freddy, who dropped back to his chair, but Simon had his hand up again.

"Ah, well, here's the problem with that argument, Liz," he said, glancing at Jackson, who gave him the nod. "You didn't invite the detective and the book club on board. I did."

She blinked back at him, blankly, so he continued:

"Jackson reminded me last night that you didn't enlist anyone's help. In fact, you did everything you could to stop them. If I hadn't been your boss, and if I hadn't already met some very capable sleuths, you probably would have succeeded, but you couldn't refuse my request, could you? You also knew that the more you protested, the more suspicious you looked, so you had to go along with it in the end. But you didn't foresee how capable the detective would be, especially when aided by my wife's *silly little book club friends.*"

"That's not true," Liz said. "I protested because I honestly thought it was a simple drowning."

"Rubbish," he fired back. "You just wanted *me* to think that. You wanted to report it as an accidental drowning. In fact, you did at first. You never meant for it to go this far. When you asked Roland to inspect Elsbeth's equipment, you told him to get back to you and only you. You did not expect him to return so quickly and mention the air valve in front of me. But it didn't really matter because you thought Roland would say the equipment was fine, that the air was still on and Elsbeth must have had an unexplained medical episode. But he didn't say that, did he? He said the opposite. He said it was *turned off*, and that meant only one thing—foul play."

"No... no," Liz spluttered, her composure cracking away. "I... I had no idea what Roland would say. He was the one in charge of the equipment. Not me."

"Ah yes, but you're the one who tampered with it."

There was another moment of shocked silence as everyone in the room tried to make sense of this fresh piece of news, some of them failing.

"I'm confused," said Connor.

"I think he's saying the captain turned Elsbeth's air off," Cindy whispered across to him.

"No!" said Liz. "That's not true. I didn't."

"But it is true," said Roland now, his voice heavy. "I'm sorry, Liz, but you and I both know the real story."

The divemaster then turned to the group to explain. "After I found Elsbeth lifeless in the water, after I somehow dragged her onto the dinghy, I checked her air and that's when I noticed the valve was turned off. And it shouldn't have been. There's no way she could have turned it off herself. I didn't think any more of it; didn't have time. I just zoomed back to the yacht where Liz was waiting for me. Together we commenced CPR, then Gary appeared and took over from Liz, but it was hopeless."

A long exhalation, a sympathetic glance at James. "I was no fan of your mother, but I did try to save her, really I did."

James just closed his eyes and dropped his head.

"Later," said Roland, "after we'd met with Mr Boulder in the captain's office, Liz asked me to check the equipment, and that's when I noticed that Elsbeth's air valve had been turned back on even though I hadn't done that. It should still have been in the Off position; it was very odd."

"No, you must have got that wrong," said Liz.

He smiled sadly at her. "You were so surprised when I came back and said the valve was off, weren't you? Like you didn't believe me. You kept asking me if I was sure, really sure, and I thought you were just trying to throw me a lifeline, trying to save my career. Now I realise it's because you had *turned that valve back on yourself.* While we were distracted doing CPR, you fiddled with it. Not to make me look innocent but to get yourself and your yacht off the hook. You didn't want there to be a suspicious death. You didn't want the truth to come out, but I couldn't lie, Liz. I had to tell the truth no matter the consequences to me. I had to confess that when I found

Elsbeth's body out there on the water, her air had been deliberately turned off."

Liz had her arms folded across her torso, was shaking her head. "That had nothing to do with me. Gary was hovering over the body too. He could have tampered with it, anyone could have in the chaos."

"Ah yes, but Gary's hair was dry, Liz, and yours was not." She flung a hand to her glossy bun as he said, "It's something I'd completely forgotten in that chaos, but when we started CPR, your cap fell off, Liz, and I noticed your hair was wet—"

"No, no, not wet!" Liz retorted, pointing at her head now. "I always slick it back. Everybody knows that. It's just argan oil."

"No, Liz, it was *dripping* wet. Dripping onto Elsbeth's face. You pushed it back up. You didn't think anyone had noticed, and I didn't think any more of it. I was too stressed trying to bring Mrs Wynter back. But then I 'fessed up to Jackson last night, and we went through it all again in minute detail. That's when I remembered your wet hair and how adamant you'd been that the valve was on. That's when I realised it had to be you. Only you."

"But... but hang on," said James, rousing again. "Why would she turn the valve *on* if she wanted my mother dead? I don't understand any of this!"

"She was covering her tracks," said Jackson after giving Roland an appreciative nod. "I never could verify your alibi, Liz, because you were alone in the bridge the whole time. Gary was sleeping off his night shift, and the crew and guests were busy with lunch. That's when you must have spotted your opportunity. After all, as you told me, the bridge has the best view in the house—180-degree view out across the water."

He shook his head at her, took a breath, then elaborated: "That first day of diving, you watched as first Claire and Simon, then the others all made their way back to the yacht for lunch. All except Elsbeth, who was swimming away, towards the second pontoon. Alone. That's when you decided to do it. There wasn't a moment to lose. You must have quickly changed into your dive gear and dashed down the staff ladder and into the water. Roland's confirmed you're a competent diver and you have your own equipment, which is stored on that side of the boat. It would not have been hard to slip into the water while everyone was at lunch. Except not everyone was at lunch, were they? You hadn't stopped long enough to see that Indya had turned back, back to follow Elsbeth."

Liz was shaking her head through all this, hands at her mouth, glaring towards Jackson.

He said, "It must have been a big shock to learn, later, that Indya had also been out at that second pontoon. There might very well be a witness. Worse, a witness who had a camera with her and took lots of photos. Might very well have taken some under the water and inadvertently captured you in the background of a shot, swimming towards Elsbeth with one thing on your mind and one thing only—murder."

"But... but *why*?" demanded James, his voice a heady mix of anger, curiosity, despair. "Why would you do such a thing to my mother? What did she ever do to you?"

Liz was now stroking her epaulet, staring up at the ceiling, refusing to speak, so Jackson spoke for her.

"It's not what your mother did to Liz," said Jackson. "It's what your mother was going to do to Freddy. Because you're a mother too, aren't you, Liz? You're a mother just as devoted as Elsbeth, except even more dangerously so."

This was yet another surprise, and the group waited for her to refute it, but again she refused to meet their eyes, and then, finally, her gaze slid down and across to the "pretty young lad" sitting beside Roland, watching proceedings with a mixture of horror and surprise in his big brown eyes.

CHAPTER 43
Mother Bears

Connor was gaping. So, too, Gary.

"Hang on a minute," the first officer spluttered. "Freddy's your *son*?"

Now Liz was smirking. "You're not as smart as you think you are, Gary."

"But… but we saw him sneak into your cabin," said Pasha, gaping so much she was practically drooling. "We thought he was your lover. You *know* that's what we thought, Liz. You never even *denied* it."

"That's because it's none of your damn business," she replied coolly.

"Is that so?" said Jackson now. "Or is it because you were hiding Freddy's real identity, masking the fact that your son is almost as nefarious as you?"

"No!" Liz roared suddenly, making several of them jump. She took a gasping breath. Then another. "My son is a good boy. He didn't do anything."

"He's nothing more than a paparazzi who preys on the rich and famous to make a living. Or at least he used to," said Jackson. "Until he went too far and got arrested after breaking into a celebrity wedding and posting the pictures on YouTube, using the pseudonym *Afraido*."

"*You're* Afraido?" said James to Freddy. "The lowlife who's been stalking half my friends?"

Freddy gave a small wave like it was something to be proud of, but his mother did not look happy.

"That's all in the past, I can assure you," she said.

"Freddy has turned his life around. That's why he changed his name. That's why he's on this yacht, starting afresh. Leaving his past behind."

"Except he didn't leave it behind, did he?" said Jackson, eyes on Sergio, who just looked deeply disappointed in the captain.

"*You* knew about Liz and Freddy?" said Pasha, eyes on Sergio too.

"I knew they were close, but that is all," Sergio replied calmly as he turned to the captain. "Oh Liz, why didn't you tell me he was your boy?"

She shrank back then, showing the first glimmer of shame.

"Why didn't you listen when I told you Freddy was trouble—"

"He's not trouble," she squeaked back. "He's my baby."

"I've heard enough of this!" roared Boulder, making them all jump. "I don't care who's related to whom on this yacht! I want to know what the hell it's got to do with the deaths of Elsbeth and Indya!"

"It has everything to do with their deaths," said Jackson. "Because Freddy was back to his old tricks, weren't you, *Afraido*? That first night when the guests all gathered for welcome drinks."

Then Jackson turned to Claire and said, "I think you're in the best position to explain this. You were there."

Claire held a hand to her breast, clearly touched by his confidence in her, then looked across at Cindy and Connor. "You guys will remember this too. Elsbeth and Boulder had just made their grand entrance up there on the stairs. James was thrilled to see his mother, but Indya sure wasn't. She was fuming, and she raced out, James fast behind her."

The Dudley-Pines nodded uncertainly, not sure where this was headed.

"What you might not have noticed," added Claire,

"was that Freddy was missing, and soon after James left, Elsbeth left the bar too. She said she was powdering her nose, but we don't think she was. We believe there was some sort of altercation with Freddy, and that's what started all of this. My guess is, Elsbeth followed James to his cabin, just like she followed him everywhere, and she probably caught Afraido secretly taping the newlyweds." A glance at James now. "Were you doing something salacious? Making up or fighting?"

He looked forlorn. "Fighting." Then a glare at Freddy. "You filmed us? Outside the room?"

Freddy scoffed. "So what?"

"Shut up, Vilfredo," said Liz, her voice low and growly, but he didn't look ashamed.

"It was nothing, Mum! I told you this already! It was lame. I would have deleted it anyway."

"So it's still on your phone?" asked Jackson casually, and Freddy shrugged, so he held out a hand. "I'd like to see that now please."

"You don't need to give that to him," warned Liz, but Freddy was already clicking it open, scrolling for the footage, handing it over.

"Chill, Mum! Sheesh, stop making a fuss! You will see."

Jackson tried not to smile as he held the phone up and they did, indeed, see.

"That 'lame' fight is not what I'm concerned with," said Jackson as they all watched a brief exchange between James and his deceased wife, just outside their cabin that fateful night.

It brought most of them to tears. Indya was still alive and kicking, or at least kicking out about Elsbeth's presence, and James was dismissing her concerns like she was a child. Then Indya cried out—loudly, clearly— "One day you're going to have to choose, and I say that day has come!"

Then they watched as she vanished into her stateroom, James following fast, not knowing he would end up losing both of them. Out of context, Freddy was right, it wasn't exactly a show-stopper, but that's not what Jackson was looking for, and now he did smile. Because one second after that door shut behind them, an elderly lady swathed in pink silk stepped around the corner. The video ended there, but Jackson knew that was only the beginning.

Claire's guess was spot-on. Elsbeth Wynter had busted Freddy illegally filming her beloved boy, and there would be consequences.

Jackson pocketed the phone and said, "I never met Mrs Wynter in person, but I know exactly how she would have reacted. Everybody agrees she was formidable, a terrifying Mother Bear. I believe she threatened Freddy's job, probably said she'd report him to the police, and that's why you had to step in, Liz. You had to stop her."

Once again, silence descended as everyone stared, aghast, at Liz, who was wrapping herself up safely behind her arms, shaking her head almost casually. "No, no, nothing like that happened." Then she smiled, oddly, towards Claire. "Don't look so proud of yourself, Ms Know-all. You know nothing. I was there. I saw the whole thing myself. And Freddy's right. It was harmless."

"You saw that?" said Freddy, astounded.

Liz nudged one shoulder. "I was on my way to the welcome drinks when I overheard that stupid woman screaming at you, threatening you like you were no one. So I waited until I got her alone, and I simply reminded her that I was in charge of this yacht, not her. That *I* was the captain and Elsbeth Wynter had no power here."

There was a surprising snigger from Simon. "And how well did that go down, hey Captain?" he called out. "People like us don't get to threaten people like Elsbeth. She's in a whole other dimension. We *need* people like Elsbeth to keep our businesses afloat— literally." He waved a palm towards the bobbing sea. "Doesn't matter where they are, they'll always hold the power. She wasn't scared of you, and she would have reminded you of that without any compunction."

"She was a bitch is what she was," spat out Liz as she swept a defiant glare towards the lawyer now. "Try to deny that, Boulder! You know exactly what I'm talking about. I saw the look of delight in your eyes when we declared Elsbeth dead out on the dive platform that day! You weren't sorry to see her go, just like Roland. You knew the world was a better place without her. She was a nasty piece of work, and she brought all this upon herself. That stupid, stupid cow threatened to expose my son, to make sure he never worked yachts again. How *dare* she? I'm the captain!"

She was becoming hysterical, and Freddy had a hand up, trying to stop her, but she was having none of it. "It wasn't just you, Freddy. She threatened to expose me too. Said we would both lose our jobs! But for what? A marital spat that lasted three seconds? Was she serious?"

"You knew she was serious," said Jackson more evenly. "That's why you went back to see her after dinner that night. Not to discuss how rude she'd been to Cindy, calling her 'shifty'. But to stand up for your son. Elsbeth couldn't have known Freddy was your boy—you kept that from everyone, even your only ally, Sergio—and so she couldn't have predicted how badly you would take that threat. Because if she had known, she might have guessed you were as ferocious a Mother Bear as she was. No, worse, because you were willing to kill to save your cub."

"I was giving her a chance!" Liz roared. "I didn't want things to get ugly, but she wasn't prepared to listen. Like *her* boy was the only one worth protecting."

"*Ina!* Mother!" said Freddy, still trying to shut her up.

But Liz would not be silenced now. "No, Vilfredo! I had no choice. I had to protect you, don't you understand?" Then, seeing shades of disgust in his eyes, she swept around to James. "*You* at least should understand. Your mother would have done *exactly* the same thing to protect you."

"Bullshit!" he yelled back. "My God are you ill? No! My mother might have overstepped, I get that now, but she would never *kill* anyone for me. Not in the name of love."

"She didn't *have* to," Liz screamed back. "She had people to do her dirty work for her." Another glower towards Boulder. "I had no one. I never have. Everything I've ever achieved is through my own hard work."

Her eyes turned towards Gary, who was watching, half-shocked, half-delighted, and she shook a finger at him. "I am so tired of you snivelling on about how you deserved the promotion more than me, like I got some kind of leg up! Ha! I earned this posting, fair and square, so why couldn't I help my son while I was here? You think James has *anything* that didn't come directly from his mother? My son had nothing and no one, just me and this job. And I wasn't going to let that stupid bitch take it from us!"

She gulped. Knew she had gone too far but she didn't seem to care now. Years of resentment at being overlooked and undermined by entitled white men like Gary needed to be aired. And he wasn't the only one. Her finger began to point around the room.

"Look at you people with your gaudy watches and your fake tans. Nothing more to stress about than what sunscreen you're using. I am sick of the lot of you! So yes, I went to see Elsbeth one last time after dinner. I tried to appeal to her as a mother. I told her Freddy's my son. Please have mercy. Forgive him this one. You know what she did? She called me a bad mother."

Liz swivelled back to glare at James again. "How *dare* your mother crash your honeymoon and then tell me *I'm* the bad one! I worked my guts out to get Vilfredo a residency visa in this country. Just because he's been living with his dad in Manila, he's treated like a foreigner. Then one small brush with the law—all over a few fuzzy wedding photos—and suddenly they're trying to deport him back. Like he was an alien. It was pure racism. But I convinced them to give him one last chance. I secured him this job, and then Elsbeth Wynter comes along and tries to rip it all from him. Like he didn't matter! I had to protect him, don't you see?"

James stood up with such ferocity, his chair went flying backwards. "How dare *you*!" he roared back. "All I see is a pathetic loser who killed my mother for a crummy job and a bit of footage! And what about Indy? Hm? What did she ever do to you?"

"Indya?" Liz looked confused now. Blinked rapidly. "No... I mean... I didn't want to hurt Indya. That wasn't part of the plan. But I *had* to. Sergio said he saw her taking pictures out there, just after she'd been speaking with Elsbeth. Just before I..."

She turned to Sergio, but he couldn't even look at her now, and she gasped. "I was scared, that's all! I thought Indya might have photographed me underwater; it was such a clear day. But I couldn't open her stupid phone to check."

"*You* stole her phone?" said James.

She shrugged like it was the least of her worries. "I saw her on the way to yoga that morning, and I just put the boat on autopilot and ducked out to ask her, very politely, did she happen to take any photos while diving. She looked at me oddly, and so I demanded to see her phone. I gave her a chance, I really did, but... the way she looked at me, James. The incrimination! Like *I* was the lunatic, not your mother! I... I couldn't have that. I just wanted to get hold of her phone. I followed her up to the sun deck, I tried to grab it, but it went flying into the jacuzzi, then she jumped in after it, and that's when I knew for certain she suspected me. She was trying to preserve the evidence! I had to stop her, see? I had to get hold of that phone..."

"The proof's not on that phone," said Jackson, now holding up a plastic bag with the waterproof camera inside.

"Indya never took that phone out diving. She had a separate waterproof camera, this one, and she hadn't yet seen the photos."

"Oh God," said Liz, dropping to her knees. "I… I thought she blamed me…"

"No," said James now, shaking his head. "Indya just loved her stupid iPhone, that's all that was. As for you?" He made a strangled sound. "She never even mentioned your name. The only person she blamed was herself."

Liz gulped at that and flung a hand to her mouth while Freddy stared at her like he didn't recognise her anymore, lips wide, tears streaming down his face.

And all the while, everyone watched on with horror and grief. But mostly it was grief for young Indya. An innocent life destroyed by the dangerous love of two overbearing mothers—one who loved her son so much she wouldn't free him to love anyone else and another who wouldn't let her son face the consequences of his own deplorable behaviour.

Silence had descended upon the group again, and Jackson let them sit in it for a moment, all eyes filled with tears, all expressions grim and distraught.

Then he cleared his throat and stepped forward.

"Liz Flinders," he called out, "I'm arresting you for the murders of Elsbeth Wynter and Indya Wynter. You do not have to say anything but—"

Liz held a hand up to interrupt him and wobbled to her feet. Then she plucked her cap from the bar top, placed it firmly on her head and said, very calmly, very professionally, "It's *Captain Flinders*, thank you very much."

EPILOGUE

The Murder Mystery Book Club were all back at the Finlay sisters' house in Sydney's Woolloomooloo, nursing cups of tea as they sat, scattered around the living room on sofas and armchairs and, in Lynette's case, a beanbag beside Max.

They weren't here to discuss a murder mystery, at least not a fictional one.

The *Living Large* had sailed into the Cairns marina soon after the grand reveal, and there they were met by a contingent of police officers and a forensic team, including a coroner and his assistant (the real deal this time).

After Captain Flinders was led away, wrists in cuffs, the passengers and crew spent the bulk of that day at the police district headquarters providing statements. Freddy's phone had been handed over as evidence, as had Indya's waterproof camera and her mobile phone, which was found hidden in plain sight under the chart table in the bridge. Unless Liz retracted her full and shocking confession, they mightn't necessarily need them.

"It's such an extraordinary story," said Missy, once the group had got her up to speed, along with Ronnie and Queenie. "And not at all what you'd expect on a luxury cruise, hey kiddoes?"

"Actually," said Alicia, "the last story we read should have prepared us for at least some of it." She smirked at Perry as she produced three fingers. "Like *The Woman in Cabin 10*, a camera *did* end up in a hot tub, there was at least one passenger masquerading as somebody else, and don't get me started on that toxic celebrity marriage."

"Well, I don't know about that," said Ronnie. "But once again I'm baffled by what people will do all in the name of love."

Perhaps she was remembering their last case, her first as a book club member at a corpse-littered mountain lodge. But Claire was still back on that yacht.

"Oh, love can send you mad," she said softly. "In completely the wrong direction."

Alicia swapped a worried look with Perry while Missy asked, "What's going to happen to Freddy now?"

"Jackson says that's in the hands of the immigration department," said Alicia, "but he couldn't care less about that. He's more focused on having the book thrown squarely at Captain Flinders. Turns out Liz had dumped Freddy as a child with his father—a Filipino barman she'd had a fling with on a cruise when she was much younger. They'd really only been reunited in the past five years, and I have to wonder if it was more about the captain's excessive pride, not to mention all that mother guilt."

"At least she had some guilt," said Claire cryptically.

Alicia frowned again. "How's Simon going, Claire? And the company? How are they coping with all this bad publicity?"

What she really wanted to know is, *how are you two*? Because she was worried for her friend and her new marriage, but she let Claire ramble about the "horrendous publicity".

And it had been horrendous.

No sooner had the club set foot on land, each of them wobbly after so many days at sea, the press descended like a storm—a swirl of flashing bulbs and screaming reporters. And they had done as they would in a storm and put their heads down and ducked for cover, fleeing Cairns for Sydney as soon as they were allowed.

But there was no cover for Simon and Living Large Enterprises. Two women had been murdered on one of his luxury holidays—rich, famous and, yes, in Elsbeth's case, powerful—and so Simon was forced to step up and meet the ferocity head-on. After multiple media releases, a sobering press conference, and a dramatic drop in the share price, they announced the MV *Living Large* would never sail again.

"That's terrible," said Perry. "They can't blame that beautiful yacht for what Liz did."

"Don't worry," said Claire. "The truth is, they're just waiting for the storm to blow over. They'll mothball it for a while, then rename the vessel, but I doubt they'll ever run honeymoon cruises again."

"Now they're blaming the *honeymooners*?"

She frowned. "Simon's superstitious like that."

Alicia nodded. She got it. A honeymoon cruise was now firmly off her bucket list too.

"What's got you worried, possum?" asked Missy, catching Alicia's frown.

"I'm just thinking of Jackson and how grumpy he was when we all showed up on the yacht to investigate." A worried look now at Missy. "Well, not all of us. We did miss you guys, but your research helped crack the case. Finding out about *Afraido* was a game-changer, Missy. As was your last-minute check of the employment records, Queenie."

The newest book club member beamed.

"I was thrilled to be able to help," said Queenie. "Yes, the files were very revealing. Not only did they show that Gary Andrews was cleared of assault by his previous employer, which helped Jackson clear him from the suspect list, but it also provided the link between Liz Flinders and Freddy. He'd used his abridged name in his application, so no one knew his background, but it was the gushing reference from Captain Flinders that secured him the butler position. The head of HR told me they never would have employed someone so inexperienced, except Liz had rung and begged them to do it. They said she was very insistent."

"Now we know why," said Ronnie, and Queenie nodded.

"She never said they were related, but Simon's putting some fresh policies in place to ensure better cross-referencing for future employees, to avoid nepotism and conflicts of interest."

Ronnie made a scoffing sound. "I'm not sure you can ever guard against a woman like Liz Flinders. She was clearly one messed-up Mother Bear." Then she shook her head. "We often think of bears as endearingly protective, but one never considers what will happen when two of them come face to face."

That sent a shudder through the rest of the group.

Later, as they went their separate ways, Alicia pulled Claire aside and said, "Can you stay for a bit? Lynette's got a night class at business school, so we were thinking of ordering takeaway from the Orient Express first. Feels kind of fitting."

"That'd be great," she said immediately. "I have something I need to tell you."

So, after the Chinese food had come and gone and Lynette had scuttled off to class, the two friends returned to the sofa with a bottle of rosé, two glasses and Max at their feet.

As Alicia poured them both a drink, she took a deep breath and said, "Tell me, Claire, now it's just the two of us. Are you and Simon really okay?"

Like Jackson, Alicia had seen the tension build up between them, so she was surprised when Claire came out in his defence.

"Simon's great, *we're* great! Better than ever." Then, noticing Alicia's frown, she added, "I know what you're all thinking. I could tell you were worried about me on the yacht, especially Jackson. It's obvious he's not a big fan of Simon's."

"It's not personal, Claire, he's just protective. We all

saw another side of Simon we hadn't seen, that's all."

"Join the club," she said, again surprising Alicia, and smiling. "Look, I know Simon's obsessed with his company, that it feels like he was putting LLE's needs first. But you know what? I don't blame him for that. The truth is I'm almost jealous."

"Jealous?"

"Yes! I'm jealous that Simon has something so important to him, so valuable, so worthy of saving." She placed her glass on the table and sat forward, stroking Max. "I know Simon loves me, I do know that, but he also loves his business and not just the business, the people behind it—Queenie, Tommo, the entire team. It's his baby, Alicia. They're his people, and I envy him that. Want to hear something even more pathetic?"

Claire reached for the glass again and took a fortifying gulp. "I was secretly envious of James Wynter back on that yacht, the way his mother adored him so much she gate-crashed his honeymoon and how his wife adored him so much she wanted him all to herself. Even Boulder, protecting him like a father would. Should! My parents… well, let's just say I never felt like they cared that much. My mother can barely raise a finger to write to me. How sad is that?"

"But you saw how dangerous that kind of obsessive love can be."

"Yes, but Simon's love for his company is not dangerous, it's not. If so, he would have helped Liz hide the truth, not bring Jackson on board to uncover it. Simon was just desperate to protect his baby but not at all costs. And who can blame him? He set that business up with Tommo thirty years ago, he's poured his whole life into it, never had kids of his own. It's his great love, but it's not mine. It's made me wonder—what about me? What do I love?"

"It's a good question, Claire," said Alicia. "What *do* you love?"

She smiled and said, "I love you."

Alicia gulped. "Me?"

She laughed. "Not like that, silly! I mean *all* of you, the book club. Like I said on the yacht, you're my people, my family. And maybe that's pathetic, but I don't have a family of my own, not really."

"It's not pathetic, Claire. Kind of scary for a brief moment there..." Alicia giggled. "But it's actually really beautiful and we love you just as much."

"And not just the club," added Claire. "I love our adventures together. I adore immersing myself in mysteries—fictional and real. Turns out, I'm pretty damn good at solving whodunnits."

"That is true," said Alicia. "So where does that leave you?"

"It leaves me in Sydney," said Claire, placing her glass down again. "I've told Simon I don't want to work up at the Rainforest Lodge anymore. It's not just because I don't want to be away from him, it's because I don't want to be away from the book club."

"Wow. You really do love us! So your marriage is okay?"

"Yes, of course. I know Simon's not perfect, but— newsflash!—neither am I, and I think that's the problem with this group. We expect perfection from everyone but each other."

Alicia frowned. "How do you mean?"

"I mean, we're cool with the fact that your mind is like a horror movie and Lynette's often a whiny princess and Missy is exhaustingly enthusiastic, and Perry can be a right bitch when he sets his mind to it. And don't get me started on Ronnie's schoolmarmishness and Queenie's pious Pollyanna perfection."

Alicia blinked back at her. "Cripes, Claire. Tell me how you really feel."

She threw a hand to her lips. "Sorry, but *I'm* not perfect either. I know I come across as cold, snobbish, a little too much of a handbrake like Anders used to be. But the fact is we forgive each other all of that, and I'm prepared to forgive Simon his obsession with LLE if he's prepared to give me you."

"And by *you*, you mean, the book club."

She laughed again. "Get over yourself, Alicia. Yes, the book club."

"Phew." Alicia winked at her now. "You're welcome to come back, Claire. We've always said that. The group will be thrilled. Although maybe don't mention any of those little flaws you just listed."

Now they both giggled and Claire said, "See? I knew you'd forgive me, and that's why I need to be back here with my true family." Then her face straightened. "You know, what's sad is how quickly I gave you all up, not to mention my vintage clothing store, which is also something I adore. It's my LLE. Took me years to build that up. I can't believe I surrendered it all so easily."

"Oh, you were just desperate for a change, Claire, and there's nothing wrong with that."

"There is when the change involves abandoning your loved ones and your true self in the process."

Alicia leaned over and clinked their wineglasses, then said, "So what happens now?"

"Now?" Claire grinned, giddily. "Now I'm going to reopen the store, and I'm going to return to the book club where I belong. So, tell me please, what riveting murder mystery is next on the list?"

"Ah…" Alicia sat forward with a giddy smile of her own. "You are going to love this one."

Then she turned to the coffee table and reached for the next book…

~~ *the end* ~~

ACKNOWLEDGEMENTS

It's been a wonderfully fruitful few years for my book club series, which has not only changed titles but has now been translated into several languages around the world, as well as converted into audio books and large-print editions. In that light, I'd like to thank my beloved brother-in-law(yer) Peter Ashton. He's always been an early and enthusiastic reader of my work, but his sage advice and counsel during this complex period have been invaluable. Thanks, Pete!

The Arts Law Centre of Australia and volunteer lawyer Katherine Giles have also gone above and beyond, trawling through contracts on my behalf, and I thank them from the bottom of my heart.

Big thanks, also, to Misa Morikawa and everyone at the Tuttle-Mori Agency, as well as translator Kyomiko Takahashi and the folk at Tokyo Sogensha (love those covers!), and to Marie Misandeau, Cécile Rauby, translator Tania Capron, and the crew at Le Cherche Midi. I cannot wait to see what you make of the series.

Thanks, as always, to my editor D.A. Sarac and my generous readers Elaine Rivers and Simone Larmer, as well as good friend Simon Harding whose advice regarding the world of scuba diving has been immensely helpful. Any errors, while inadvertent, are all my own.

Finally, a big thank you to my beautiful family for their boundless support, especially Christian, Felix and Nimo (talk about stunning covers!), as well as you, dear readers, for lapping up this series, reviewing it so keenly, and enabling me to write more.

Without all of you, I'm just a suspicious creature conjuring up stories in her sunroom...

ALSO BY C.A. LARMER

After the Ferry: A Psychological Novel

IT'S THE 1990s, pre-mobile phones, and a young traveller must make a terrifying choice: Will she jump ship with a seductive stranger? Or stay cocooned on the Greek ferry with friends and miss what could be the love of her life?

One choice leads to true love.
One choice leads to murder.
But which is which?

"Larmer's plot is a clever one...The characters are finely honed and credible, and Amelia's contrasting lives and personalities are brilliantly rendered and made plausible."
Jack Magnus, Readers Favorite

Killer Twist (Ghostwriter Mystery 1)

KILLER TWIST is the first stand-alone mystery in the popular 'amateur women sleuths' series featuring feisty ghostwriter Roxy Parker.

"A fun read with a well defined protagonist, interesting secondary characters and an easy style. Lots of local flavour which catches the imagination."
Parents' Little Black Book @ Amazon

"Roxy Parker is a compelling character and I couldn't help but adore her. She's 30, hip, very inquisitive, and fiercely independent. A great cozy. I enjoyed it immensely and will be ordering the second in the series."
Rhonda @Amazon

Blind Men Don't Dial Zero
(Sleuths of Last Resort 1)

POLICE say the case is open-and-shut. The heir to a massive fortune, Heath, slaughters his parents, confesses to the crimes, then turns the gun on himself. Heath's grandfather says, "Not so fast." With the case now closed, Sir George assembles his own crack team of detectives—five amateur sleuths with a nose for mystery and a need to prove themselves—then pits them against each other to solve it. They have just two weeks…

"This is a fantastic read! lots of twists and turns and a real page turner! Quirky, interesting and complex characters fill this interesting adventure! I loved the book!"
Charlene @Amazon

"Will have even the most seasoned sleuth baffled as these amateurs tackle a wealthy family, loyal employees, and unsavoury boyfriends. You will find this action-filled journey unforgettable and hard to put down"
Peggy Jo Wipf for Readers' Favorite

calarmer.com

Made in the USA
Middletown, DE
29 December 2023

46976626R00189